# the Killer Enigma

## Breakfield and Burkey

**The Killer Enigma**
Charles V Breakfield and Roxanne E Burkey
© Copyright 2023
ALL RIGHTS RESERVED

With certain exceptions, no part of this book may be reproduced in any written, electronic, recording, or photocopying form without written permission of the publisher or author. The exceptions would be in the case of brief quotations embodied in critical articles or reviews and pages where permission is specifically granted in writing by the author or publisher and where authorship/source is acknowledged in the quoted materials.

This book is a work of fiction. All names, characters, places, and incidents are the products of the authors' imaginations or are used fictitiously. Any resemblance to actual events, locales, or people living or dead is coincidental.

Published by

ICABOD Press

ISBN: 978-1- 946858-68-9 (paperback)
ISBN: 978-1- 946858-67-2 (e-book)

Library of Congress Control Number: 2023908292
Interior and eBook design: F + P Graphic Design, FPGD.com

First Edition
Printed in the United States

MYSTERY | CRIME | SUSPENSE

N
W
E
S
Hayden's Resort west side of reservoir
28 TEXAS
Doyle's Garage
O'Gara'S Bar
LouEllin's Lounge
Corral 44
Doyle's General Store
Piggly Wiggly
Pickle Dilly Bait & Tackle
City Hall
Olivia's Pizza
Main Street
Fernhope Hardware Store
Luby's
Dept's Parks & Wildlife
Junior High Middle School
Flower B & B
Bluff Pharmacy
113 TEXAS
Magnolia Bluff High School
Library
Methodist Church
Baptist Church
Merricks Doyle's Memorial Park
Presbyterian Church
Cozy Corners Motel
Lutheran Church
Reservoir
Catholic Church
28 TEXAS
Magnolia Bluff Collage
Schiff's Funeral Home & Flow's Flower Shop
Magnolia Bluff Cemetery
38 TEXAS
Magnolia Bluff

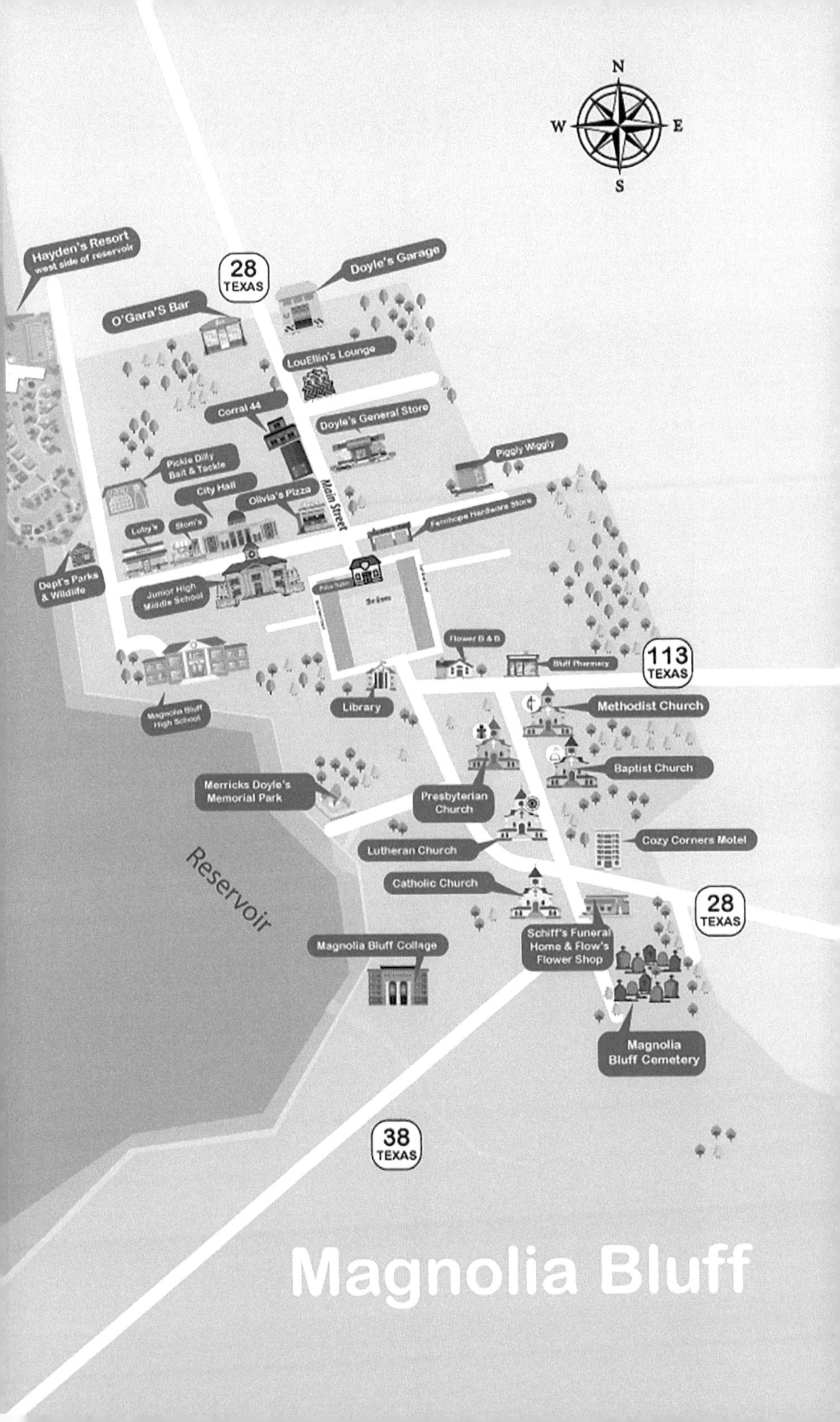

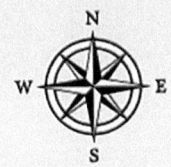

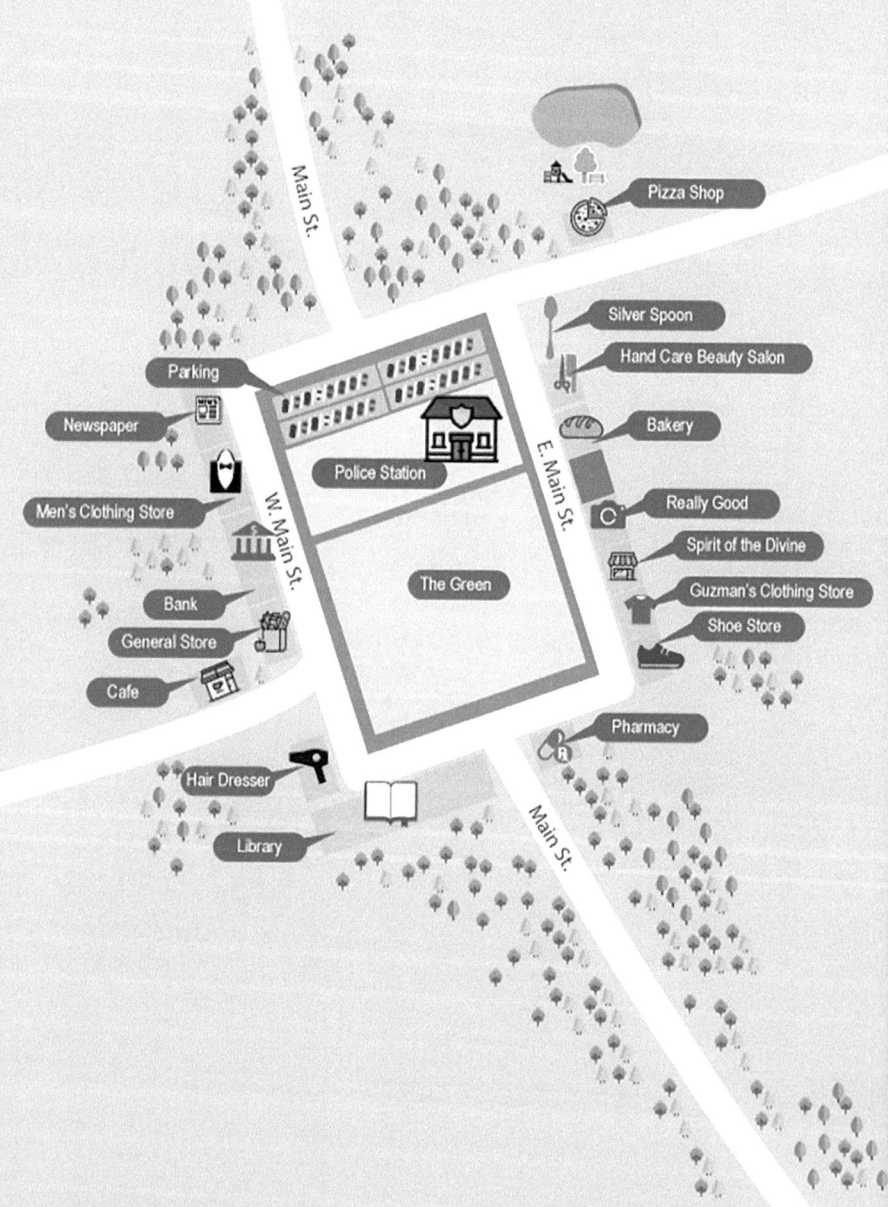

## CHAPTER 1

# Dinner Out, Not So Easy...

JJ stopped his silver Porsche Carrera at the valet station of Mama Elise's Ristorante. He got out and grinned at the attendants who crowded to the front of the car. "Her name's Sophia. She hates getting scratched," he added when he pitched the keys. The tallest attendant caught the ring and held it high as the group vied to park it. JJ circled the car to the passenger side. "Can you drive a standard clutch without stalling it?"

The hand-off of the keys to the attendant who commented he could, resulted in another chuckle.

"Sophia is a Tiptronic with both manual mode and automatic capabilities. Use the automatic mode, guys." Fingering his black longish hair away from his forehead, he hoped the argument over who would park his car might continue for a few more minutes.

JJ circled the car to the passenger side. He lifted the handle and soundlessly opened the door to reveal the long, sculpted legs of the girl of his dreams. Jo reached his offered hand, wrapping her soft fingers with the French-tipped manicure around his fingers to secure her grip. She tugged on the hem of her short red leather skirt to prevent it from riding too high as her legs hit the pavement.

"Sweetheart, I wouldn't mind seeing more of your legs," he whispered.

"I know, but later, honey," she giggled, and gracefully stood in one fluid motion. At the last second, she grasped her beautiful red chapeau, letting her mane of wavy, ebony hair tumble down her back.

A couple of inches taller than her lithe five foot nine, JJ scooted his hand around her waist, brushing her bare back. "You look beautiful."

He felt her gentle elbowing in his side. "You always say that. I feel perfect with you. Let's duck inside before someone spots us."

They walked to the front door. JJ pulled it open and escorted her toward the hostess desk. The rich Italian seasonings of garlic, onions, and bread assaulted his nose. He heard the piano near the bar playing easy listening jazz. Mama Elise's Ristorante was a favorite destination when they escaped their busy work demands. Like teenagers, they held hands waiting their turn.

A pretty young girl, looking way too grown up in her evening gown, with her perfect makeup and dark hair pulled into a bun, raised her eyes and grinned from behind the hostess station.

"Evening, Cecilia, you look lovely," JJ commented. "I know your Granma is delighted you're working here. We have reservations, and I hope Mama reserved the back table I requested."

"Of course, she did. Do you need menus tonight?"

Swaying beside JJ to the music, Jo licked her lips. "I always like to look and see if something piques my tastebuds, so yes."

Cecilia picked up a couple. "Right this way, please."

"Cecilia, did you speak to your Granma about your desire to try modeling?" Jo asked while they walked toward their table. I'm still willing to make the introductions to Lara if you get her approval."

Setting the menus on the table, the girl looked up, a twinkle in her eyes. "Not yet. I still want to work with you at Destiny Fashions, though I doubt I'll get as popular and well-known as you. My sixteenth birthday is a little over a month away. I plan to ask her that morning."

JJ pushed in Jo's chair as she sat. Jo patted the girl's arm and smiled at her. "Let me know when to speak to Lara. If it works out, I will watch over you, too. You must keep up with your studies, no matter what."

Cecilia's face burst into a grin. "Yes, ma'am, I will. Enjoy your dinner. Oh, and we have your Italian style escargot in wine sauce this evening."

Jo opened the menu and peered at JJ over the top. "At least I know my appetizer order. I'm so glad we made time to enjoy a dinner out. I do love this place, honey."

"I agree. The atmosphere is perfect, food delicious, and service impeccable. Maybe you will join me in a dance later before dessert?"

The waiter appeared and took their orders. He replaced the menus with a warm basket of soft breadsticks and butter. They each broke off a small sample, enjoying the melt-in-your-mouth texture.

"These are dangerous to me," Jo announced, pushing the basket toward him.

He curved his lips as he noticed the love reflected in her eyes, and his heart swelled. "You know it is nearly our first anniversary. I hope you can arrange time off to celebrate before the holidays."

"I asked Lara the schedule for the next couple of months. I'm sure she'll let me know soon.

The music shifted from jazz to traditional Italian, causing them to look toward the bar. JJ noted the enormous fig tree with its massive branches appearing to sustain the roof. Strings of red, white, and green lights flickered into the bar and danced on the glasses as they were transported by staff to the diners. He heard fragments of intimate conversations between the seated couples.

Their wine arrived, and JJ toasted to their health and love. The sweet tone of their glasses touching punctuated his statement.

Jo sipped the wine and expelled a groan of appreciation that put a smile on her well-known face. "Honey, I received another letter from Lily."

"And what did our favorite Texas proprietress have to say? Is she well? Any news of the girls?"

"Of course, she misses us and has a room available whenever we want to return. Renata is learning additional recipes and planning the breakfast menus. Lily says she's excelling at math and art." Jo chuckled. "Apparently, Renata still flips between English and Spanish when excited. Lily says her Spanish is improving, but she still helps with Renata's English per Ann's request. She sent along thanks for the language software app you provided."

"Excellent. What else?"

"A few more incidents happened in town, keeping the gossipers happy and the sheriff busy. Camila's in some of Renata's classes in high school. Hank and Ann finally finished their formal adoption. The girls have secured a loving home and part-time jobs they love. After school, Camila helps with caring for their horses and has convinced Hank to offer riding lessons."

"That means the next time we get to visit we'll see them both. Good. I know you miss them, sweetheart, but we need at least a week, preferably two to enjoy that trip. Should we add that destination in the hat for our anniversary getaway?" JJ asked.

"Maybe. But then we don't get the alone-time you wanted. Staying at The Flower is not exactly quiet romance time. I thought you wanted…"

"There she is!" a loud voice announced.

Flashbulbs strobed into their secluded corner. A man, microphone in hand, rushed past the waiters with a cameraman on his heels. JJ stood, blocking the intruders' direct access to Jo. Other diners looked on with interest but remained seated. The obnoxious pair moved like boxers in a ring, bobbing and weaving to close on their quarry.

The man with the microphone launched into a barrage of questions with the cameraman filming. "Jo W of Destiny Fashions, how does it feel to be adored by millions? Who's with you? Someone said you got married, but this can't be the guy. He's not a well-known celebrity. Are you cheating on your husband? Harold, get a shot of this loser. We might find out who he is and do an exposé."

Without enough room to do anything but keep them from getting too close, JJ slammed the palm of his hand on the table. It sounded like a gunshot. He pushed the guy with the camera, resulting in the device falling to the floor. He stomped on it while that man protested, "My equipment, man."

"Tough luck, buddy. Get outta here and take that fool with you," JJ demanded, shaking with anger.

The waitstaff formed a line that encircled the paparazzi and herded them toward the door for ejection. Jo covered her face with her hands, her shoulders shuddering in what JJ knew were tears.

He reached her side and pulled her close, to escape into the kitchen. The interviewer evaded the wedge of the waiters and rushed behind them. "Jo W, where's your next fashion shoot? I need an exclusive." He grabbed Jo's sleeve, tearing it.

Jo screamed, "No comment!"

JJ latched onto the microphone and ripped it from the guy's hand. "No more chances, idiot," he growled as he slammed the device into the owner's gut and broke it in two. A sidekick connected and put the man on the floor moaning.

Cecilia motioned from the door to the kitchen. Resounding applause was heard as JJ escorted Jo to their freedom.

JJ inhaled shakily. "Thanks, Cecilia, for saving us. We need to leave but clearly not via the front door."

Mama Elise stomped into the kitchen. "JJ, the front of the restaurant is surrounded by fans and reporters. I've called the police, but it will take time before they arrive."

JJ looked upward as if for divine intervention, then placed a call.

"Hey, JJ," Brayson answered. "Your security application is indicating you and Jo have drawn a crowd. The satellite view suggests cameras and live transmissions. Were you serenading her in the street, man?" Brayson jested.

"No," JJ replied through clenched teeth. "I'm not certain who alerted them. Mama usually keeps our arrivals under cover."

"The restaurant event is uploading real-time reporting comments. I was able to redirect the upload of the film clips and photos. I destroyed them and have a temporary block in place. The editor will think the camera guy messed up."

"Brayson, how close is your Timothy Project to reality?" JJ shot a loving look in Jo's direction.

"I was remote testing Timothy before your application went nuts. I don't have enough control to maneuver it around that sort of crowd. Without a driver, the vehicle might attract more attention if the bright lights hit it wrong."

"Agreed, but if you can get it to the back entrance of this place, I might have an idea."

"I can remote control it to the door. The keys are under the mat if you want manual control. Enter the passcode on the keypad."

"Let's do it. We'll add a case study for your efforts and proof points. You kept the tinted windows, right?"

"Of course. But stay away from the filming lights. It's still illegal to have unregistered driverless vehicles on public streets."

"I don't think we have a choice if we want to escape without Jo getting injured. If you can get it here, it won't be driverless for long."

Silence ensued. "Okay, boss. Fifteen minutes. I'll text you."

The roar of the growing crowd echoed in the kitchen.

"We need to leave," Jo said, with fear reflected in her eyes.

"Working on it, honey. Give me a few minutes." JJ turned toward Cecilia.

"Cecilia, can you drive the Porsche?"

"You know I can. Granma has me drive hers all the time."

"Put on Jo's hat, saunter out the front, and present the ticket for my Porsche from the valet. Show your face so they won't attack you thinking you're Jo, though your body size and hair are a close match. Keep your hair in the twist. Drive off and weave around a few streets to give the reporters the brushoff. Then return to the back of the restaurant. I think thirty minutes should do it. Let the valet park it. I'll get it later." He cleared his throat and turned back to Mama.

Cecilia nodded and disappeared to change.

Mama Elise embraced Jo with tears welling in her eyes. "I apologize your meal got interrupted. That back table is typically secure, but I should have added extra guards at the door. I will next time."

Jo sniffled and wiped her eyes. "Not your fault, Mama. But I was so looking forward to your food tonight."

Mama patted her shoulder and pinched JJ's cheek. "I told my head chef to make it to-go. I held his hand, promising him you'd love it regardless of the container it's served in. I added a couple of wine bottles to complement the flavors; he insisted on the perfect wine. There's no charge for the meal or extra entertainment."

"Don't be silly, Mama," JJ said, then added a hug. "It's no one's fault." He provided payment and pressed it into her hand.

"Next time I'll ask you to close the restaurant and buy all the tables. Please convey our gratitude to your entire staff."

He faced Mama, but continued holding Jo's hand. "Are the guests tonight friends of yours?"

"Of course. I only allow close friends when you dine here."

"Do you think you can get them to help with a ruse?"

"What do you want done? I'll tell them myself."

"I need you to tell a few of the guests to please start out the doors as if finished eating, and three minutes later, shout that we escaped dressed as waiters."

Mama grinned. "I'll make it so." She strode out the door to the main dining room and returned several minutes later with a smug look on her face. She picked up their bagged meal.

A waiter approached Mama, and she whispered into his ear.

"We are ready, and the waiters are leaving." Mama said. "Cecilia grabbed the car and is taking it to my home. You can retrieve it anytime you wish. No one followed her."

JJ pulled Jo close and promised, "Come on, sweetheart. Dinner will be served shortly on our patio table. I'll even play soft Italian jazz."

Jo hugged Mama, and the two left.

Enclosed in Timothy, Jo mumbled, "I don't like pushy reporters. Thank heavens on the shoots we use extra security."

JJ patted her knee. "I know how hard it is for you, sweetheart. It'll be okay."

CHAPTER 2

# Planning Life-Work's in the Way

Early the next morning, JJ slipped from bed and went to his office at their home in São Paulo. Jo planned to sleep late to recover from the reporter invasion they endured the prior evening. He powered up his computer and frowned at the email avalanche received overnight. Ordinarily it was standard business as usual, but the events at dinner and his bride's restlessness through the night resulted in his distraction. The good and bad sides of success left him wanting to make this first anniversary celebration memorable. They designated October, even though the real date was December, to avoid competing with the Christmas season. The family agreed to honor their wishes.

The savory, strong Indonesian blended coffee was normally able to launch his mental faculties into overdrive, but his thoughts were unable to advance from neutral. The handle of the cup swaying between his thumb and forefinger moved but went nowhere. The text window beeped an inbound message. He opened the exchange sent by Brayson Morris, his right-hand support.

> JJ, you're not replying to my urgent email. You want to talk about it? You can push your coffee handle around, but we need to get some business done.

JJ ground his teeth, annoyed at his transparency. He jammed the icon to escalate the chat message to a voice/video call.

"Morning, JJ," greeted Brayson. "I suspect the paparazzi debacle left a cloud over your entire night. I'm the poster child for CATS' emotional rescue division, ready to offer high-spirited motivational counsel, pithy sayings, stale advice, and, if irrelevant, musically recount bawdy lyrical humor pilfered from tunes penned by the musical genius of Lonny Lupnerder."

JJ frowned, digesting the teasing for a few heartbeats, and then he chuckled, which evolved into a boisterous laugh.

Brayson grinned and his eyes sparkled as if waiting for JJ's control to return.

"Thanks, Brayson," JJ said, after regaining his composure. "I needed a diversion. Jo is a mix of mad and frustrated. She loves the work and the fame, but a little privacy would be nice now and again. We wanted a relaxing night out before her next shoot in Mexico. She leaves early tomorrow morning and wanted to plan our anniversary celebration. Our work schedules are messing with her newlywed glow, which worries me. I see the maelstrom of new requests for CATS' support to defeat the new cyber onslaughts. I need to focus before we commit the team, but my mind is going in circles."

"I'm glad you're not signing before reading. One of those is a doozy; we may need new hires to complete the assignment. We can talk through them faster." Brayson made an odd face and cleared his throat. "Burn out. Boss, we've seen it in our clients and contractors. Left untreated, it wreaks havoc and doesn't end well."

"I don't work hard, man," JJ countered.

"You work at racing speeds. You also push the limits of two to three hours of rest when Jo's home so she can rest. Noble, but lack of sleep can take a toll."

JJ tilted his head and twisted his mouth, considering denying the comments. "I want to be an innovative leader of this team and a dynamite partner for a gorgeous supermodel."

"You ARE," reassured Brayson. "You both deserve a break. Perhaps you need to get serious about combining your anniversary with a vacation. Jo works a grueling schedule when there's a shoot. She'd enjoy time away. You need to unplug for a week, or even a month, if her schedule permits."

JJ caught the flash of a smirk across the face of his friend and second in command. He remembered the history of Brayson climbing out of the dismal hole of his life before he'd married Marian. The two of them balanced life and work, but it was an ongoing effort. "You're right."

"Let's face it, you two didn't have much alone time when you went to Texas, but you ended up getting closer. Strictly speaking, you never had a honeymoon. Make plans with Jo for your getaway, including the where and how long. Focus on you as a couple. It helps, man. Oh, you made me take off after the last huge case because you recognized my stress level reached the outer limits. I'll cover the work. Though I might hand out raises or bonuses while you're gone."

JJ clucked his tongue in disapproval. "Brayson, why the generous streak? The next thing you'll want is a lunch HOUR and paid vacations. We've a business to run. Any vacation I take impacts revenue."

Brayson laughed. "You know I oversee the books. I did notice we're way ahead of your profit target for the year with three months remaining. I maintain that success at the cost of mental health is failure. You both need some time to help one another."

JJ sighed and only nodded.

Brayson petitioned, "Just remember. After you get back, I may want some married couple time off too. We all need to get away now and then. You and Jo need to be at your peak and you can't on your current trajectory."

JJ smiled. "Sound advice, my friend. Now where to go?"

Brayson laughed. "That's the easy part. Just go where she tells you."

CHAPTER 3

# You Want to go Where?

Their evening dinner, including reheated leftovers from Mama's, filled the emptiness. Their outdoor garden patio, in full bloom with floral scents and brilliant color, allowed fun conversation. JJ enjoyed the times when Jo tended the flowers with amazing results displayed in all their glory, season after season. JJ handled watering and trimming while she traveled. He planted new shrubs as requested by his master gardener. Between their brightly decorated rooms reflecting the colors of Brazil, and this outdoor haven, home called to them both with its peace and harmony.

JJ and Jo's dinner conversation seemed to assume a life of its own.

"I'll take better care of security next time we plan a night out," JJ promised.

"It's hard when we are here in Brazil, JJ." Jo wrinkled her nose. "People here seem to recognize me more often."

"Jo, even though our home is lovely," he said with a sweep of his arm at the romantic garden setting with its array of colors and fragrances, "I think we need to spend time together to relax and enjoy us. You pick the location. Tell me where and when you want to go. My only stipulation is we're gone at least two weeks, preferably a month."

The way she bounded up and danced around like a kid with a new toy, he suspected a hidden spring ejected her from her chair. The hug and kiss that followed her excited display got filed in *the best ways to delight your bride folder* in his mind. His mind raced between her enjoyment and worries about the logistics of keeping the media in the dark about their plans. His relief was palatable when Brayson succeeded in eliminating last evening's pictures from social media. He authorized a bonus to the man's next paycheck.

Jo's giddiness between her dancing, clapping, and sing-song, fragmented her speech on all the things she wanted to experience on their trip. JJ was glad he'd made her decide, as she alternated between kisses and hugs, so he added his own, plus a fanny pat.

"Sweetheart, are you certain Magnolia Bluff is the place to spend our first anniversary? Are you planning to test your frying pan swinging skills like when we helped stop the human trafficking mobster? We could go to a private beach with water sports. I'd get us a boat for skiing or fishing if you want. The Mediterranean, or even Europe, provides us privacy in certain locations." He watched part of her exuberance deflate before his eyes.

"Honey, those places are like going to work. Exotic destinations for backdrops to the latest fashions. Unless you prefer them, I'd rather not go where all the rich and famous hang. I'll get spotted. I'd rather avoid getting mobbed and questioned to death. In Magnolia Bluff, only Lily knows me, and she's sworn to secrecy. Plus, we have actual friends, and I'd like to see how Camila and Renata have changed."

Seeing the light in her eyes and the bounce in her step convinced JJ. "If it's what you want, then great. We have friends and it is quiet."

"Wouldn't it be fun to ride horses around the Texas Hill Country from Ann and Hank's ranch again?" Jo grabbed her thick hair into a tie and kicked up her heels. "We can swim in the reservoir, and I can show you my new bikini."

JJ waggled his eyebrows and pulled her into his lap, wrapping his arms around his best girl. "I love you, Jo." He nuzzled her neck and hit his target.

She wiggled like crazy. "Stop, Hee! Hee! Hee!" she chortled.

"If you're happy then I'm on it. Get the dates from Aunt Lara, and I'll make arrangements."

"I'll press her tomorrow. I know she'll be happy for us."

JJ snorted, "I agree. I had some reservations, but your excitement is contagious. Disaster doesn't strike twice in the same location, so we'll get the nice quiet vacation we deserve."

"Thanks, honey." She gave him a last hug. "Let's go work out, then crash. I have an early call time."

CHAPTER 4

# Media Stalking

Chief Editor Rosen snarled, "Why do you bring me social media videos at this time in our hour of need? We lost the best chance at the scoop of the year due to clumsy resources in Paris. Insider information doesn't hit this desk often enough to squander."

"I know, Boss," the junior editor persisted. "Look who our competition nearly had. It's JoW the Brazilian supermodel and an escort in a small restaurant outside of São Paulo. An exclusive on her could easily shoot us to the top for the year."

The chief reviewed the photo. "So, where'd you get this?"

"My cousin got a job doing valet services in the area. A guy drove her in, but they must-a had a fight because she drove out alone. He said there was some other issue going on in the restaurant, and they threw out a reporter before she took off."

"Okay, you have my attention. What do we have besides a cell phone shot?"

The younger man grinned. "I have a license plate for a pretty Porsche getting traced to the Bernardes estate not too far away. That's where JoW calls home. Plus, gossip columnists around Brazil suggest she got married in a private ceremony, but no one can confirm the marriage, or her husband's identity."

"Yay. So?"

"Rumor has it that Destiny Fashions has another shoot occurring, but no one has nailed the location. I think if we stake out the estate, we might get what we want."

Rosen tapped his chin with his fingers, considering the possibilities. "All right, put the prettiest two girls we have on it. Maybe they can seek an extra spot in a background picture. Marie has the look; make her one of them."

"On it, boss," he said as he turned to leave the office.

"And," Rosen added, "an extra bonus for you and the girls if we get an in."

Jo stood with the models, her hair and makeup complementing her oval face, big-brown eyes and perfect cheekbones, or so Lara kept telling her. The dress fit to perfection with a new style she already loved, but the world hadn't yet seen. Lara's collection this season rose above last year's. The rugged hillside backdrop on one side, with ocean on the other, along with special lighting enhancements by Miguel the head photographer would highlight the mood of the dazzling designs.

Lara organized the order of appearance by the models to help each achieve the pinnacle of excellence. "All right, team, this is the second most important shoot of the season. Leave the calories on the plates, not in your behinds. I need your best efforts here in Mexico before the shoot next month. I don't want second thoughts on your faces."

Even the hardened veterans of Destiny Fashions snickered at her all-too-familiar comments. Jo felt apprehensive at approaching Lara with her request while in the midst of the shoot. Since her turn in the schedule was targeted near the end, she decided she had time to speak to Carlos.

Jo sidled up to her stepfather, an older version of her husband, with greying black hair, tall lithe form, and chiseled features. Her hand rested for a second on his arm, gaining his attention. "Good morning, Carlos. Can you help me find the right moment to ask Lara for time off? JJ and I are hoping for a break to celebrate our anniversary." She caught the twinkle in his chocolate-brown eyes. "I want to minimize the bite marks on my arm this time."

Carlos chuckled. "We can't have bite marks before the final shoot of the season. Don't fret. I'll lay down suppressive fire from the howitzers, have aircraft drop smoke canisters from a fast low-level pass, then you run in to make your request. Remember to say please and thank you. She'll storm, stare at me, then smirk at both of us with a nod. If that doesn't happen, you run, and I'll sweet talk her."

Jo stared uneasily into Carlos's eyes and grinned. "I'm never sure if we're on a photo shoot or on a mission attacking an enemy position. You'll help, right?"

"Yes, honey," he chortled. "I'll help secure your request." He pulled her close, careful of the outfit and extended a light fatherly kiss on her forehead to confirm.

The moment Lara gave the crew ten, Carlos raised his arm. "I'd like a moment, General Lara."

Lara turned and made a face, leaving no doubts Carlos derailed her thoughts. She resolutely nodded as the pair joined her.

CHAPTER 5

# It's Work with Some Fun

Jo grinned following the spirited discussion with Lara. Her adoptive parents were behind her desire to take a full holiday to celebrate her and JJ's anniversary. She sent a quick text message to JJ with the details.

> Honey—Got the time off! Come get me in Mexico and we can drive to Austin. I promised to be on time to the final shoot for this season in Hawaii.
> You can join me there too. We get a month!

Jo sensed his laughter and delight in his rapid response.

> Okay, babe. I'll do an emergency evac to get off faster rather than wait for the jet to dock at the gate. Be there day after tomorrow. LYL.

Jo danced a quick soft-shoe and rejoined the models for the day's shoot.

"You out on another vacation with your dreamboat male hunk?" remarked Lorena. "With things going your way, I don't understand why you work so hard at this line of work. I mean if it were me, I'd be riding off in the sunset planning the baby thing."

"Not ready for that yet. I love JJ." Jo patted her co-worker's arm. "And I love my job because of great friends like you."

Sometimes Jo worried about her role as Destiny Fashions' top model. She cheered for all the models when the shots worked, especially the first time. Jealousy could mess with her head if she permitted those thoughts. Not today, she thought with a shake of her head. Bubbling with excitement for her getaway, she added, "We got this, Lorena. Let's show the world."

Jo squared her shoulders while Lorena went for a final touch up on her lipstick and shadow. Being confrontational was not in Jo's heart.

Morgan overhead the comments. "Jo," she whispered, "Lorena hopes you'll retire so she can take your position."

"She wants to make it to the top. I get it." Jo liked Morgan, who looked like an older sister from the same gene pool. They teased one another that in the right lighting with the same outfits, they could switch, with no one the wiser. "Don't worry, there's enough for all of us to succeed, even the new girl who begged for a stand-in shot. Lara knows what she wants in presenting her latest clothing."

Morgan hugged Jo. "All right. But I think Lorena's a bit too manipulative. Nice to look at, not pretty on the inside like you."

"We are all better together." Jo hip-bumped Morgan.

"Ladies," Lara announced, "Carlos intercepted a security problem. A couple of pushy operators tried to access the shooting area with job offers. Hotel security sent them packing. If you leave the hotel without our security, you might be accosted. Tell our team where you're headed if you leave the grounds. You're under our care. I don't want my stars grabbed for who-knows-what."

The new model walked next to Morgan and Jo after the final touchups from their make-up artist. Marie strode over wearing the printed casual loungewear outfit, one of the show pieces.

"Wow, Marie," Jo complimented. "You look terrific. I'm sure Lara will agree."

Marie blushed and prattled, "I had no idea when I pleaded for a chance that I'd meet JoW." She twirled around, and asked, "It feels so nice. I never thought I might be in print."

"You're lovely and graceful," Morgan said. "It's the camera who must pull out the sparkle in your eyes and confidence in your stance."

"We need to get this right the first time, girls," Jo insisted. "I get to take a four-week vacay. So, let's do this."

Jo's name was called. She went to her mark and posed as directed. She overheard Marie's comments.

"Morgan, where's JoW going on holiday? Is she going with that hunk Lorena mentioned?"

"I'm not sure, Marie," said Morgan. "Her itinerary's kept fairly quiet. Lara and Carlos maintain a close eye on their daughter. She deserves to enjoy time out of limelight," Morgan added, before heading to her spot on the set.

Lighting and setting worked to make this one of the easiest sessions from this season. Jo sidled up to Morgan as the models headed back toward the hotel to change and eat.

"Morgan, can we chat in my room after dinner? I think I need your help," Jo asked.

Linking an arm around Jo, she said, "Sure."

CHAPTER 6

# Help Comes in Two Flavors

The plane touched down at General Servando Canales International Airport without a hitch. JJ grabbed his bags and proceeded to the rental car area to pick up his reserved vehicle. His only thought was to get to the hotel in Matamoros, meet with his Aunt Lara and Uncle Carlos for breakfast, then escape with his wife to Magnolia Bluff. He felt the job stress melting and anticipation growing at seeing Jo. *Ah, this getaway is going to be great,*" he mumbled.

He programmed the directions to the hotel into his rental. Forty minutes jived with his expectations, leaving him enough time to call the office and verify the plans. He placed a call. "Hey, Brayson, I arrived, and all is good. Driving this Mustang is going to be fun. Jo will love it, thanks."

"Of course. Everything here is fine and handled. We won't be bothering you for any work items, so go relax."

"I intend to do just that." JJ squinted, searching the road for local farmers in their donkey-pulled wagons or bikers.

"There is one small thing, boss. Jo called me after your plane took off because you were out of service. Let her know she was spot on. Her plan is a riot."

JJ felt his stomach roll. "Something I need to do?"

"Nope. Believe it or not, she's a smart lady."

"I know that. But what was the problem that you could handle instead of me?"

"JJ, believe it or not, we adults can handle some things. With this one, I think you'll enjoy the story she promised to tell you on the way to your destination. I'm still chuckling."

"Now I'm unnecessary?"

"Not at all. Now you get time with a smart, pretty girl who loves you. All good, bro. All good."

JJ planned to speed up but he caught sight of several bicyclists and kept his anxiety in check.

His Uncle Carlos met him at the security checkpoint in the underground parking area. JJ got out, pocketed the keys, and shook hands with the man he resembled. "Hi, Uncle. Thanks for meeting me. I didn't want to wander the halls. I figured security would take me for a stalker."

"Right you are, JJ." Carlos looped an arm around him then provided a ballcap and sunglasses. "Nice to see you."

"The car I parked next to looks just like my rental. It must be the popular model."

Carlos laughed. "Something like that. Let's go find your bride and aunt. We have time for a nice private breakfast before you take off."

The elevator stopped at the top floor. As they exited, JJ caught sight of a lady who looked a lot like Jo, walking with someone who appeared a lot like him…in the same ballcap, too. "Honey," he called.

"JJ, that's not her. Let's go have breakfast," said Carlos.

The door to the suite opened with Carlos's card. Jo rushed into JJ's arms. "Honey, you're here. Right on time. Come in. Lara, he's here."

"So I gathered with your squealing and running." Lara chuckled.

Lara hugged her nephew and pulled him toward the patio where breakfast was laid out in the morning light. Bright colors of linens and dishes reminded him they were in Mexico. "Are you famished?"

"I am, actually. I was in such a hurry to catch the flight and then drive here early, I figured I wait to eat with you."

"Good. We have enough for ten rather than the four that are here."

"Aunt Lara, did you have a meeting this morning as I was arriving? I mistook the lady taking the elevator for Jo."

He pushed in Lara's chair then repeated the courtesy for Jo, adding a kiss to her cheek. "The lady was wearing exactly the same outfit you're wearing. I notice the small details. Did you have another shoot this morning?"

Jo grinned and patted his arm. "No, honey. I discovered a fox in the henhouse. I decided rather than evicting the model wannabe pest, I'd get Brayson and Uncle Carlos to send her on a wild goose chase. Plus, Morgan asked for a free getaway to Cancun for four weeks with her favorite photographer, Miguel, who needed time off too." She added items to her plate from the serving dishes. "Come on, let's eat. I'll give you all the details on the drive."

"Yes, honey. Brayson told me you were smart, and I agreed. Aunt Lara, this food smells and looks delicious."

An hour later, JJ carried Jo's bags with Lara and Carlos walking along to the garage. JJ raised an eyebrow with his uncle's response to a call in which he heard one side of the conversation.

"Good job. Keep the surveillance going until they reach Cancun and let me know if they leave." Carlos ended the conversation, and said, "Jo, they took the bait. Not only was the fair

Marie in the chase vehicle but also another pretty lady and a guy carrying camera bags. You'll be over the border before they figure out it's not you."

Jo hugged Carlos. "Thank you for your help." She moved into Lara's embrace. "I am so glad we get a chance to just enjoy. I appreciate you letting me take the time off. I promise I won't gain an ounce."

"You two enjoy." Lara dabbed a hankie on her eyes. "I'll miss you. Please be careful."

JJ opened the door and kissed Jo before she sat. He walked around to the driver's side and fastened his seatbelt. "Honey, we are going to love this Mustang convertible. Fast and comfortable." He reached into the glove box. "I grabbed this for you to wear."

Jo added the cap and waved as the car made its way to the exit. "Honey, let's enjoy our time together." With both arms raised to the sky as they cleared the garage, she yelled, "Woo-hoo!" loud enough to turn the heads of those mingling in the lawn area on benches enjoying the flowers.

JJ patted her leg and leaned over for a quick kiss as he stopped for a guest walking toward the pool. "Nice, honey."

"You're right, it is a nice hotel."

"Not that—you, sweetheart." He noticed a man taking a selfie with them in the background. He couldn't put his finger on why the man caught his attention, other than he was dressed in a suit that wasn't tourist-casual.

Jo leaned in for another kiss and squeezed his hand, distracting his thoughts. He put the car into gear and maneuvered onto their route to her desired destination.

CHAPTER 7

# Welcome Home

**JJ** and Jo beamed at each other during the drive from Austin to Magnolia Bluff on Texas Highway 28. The sun lit up the green countryside, lush and blooming from recent rains that teased out the purple and yellow wildflowers of fall. The sun's warm glow kissed their skin as the open-air convertible teased Jo's hair and wisps of brown tendrils sailed around her face. Even JJ's hair joined in the unruly behavior. The conversation and Jo's singing offkey with the radio had them giggling.

"I do love being in love with you, sweetheart," JJ said, "but we're going to spend a lot of time at Lily's B&B to get these tangles out. I should have grabbed two ballcaps before accepting this rental."

"JJ, I'm not complaining. I'm glad you don't have to worry about work for a couple of weeks. It's a bright, autumn sunshiny day, and the open-air ride is fun." She patted his leg. "I'm with my man. I'll forget the hair tangles and only recall I'm having the time of my life with you."

"Honey, I wasn't grousing," JJ grinned, squeezing her hand. "I wish I'd bought two Texas Longhorn ballcaps." Smiling he added, "Your beautiful ebony hair looks great with that burnt orange colored hat."

Jo pointed excitedly at the white and green sign on the side of the road. "Oh, look. We're coming into Magnolia Bluff. I just love seeing welcome signs for Texas towns and the population numbers. But what does it mean when they say home to 9,825 friendly souls and 12 authors?"

"A good question. We'll have to ask. We are only a few minutes from Flower B&B. I'll park; you head in the back way and go upstairs to our assigned room. I am glad her business is so good that she has a phone app to confirm reservations. When we get settled, we'll plan our play time, sweetheart."

Jo laughed. "I want a massage at the spa Lily mentioned on her website. I think it was Bluff Spa and Salt Cave. After looking at all the services they offer, I might be gone the whole day."

"Hey." JJ frowned. "I'm not sure I want someone else's hands on your gorgeous bod where I can't get to it."

Jo leaned over and provided a reassuring kiss to his cheek. "Honey, I wasn't going without you. They do couples, but you'll have to behave yourself until we get back to the B&B."

"All right," JJ mumbled, "but…not right away. Say like the next time we come back, perhaps? Don't forget we have an in-room hot tub where I don't have to behave myself." Jo's disapproving glare was enough to get him to admit, "Uh, what I mean is yes, dear. Whatever you want, dear. Happy to do the couples spa thing and behave myself until we get back to our room, dear."

Jo giggled.

"We're here," JJ announced. "Let me park in the back and put the top up. Then we get to see Lily. I hope she has some snacks ready for us. I'm hungry."

Jo waited until the convertible got situated before she helped secure their luggage.

JJ took a deep breath and flung his arms wide. "Hurray, the peace and quiet of a B&B in the sleepy town of Magnolia Bluff. Maybe tomorrow we can drop in on some of our friends here and do a little catch up."

Jo's hair under the ballcap bounced as she nodded.

In no great hurry, they marched up the back steps and lazily reached for the door handle to enter. Lily appeared in the opening, beaming from ear to ear. She bellowed over her shoulder, "I told you they'd arrive today. Now you two drop those bags." She pointed an index finger to inside the kitchen. "Come let us greet you as town heroes we've never forgotten."

JJ and Jo stoically surveyed the throng of people eager to shake hands, hug, and air-kiss the town celebrities in true Texas fashion: with lots of noise.

JJ asked out of the side of his mouth, "Honey, you did tell Lily we were coming for peace and quiet? And that she shouldn't make a big fuss about us coming back, right?"

Jo appeared in shock and mumbled, "Uh-uh..."

Lily, ever the boisterous and loud hostess, pushed back a strand of jet-black hair from her face, and announced, "In case you've forgotten, this pair helped stop a human trafficking operation. And this young man—" she patted him on the arm— "saved our podcasting event more than once last year. He also single-handedly waxed ten ruffians who tried to get him to stop. Then, when I got jumped in the kitchen, this pretty, fresh-scrubbed-faced girl came to my aid. Armed with nothing more than a cast iron skillet, Jo laid out the attackers. I've got a dented skillet to prove it. Give them a quick greeting, then we can let them settle down for their quiet getaway. You might see 'em around, but they want time for romance. I know y'all understand."

JJ saw the dining room, sitting room, and foyer were packed with people waiting to greet them. He breathed in and out to reduce his anxiety at the near mob scene ready to descend. JJ sarcastically croaked into Jo's ear, "What, no high school marching band?"

Lily chuckled. "No, JJ. I don't have room for the band. I brought our two best trumpet players though. They're going to perform their rendition of Lonny Lupnerder's hit *It's Only a Lonely Bull*."

JJ swallowed hard at the pending serenade. Two young men came forward to introduce themselves. One stammered his name in awe of the two urban legends of Magnolia Bluff.

Jo glanced at JJ for reassurance. "We'd be honored to listen to your rendition, right, JJ? After dinner?"

Lily hollered, "Nah, Jo, they've been practicing. Hit it, guys—with feeling."

JJ and Jo shook hands or exchanged hugs with the well-wishers as the two musicians worked to hit the same notes from the sheet music that rustled with the dense movement of the crowd.

After an eternity of two minutes into their song, Jo gathered the boys into a quick thank-you hug.

JJ eyed Lily as she folded her arms.

Lily cleared her throat, and announced, "Okay, folks, time to go. These two need a break." She winked at JJ, and added, "We'll plan something else while they're in town."

Once in their room, JJ and Jo dropped into chairs, reveling in the blissful quiet. JJ patted his right ear to shake off the ringing of the trumpets. "I don't see us sneaking up on anybody around here," he commented. "Any idea what else Lily might be planning? We could barricade ourselves in here." With a sly look of amorous intent, he leaned forward. "I can see some advantages there."

"We're going to visit friends like Hank and Ann" Jo chided. "We'll keep our agenda a secret, to avoid ambush. I'll ask Lily to limit the events here. At least they didn't hound me for an interview, photos, or autographs. They like us as people."

JJ reached over and took her hand. "I know. I'd probably be disappointed if they hadn't done something to welcome us."

Jo looked at the familiar surroundings. Her favorite part of this B&B was the light flower décor and blooms bursting outdoors, visible through the window.

"I'm glad Lily kept the room the same. We had some delightful conversations in this suite. I wonder if the bathtub is as inviting as before."

"We could try it now if you like, sweetheart."

"I'd like to unpack and have a snack before, so I can relax with you."

JJ squeezed her hand and rubbed his thumb across her soft skin. "You were right, Jo. Magnolia Bluff was our best destination because no one knows about our work lives."

Jo reached over and smoothed JJ's hair back over his ear, but the moment got lost by a knock on the door. "Kids, I hope I'm not interrupting," Lily called, "brought up some snacks and a little vino to help get you in the mood." She laughed. "If I'm not already too late."

JJ winked at Jo. "Great, snacks. Wait a second, Lily, I gotta put something on before I open the door."

He heard Lily grumble, "I'm always up for a floor show, and you are a darling. I'll just leave this tray by the door and skedaddle. Talk later." JJ heard her last complaint. "I wonder if he was funning me." Then footfalls headed toward the stairs.

Jo swatted his arm and they laughed.

CHAPTER 8

# Vacation Mornings

**JJ** rested on one elbow dreamily studying Jo's features as the early morning light built in the room. He watched her breathing and resisted the temptation to touch and caress her features for fear of waking her. He moved his gaze to the lace curtains over the window, briefly watching the morning sun brighten.

Jo's eyes fluttered open, and she caught his gaze.

"Good morning, sweetheart." JJ whispered then added a kiss to her cheek. "Did you rest well?"

"I did. Why are you staring at me?"

"Just enjoying an unhurried view of my pretty lady. I trust the massage and lotion I used helped your rest. You sank into sleep with a heavy sigh."

Jo frowned, as she stretched. "Oh dear, I'm sorry I conked out and was less than amorous. I'll make it up to you. How early is it?"

"Judging from the noise echoing from the kitchen, I'd say time to get dressed and see what's for breakfast. The snack was great." He patted his tumbling stomach. "But I'm hungry and I bet you are too. I hope Renata is on duty."

Jo got wide-eyed and bolted to a sitting position. "You're right, and I didn't see her last night. I can't wait. Let's get dressed and head down. I want to see how she and Lily interact." She kissed him soundly. "More us time tonight."

"Yes, good idea. It'll be fun to explore the outdoors."

"After breakfast, we can go to Hank and Ann's, see Camila and rent horses to ride around the reservoir."

"Sounds good. I'll ask Lily if she can pack a picnic, with a couple of apples for the horses. I'll bring a swimsuit, if you will join me in the water."

"Yes," she crowed. "When we get back, we'll need the spa and rubdown shown on the website and…"

"Honey, let's not stuff a whole week into just one day." He hugged her. "We're here to relax and have fun each day, right?"

Jo looked so adorable with her sheepish grin, he had to kiss her again to put the smile back.

She added, "Sorry, yes, my love. Come on, let's get ready. I need coffee."

"I hogged the bathroom first the last time. Now it's your turn. If we go in together, we won't leave the room for hours."

Jo giggled and glided toward the open door, stopping long enough to grab her clothes.

They held hands down the stairs, inhaling the fresh scents of brewed coffee, sausages, bacon, and cinnamon. JJ asked, "Do you think breakfast tacos or waffles are this morning's special?"

"I don't care as long as it tastes as appetizing as it smells."

"And coffee."

"Yes, honey, coffee," she agreed.

At the landing, they turned toward the dining room. JJ noticed Lily in an animated conversation with a nicely dressed lady, who nodded at the standard Lily-barrage of questions.

Jo leaned in, and whispered, "She looks like a businesswoman with that styled hair and great shoes."

JJ chuckled. "Glad you notice those types of things." He tugged Jo's hand and tried to sneak behind the ladies.

Lily spun around. "These are the heroes I mentioned, Joyce. Kids, this is Joyce Blackstone, a new realtor working for the Magnolia Bluff Real Estate Agency. Joyce moved here with her son Jason a while back. I wanted to bring her up to speed on your selfless heroism on the town's behalf."

Joyce reached out to shake hands with Jo then JJ. She smiled. "I'm getting off the ground with my new sales role at the agency. They're teaching me from the ground up. If you need a realtor, I'd consider it an honor to help you find property here in our sleepy little town."

"Good to know," JJ replied. "Thanks." He reached an arm around Jo's waist to guide her to the dining room, but Jo had something else in mind.

"Real estate?" she asked. "As in something with property near the reservoir for swimming and camping?"

Stunned, JJ stood speechless. He watched the three women discussing possible properties for their consideration.

"We would need enough room for a couple of horses. We love to ride," added Jo.

JJ's heart leapt to his throat when Jo bubbled about access to town, roads, and new versus older homes. He chuckled at her antics and her genuine enthusiasm. He kissed her cheek, certain she didn't notice, and, after securing coffee and snagging a mini-muffin on a plate, headed to an open table beside a window with a view of the gardens he knew Jo would appreciate.

He studied the group and added the realtor's name to his phone to check on her background later.

Renata entered through the swinging doorway from the kitchen with items to add to the buffet. When she saw JJ, she gasped and nearly dropped the tray. She rushed to give him a hug, which he rose to receive.

JJ held Renata at arm's length. "You're certainly not the scared little girl I met last year. You've grown and are even prettier than I remember."

Renata blushed.

JJ heard the conversation from the foyer abruptly end, followed by Jo's steps and exclamation in Spanish, "Renata, I'm glad to see you!" She added a warm hug and laughed with the teen several times. "JJ and I hoped you'd be working this morning."

"I work every breakfast before school and several meals over the weekend when Lily asks."

Lily sidled up to Renata. "Okay, Ms. Renata," she insisted. "Let's allow these two to eat before the food gets cold. We've other guests to keep happy. Visiting needs to wait until after our chores. JJ, do you want breakfast burritos or waffles and eggs to quieten down that stomach I keep hearing?"

JJ looked at Jo and giggled. "Please, bring us both, Lily. Jo, I'll pour you some coffee."

"No, sir," Lily growled. "I'll get that. You two enjoy the garden view. The pink bougainvillea are growing wild this year; the hummingbirds love 'em."

She turned to fetch the coffee and shooed Renata back to the kitchen.

"Sweetheart, you seemed to like Joyce. What was the talk about property here in Magnolia Bluff for us to look at?"

Jo got almost as excited as she'd been in the foyer. "My imagination is running in overdrive, honey. I love the idea of a place big enough for a couple of horses, warm nights under the Texas stars, and escaping to the reservoir for picnics. Joyce seems like a nice lady. Maybe it won't hurt to look at what she might find." She inhaled and sipped her aromatic coffee and grinned. "I thought I'd die laughing when Lily stated that we'd need enough land for privacy so we could run to the reservoir naked for swimming. It reminded me of Ann and Hank's midnight secrets at their ranch."

Snickering slowly erased his objection to the idea. "There's no harm in looking, my love, and we'll see what she comes back with. As a newbie, I suspect she's anxious for a sale."

"Thanks, JJ. It could be a fun idea."

"Let's finish breakfast and visit Hank, Ann, and Camila. We both are looking forward to seeing them. I recommend we take swim gear and dress for riding. Did you bring your string bikini again this trip?"

"Nope. Something you'll like better. Lara gave it to me to test before the Hawaii shoot."

CHAPTER 9

# Visiting the Ranch

The other B&B guests kept Lily busy, and gave JJ and Jo time to enjoy their breakfast without the mother-hen-hovering routine.

"Honest, Lily, your food took away my appetite." JJ remarked when she paused for the fifth time.

"He's right, Lily. As delicious as we remembered. Thank you."

Lily beamed and slapped the table with glee. "What do you two love birds have in mind for today? Is there anything I can help with?"

JJ nodded. "Ms. Lily, we want to head over to Hank's ranch and maybe go for a picnic, if he can loan us some horses."

"Since the girls' adoption is finalized, JJ and I want to see Camila and how she's doing with her new family. We'd really like to ride the same horses we had before—Midnight and Lucy—and head to the reservoir for a swim. Can you please call and alert them?" Jo asked sweetly.

Lily's hand dove into her apron pocket for her phone. "Oh right, kids. I better call them so they don't shoot at you when you drive up. They've become extra fussy about visitors ever since they adopted the girls. Wished I'd thought to tell Hank that you'd like to come out when he dropped Renata off to work this morning."

"We thought we'd leave within the hour. If they're busy we can drive around, no problem. Can we take Renata home for you?"

"Actually, I need her here to help prepare the B&B ready for the fall season. School starts back soon, and I won't have hours available from her then. I'll bring her home later."

The call connected, and Lily punched the speaker button.

Hank answered, "Whatever you're selling, we don't need it. If this is about money I owe, leave a message at the tone, and we'll git back to you when I've got something to give you. If this is…"

JJ watched Lily's face contort into a disgusted glare at the phone.

"Hank, when are you going to get a decent phone that shows caller-ID? It's me, Lily." Lily pressed the mute button then looked at the couple. "He still uses that princess phone on the wall from the last century." Lily pressed to unmute. "I'm calling to tell you visitors will arrive at the ranch within the hour. They want to see Ann and Camila, maybe even you. Don't do your silly routine with your .45 Colt—*BANG, BANG, BANG—halt who goes there*—when Jo and JJ show up."

"No kidding?" he excitedly, replied. "Why didn't somebody say something about them being here?"

"If you'd answer your emails, Hank, you'd-a known." She sarcastically added, "Oh, that's right, you'd have to have an email account to do that, wouldn't you? They'll be there in a while and maybe rent some horses from you so you can pay your bills."

Lily disconnected, threw her hands to her sides with clenched fists, and stomped her feet. "For every one of us trying to keep up with the times and new technology, we gotta have some bonehead Luddite trying to cling to the last century."

"Lily, thanks for not letting us get shot going to Hank's," JJ deadpanned.

"That ain't happening on my watch, young'uns." Lily patted Jo's arm affectionately. "Now scoot so Renata and me can finish the chores."

JJ slowly pulled the car near the front porch and parked. Before the engine stopped, Camila and Ann boiled from the door. Hank limped behind using a walking stick for balance.

Jo was smothered first with hugs and affection from the girls, then by Hank. JJ got engulfed by both girls and cocked his head to shake hands with Hank.

"Hank, I can't help but notice you seem to be favoring your left leg. I hope it's nothing too serious."

"The old coot's been limping for almost a week," Ann snapped. "One of the horses stepped on his foot, but he won't see the doctor to find out how bad it really is. He'd much rather find what he can get over the counter at the pharmacy for a crushed foot. Stubborn old man."

Hank looked at his feet for a moment then pointedly looked at Ann as if to start a heated debate. JJ said, "Let me know if I can take you to the doc, Hank."

Jo looked at JJ and changed the subject. "We met a realtor named Joyce Blackstone at the B&B who said she would search for some property for us while we are here. I think Lily goaded her, but I like the idea of looking, and so does JJ."

"Jo, I don't think they're interested in our notions. We were hoping to rent the two horses, Hank, if they are available."

"Camila, are Midnight and Lucy up for riding today?"

She nodded with a smile, her glossy curls bouncing. "Yes. Can I go along?"

"Not today," Ann interjected. "But you could saddle them up. Hank would take forever to walk to the corral."

Camila raced off. JJ marveled about how healthy and happy she appeared. He sent a knowing smile to Jo about the teen.

Hank limped closer and leaned on his walking stick. "Paying a realtor six-percent commission is like paying an escort service a commission for introductions to a… You know what I mean, young man."

Ann smacked the hand on top of the stick, and hissed, "Hank, none of that in front of Jo. I'm glad Camila took off."

"What I meant to say…" Hank cleared his throat. "You might take a look while you're riding to the reservoir. There's a piece of property across the road adjacent to ours. It recently came on the market. No one's lived there in over twenty years, maybe twenty-five. Someone mentioned the taxes stopped getting paid a couple of months ago. If it goes on the market, it'll be at a discount to get the taxes paid and property renovated. I haven't been on the land in a long time, but I recall lots of holes, like someone pulled out trees or maybe tried to put in fence posts closer to the ranch building. It's fairly rundown and would need to get leveled, but the barn might be worth salvaging."

JJ noticed Jo's grin and enthusiasm making her eyes brighten. "Hank, that's a great thought. We'll try to take a look and maybe get some pictures. If we're interested, we'll need a sketch of the boundaries, and maybe your thoughts on what it's value should be."

"I'll work on a sketch while you're out riding. I used to have drawings of the neighboring tracts. I'll try to find them."

They walked to the corral, moving slow so Hank could keep up.

"Hank, would you recommend they buy that parcel with a ramshackle building? I thought you liked this couple."

"I do like them. They'd be close for the girls, and someone would be living there rather than the squatters which sometimes show up in the summer. You've seen them."

Ann looped her arm through his. "I knew you cared about them."

CHAPTER 10

# Looking for a Dream

**JJ** and Jo added bathing suits and lunch into the saddlebags. Grinning like Cheshire Cats, they mounted their favorite rides and waved see-ya later, as they guided the horses out of the gate. The clopping of the hooves sounded like drumbeats for a song. The weather was warm with a gentle breeze that rustled the leaves and let the clouds meander across the blue sky.

JJ waved his right hand with open palm over the scenery peeking through the trees. "The countryside is beautiful."

"It is. If we get into the foothills a bit higher in elevation, I bet the vistas are heart-stopping. Thank you, honey, for letting me talk you into Magnolia Bluff. I feel peaceful here. And I love to ride." Jo used the ends of the reins and flicked them. "Ya, ya, Midnight," she added. And the race was on.

JJ realized her slight head start might prevent him from catching let alone beating her. Her skills were superb, riding Midnight like they were one. He admired the view for a moment. "Giddy-up, let's get 'em, Lucy." JJ hated inhaling the dust behind her and kept to one side. When they reached the intersection and she slowed to a stop, he shortened her lead.

JJ noticed her look toward the heavy wrought-iron gate that opened to the former ranch belonging to Mateo Hernandez. The stronghold had housed youngsters trafficked by his cartel until it got busted up on their last trip here.

He stopped beside her. "Jo, are you all right, sweetheart?"

"Yes, I am recalling that part of our visit. It was horrific, but we helped put them out of business." She looked at him her eyes heavy with moisture. She brushed away the tears. "We saved Camila and Renata too."

"Yes, we did good together." He watched to see if she broke down.

Jo held her chin high. "It's a shame Madison had to face her ordeal with those monsters. Lily shared pieces of the story, but it must have nearly broken her. She's one tough lady."

"Madison sure is. I hope we get the chance to see her. She had Hernandez sent to the supermax prison in Colorado. The place from which no escape is possible. Too bad he bought his way back to Beaumont and escaped from there. The man's got friends in high places."

They nudged the horses down the trail toward the reservoir.

"I did ask around while I was in Matamoros but got nothing specific. I was told it might take a while to receive information on him. We won't tell Madison he got free, will we?"

"Sooner or later, Mateo will make a mistake, and he'll pay for his crimes. However, my dear, we have some property to scan, which I think is on the left."

JJ spotted the signs for No Trespassing and Private Property. "Honey, it appears we won't get in without breaking the locks on the gate. Plus, with those signs, we could end up seeing Chief Tommy Jager under the wrong circumstances."

Jo dismounted and looped the reins around a tree. She took out her phone and started clicking. "JJ, do you see a building over there? It sure is tough with the wild overgrown mess."

JJ stood in the stirrups; Lucy stepped sideways at the weight shift. "Easy, girl. Hold on." He grabbed his phone and snapped some pictures.

Jo mounted Midnight. "Let's ride down the fence line and take more shots. I like your idea of getting photos from different vantage points."

They rode down the trail aligned to the property, catching different angles. "I like the openness, JJ. It needs a lot of work. Any idea how much land is here?"

"Maybe ten acres or a little over four hectares, but it's hard to tell without the plat map. Hank may have that when we return. Check out the house with the flattened roof."

"I'd say it's about two hundred meters from the gate."

"Right. The adjacent building, which might be the barn, seems intact but weathered."

Jo stopped and stared at JJ. "Do you recall the antique store in town last year? They had signs painted and carved on weathered wood from old buildings. Maybe that's a popular artform here."

"I do remember seeing a couple of hysterical sayings, like *'One drink away from telling everybody what I really think!'* struck me.

They laughed and snapped a few more shots at the corner of the parcel. "Let's find that water and enjoy a swim," JJ announced. "Every reservoir has a dam to control the water intake. At some point a hike might be in order to see it."

"I'm hungry, too. The way Midnight is pawing the dirt, I think he smells water." Jo patted the horse's neck. "Midnight, let's go." They took off at an easy trot.

Both horses headed to the water's edge and bent for refreshment, slurping the liquid over their bits. JJ watched Jo slide off her saddle and gather towels wrapped around the wine bottle. There was nothing he enjoyed more than watching his pretty wife. He dismounted then pulled out their food and some oats for the horses packed in feedbags.

"You got the horses, JJ? I'll go find a spot for them…and us."

"Yep. Got 'em." He held the reins. Once they drank their fill, they shook their heads sending a spray of droplets in all directions. He secured them to trees in the shady area where Jo had set up camp. He turned in time to see the pile of her jeans and tee shirt on the ground. His breath caught and jaw dropped when she turned.

Jo pirouetted. "You like, honey?"

The cat caught his tongue, so he nodded, captivated by the sight. JJ appreciated her in any outfit, or nothing at all.

She stomped her foot with the pretty glittery-pink toenails catching the sun. "Please say something."

JJ cleared his throat. "Sweetheart, you're lovely. Four perfectly cut triangles of brown and black geometric shapes, connected by translucent ties, showing every possible square inch of skin, yet decency maintained, complements your bronzed skin, perfectly. How's that?"

Jo laughed then scampered toward the water, her dark hair waving on her back. She looked over her shoulder. "That is exactly the sort of sweet talk I was hoping you'd say. Come on, and please, bring a towel. I forgot." She squealed when she splashed into the water.

JJ skimmed off his pants and shirt, stacking them neatly by her clothes, then dashed after her. Walking into the tepid water he noticed it felt wonderful against his skin. He looked at Jo and didn't notice goosebumps so assumed she felt the same. They swam a bit, splashed, laughed, and enjoyed the refreshment.

"How 'bout we dry off some and eat? I'm hungry," JJ suggested.

"Good idea." She playfully jumped on his back piggy-back style. "Carry me out and we can look at our photos while we eat."

He set her down, then grabbed the towel and wrapped it around her. JJ shook his head, tossing drops everywhere, and pushed the strands out of his face. Jo toweled off and wiped down his back as they walked toward the horses. They received a whinnied welcome.

JJ attached the oat feedbags to the horses while Jo set up the blanket and laid out the food.

"Honey, open the wine, please."

JJ grabbed the bottle and corkscrew, making short work of the easy task. They sat on the blanket, and he poured the wine.

Jo raised her glass. "To us, and maybe a new vacation home."

JJ touched her glass and kissed her. "To a fun future. You always have great ideas."

They munched and sipped. Jo reviewed her photos. "JJ, if we cleared the brush, we could have both a vegetable and flower garden."

"We could, but because of the huge deer population, we need to build some tough fences. I don't know exactly how it would be maintained while we're away."

She frowned. "Oh, right. I hadn't thought about that. I'm just dreaming. Oh, but hey, this near to Hank and Ann, perhaps we could have Camila as the caretaker while we are away."

He hugged her close. "Dreams are good. I think the house needs removal. It doesn't seem like there's enough to salvage. What sort of house would you like? One story, or two?"

She giggled. "Is this a *maybe we could build something*? If so, then two."

"Okay, but only if we have the bright colors like our home in Brazil. It makes me happy to walk inside every day. I'd like a similar look and feel."

"I can do that." She chewed on the crackers and cheese. "A nice relaxing spot, honey."

"I agree. We need to finish here and get the horses back. If you'll pick up, I'll take the them for another drink. Uh, you want to wear that back to the ranch? It looks good."

She laughed and kissed his cheek. "But not comfortable when I take off at a gallop to reach the ranch first."

"Oh, you're on, baby. An even start this time, and you can eat my dust."

## CHAPTER 11

# Weighing the Options

JJ and Jo tied in the race back to the ranch. Camila accepted the horses, promising them both a good rubdown and brushing.

"Good race, honey," JJ said, with a smug facial expression. "We tied."

"It was a blast." Jo patted his arm. "Next time I won't let you win." Camila tugged the reins to coax the animals towards the corral. "Thank you, Camila," Jo said with a quick hug. "Midnight is amazing."

Camila grinned. "He's my favorite too."

"Glad you packed the oats," JJ added. "They enjoyed every morsel, and the apples made them whinny."

Hank hobbled onto the porch with a roll of paper held loosely in one hand. "Come into the shade. Ann's bringing out some fresh lemonade." He sat in the closest chair to the rectangular table, and unrolled the paper. "Kids, I found the plat maps with my tract, and those in the near vicinity. Come take a look."

JJ pulled up a chair. He reached for a couple of stones on the ground to help hold the map corners. Jo sat on the other side of Hank.

Ann arrived with a tray. She poured glasses of sweet and sour lemonade. "Fresh-squeezed, Jo. Let me know what you think." She set the tray on the side table, then took the seat across from

Hank. "Our spread is the spot lined off in the middle of the map," she announced with a hint of pride.

JJ traced some of the lines with his finger. Based on the notations, he mentally calculated the size of the property. "It appears like your parcel is around twelve or thirteen hectares or, as you would say, about thirty acres. Was that the standard division of the land?"

"You're right, son, we have just over thirty acres. These parcels each contained five acres. We bought the adjoining pieces to get the water. Ann liked this view for the house with the road close for mail and such." He swept his arm toward his wife. "Our borders extend another twenty acres into the west behind Ann. We keep a modest number of cows on that land and rotate them between pastures for grazing."

"Ten acres seems like an enormous amount of property to maintain, Jo."

Jo pulled her bottom lip under her front teeth as if chewing on it, then wrinkled her nose. "It is, especially if we are thinking of a getaway location, not fulltime. But I do like the open space. We aren't grazing cows."

JJ sipped the chilled glass and licked his lips. "Ann, this is mouth-puckering delicious with a sweet kick." He took another taste. "I agree, Jo. Hank, do you know anything about the owners of the property? We took a bunch of pictures from many angles, but what appears to have been the house is definitely toast. The other building seems salvageable, but until we look around, we won't know. Do you know anything about the prior residents?" JJ watched Ann and Hank, hoping they'd share the history.

Hank leaned back in his chair and stretched out his legs. His head tilted as if recalling. "Thomas Stevens, and his pretty bride Marissa, lived there as newlyweds. Thomas was a nice enough lad, handy around the place. He worked at the bank as an auditor, I think. Is that right, Ann?"

"It is. They helped build that place probably thirty-five years ago. The whole community raised the barn, but a contractor built the house. I liked little Marissa. Not even twenty when they moved here. I think she said they married when she turned legal." Ann poured a refill and grinned after a sip. "That girl had a green thumb. All the flowers bloomed in a multitude of colors—like a rainbow it was. The area was always well tended. We'd talk now and then. They invited folks over for barbequing in the summer. Always a nice spread, good company. It was her friendliness and his desire to be open with the community for the financial aspect. Their life was perfect until she got so sick."

JJ looked from one to the other and noticed Jo looking sad. "What was the matter?"

Hank nodded then shook his head with an expression of sadness. "Marissa was diagnosed with ovarian cancer, Stage 4. It was so far along the doctors said *Try to make her comfortable*. So, he did. Thomas spent every waking hour working at the bank then caring for Marissa in the evenings. Like us, they weren't blessed with children either." He scratched his head. "Ann, didn't he get some help while he worked as well?"

"Yep, the ladies in the community joined together. People signed up to deliver meals daily, and groceries when needed, but Annie sat by Marissa's side every day. I don't recall where Annie went after Marissa passed. I know she often stayed on a cot in the extra room so Thomas could wake her when he went to work." Ann looked out toward an unseen memory then nodded as if watching the scene unfold like a movie. "Flagstone, I believe was her last name. Showed up in town one day and worked part time at the café as a waitress. She was younger than Marissa. She helped with some of the barbeques Marissa offered for her husband's bank customers. The two were quite close. Annie was broken up at the end. Hank, didn't Thomas disappear not too long after Marissa died?"

Hank leaned forward, putting his elbows on the table and palms crossed. "It was kind-a strange. After the funeral, he holed up in his house, taking a leave from the bank. I heard a week or so after, he went to work for maybe a month then one day never returned. Can't say about Annie, but, Ann, didn't the ladies help that poor child after the service at the cemetery to get a ride into town?"

Ann sat straighter and cocked her head. "Several ladies, including Mary Lou Fight, checked on Annie for a few days, then I think the girl rode a bus out of town. I haven't heard any more about her. The community took it hard. We were all sad."

Jo perked up. "So, with all that, why didn't someone buy the place?"

Hank outlined the Stevens' parcel with his finger. "A couple of years after, I went to the bank and asked if it would be available. I was told the property remained in the Stevens' name, and taxes were paid annually. We figured he might come back someday. As long as the taxes got paid, it was unsellable. A couple of months ago, the payment for taxes stopped. Gunter Fight at First National Bank of Magnolia Bluff is looking at options. I know this because we grab lunch in town together once or twice a month. Gunter knows I wanted the parcel, so he tells me things."

"JJ, what do you think?" Jo asked, with bright eyes and that smile he loved.

"I think we've learned more than we expected. Let's take ourselves back to Flower and talk about the options. Plus, you still have possible options from Joyce Blackstone." He stood and reached a hand toward Hank, who also rose. "Hank, thank you for the information. May I snap a picture of the layout?"

"No, just take the plat with you. Bring it back next time you visit."

Jo hugged Ann. "Thank you, Ann. Sorry you lost your friend."

Ann smiled and patted Jo's arm. "We have the girls, we're all good. Maybe you'll move to Magnolia Bluff and we'll be neighbors. Camila, honey, they're leaving. Come say goodbye."

Camila trotted over. "Nice to see you. Next time, I'll ride with you and show you some awesome spots."

Jo ruffled her hair. "Great idea. I love this area and want more memories."

JJ opened the car door for Jo, placed the rolled maps in back, then went to the driver's side. They waved as they drove away.

Laughing, Jo remarked, "What a fascinating story. I think we need to conduct some research."

JJ patted her knee. "I could not agree more. We'll talk over wine and dinner."

"Deal." She leaned over and kissed him.

After returning from Hank and Ann's, they walked into the B&B, the scent of roasted garlic and fresh bread promised a pasta dinner. JJ and Jo decided dinner at Flower made sense.

"Jo." He placed his hand on her back to guide her upstairs. "Lily always seems to hit the right combination of meals."

Jo laughed. "She does. Her pasta is mouthwatering. Let's get changed and enjoy a nice glass of wine with dinner."

At the landing, JJ nuzzled her neck and tapped her hip with the rolled map. "Afterwards, how about we have a slice or two of cheesecake and coffee upstairs while we look through the pictures."

"Great idea. Maybe relax in that claw foot tub." She danced to the door. "I want to schedule spa stuff for tomorrow morning after breakfast, if you'll join me. You know, set up a mani-pedi, and massage for two."

"Not certain about the first two, but in for the third, for sure."

Jo changed into a short pink skirt and printed silk blouse. JJ enjoyed watching her to the point he failed to change. Jo kissed him quick. "Sorry to distract you, honey. I'll call Bluff Spa and Salt Cave to see if we can do all of that, plus that renowned salt session. Great for the skin." Grinning, she gave him a smug look, then called.

JJ hadn't heard all the conversation, but watching her animated expression, he knew success when she nodded, saying *Thank you*. "I'm ready, Jo. Are we on for the morning?"

"Yep, and I can have my legs waxed too."

"I'm sure that's a good thing." Looping an arm around her he added, "Let's go get supper. I have another idea for later. I'll share with you after dessert."

"Hmmm."

Lily spotted the pair as they entered the dining area. She clapped. "I was hoping my pasta could tempt you to eat here. I reserved the table by the window. I'll light fresh candles after you sit. I have three different pasta styles tonight that Renata and I made earlier today. There's fusilli, farfalle, and macaroni. You should have seen how excited she was to learn how to make each style. She did a great job." Pulling Jo along toward the table, she inhaled ever so slightly. "We can use either a traditional mushroom marinara, creamy Alfredo, or pesto sauces. I also have grilled chicken because I knew you liked that with your pasta." She swept her arm indicating they should sit.

JJ pushed in Jo's chair while Lily lit the candles. "Lily, this is lovely. Thank you so much."

"Lily, based on the smells floating in the air the moment we walked in, JJ and I knew no other place would be as delicious."

Lily leaned over and patted Jo's arm like a doting mom. "I made some cheesecake and crème brûlée for dessert, if you are interested. Did you want red or white wine?"

"Lily, red tonight," JJ replied.

"I'll get the wine and grab some warm breadsticks for you. Then I want to hear about your day." Lily rushed off, disappearing through the door to the kitchen.

They both laughed. "She has more energy when she talks than any kid." Jo giggled. "I'm glad Renata is working with her. I guess they overcame the language barrier with a mixture of English and Spanish. I noticed both girls doing well with their English."

Lily appeared with filled glasses in hand and warm bread wrapped in a toweled basket. A small metal container brimmed with fresh-whipped butter. "Here you go. Now what can I get you two?"

JJ gestured Jo should start. "I think I'll take the Alfredo sauce over the farfalle with chicken on the side. Maybe a small salad with Italian dressing, if it's not too much trouble."

"Sounds good, Jo, and I may sample, but I'd like the mushroom marinara with chicken over traditional macaroni, please. And a salad like Jo's."

"Gotcha. I'll get the salads out shortly. I need to take the order from Mr. Montgomery and Ms. Duncan, so it might be a minute. He's a financial investor, and she is his auditor, I think he said. They aren't a couple, at least as far as the rooms are concerned. He's planning to speak to Gunter tomorrow." She tapped her chin and squinted. "I wish I knew why, but I'll find out sooner or later."

JJ noticed the pair. Mr. Montgomery, early forties, was well over six feet, close-cropped black hair, dark eyes, and generous mouth. Even in jeans and tee shirt, he appeared fit. His biceps, and narrow waist, visible with the tucked in tee shirt suggesting an athlete. Ms. Duncan looked closer to fifty with short greying hair styled nicely. Her longer shorts and tailored blouse indicated her good taste in clothes.

"Cheers, honey." JJ lifted his glass.

"To us," she added after their glasses touched with a familiar ring. "Ms. Duncan has great taste in casual wear. That's one of Destiny Fashions' designs." She broke off a piece of her breadstick and sampled it. "Glad I didn't bring the same outfit with me. And she has a definite preference for gold jewelry. A professional look even at dinner. Impressive."

Lily was bubbly as always when she talked. She was a part of the atmosphere. JJ noticed there were only the two tables occupied, so Lily would be able to get the information if available. JJ was curious now but tucked it away to mull over later.

JJ and Jo chatted while enjoying the delicious meal and Lily's commentary as she served.

"Lily, as usual your food spoiled our appetites."

"But," Jo grinned and giggled. "JJ and I would like a plain cheesecake and crème brûlée to take to our room." Leaning over, she added, "And maybe a bottle of that delicious red wine."

"Sure thing. Coming right up. JJ, can you carry everything?"

"Yes, ma'am. I got this. Thank you."

When they started out the door to the stairs, JJ overheard Ms. Duncan say, "Calvin, we want to get a look at the records if possible. The bank holds the paper at this point."

Since JJ had no frame of reference, he filed it to consider later.

"Come on, Jo. We have pictures to review and plans to discuss."

CHAPTER 12

# What's Wrong with This Picture?

Morning's sunrise brightened the room by degrees. With dawn, the breeze through the open window carried the fragrance of flowers from Lily's gardens. Jo overheard the birds greeting one another and grinned when she saw JJ still slumbering beside her. She recalled their discussion of the property. The pictures allowed their imaginations to overflow with the lure of a place to relax—to enjoy community. It appealed to Jo, but she wasn't sure if JJ saw advantages in a less stressful place. She eased from bed like a swan through water with no ripple. She collected the outfit sitting on the chair and disappeared into the bathroom.

The running water hid her humming a little tune, as she looked forward to the salt cave. She toweled off, smoothed on lotion, dressed, and applied a little mascara. Smiling into the mirror, she approved the results. In seconds she twisted her hair into a chignon to keep it off her neck. Small ear studs, her wedding ring, and a squirt of perfume finished her morning ritual.

JJ was smiling. "I can't believe you can wake up, sneak out of bed and get yourself together without me hearing you." He reached for her hand and pulled her into his lap. "You look perfect and rested."

She gave him a sweet kiss that promised more later. "I feel terrific. But, honey, we need to head down to enjoy breakfast before we leave for the spa."

"Won't take a moment, unless you want to move our appointment to this afternoon." His smoldering eyes indicated he was all for it.

"You and I both think it's rude to change an appointment on short notice." She rose. "I'll wait here while you get ready, and we'll eat. Can we have breakfast mimosas?"

"I like it. Sure."

JJ emerged from the bathroom dressed in comfortable shorts and button-down shirt with short sleeves. He added his sandals. "Let's go. I'll carry the dishes to the kitchen."

She took his free hand. "I liked our talk last night. Do you think this might work as a destination target for staycations? I do worry that the photographers might find us. It wouldn't be as secure as São Paulo, but to be honest I like that aspect."

"It's something we need to look at seriously. With a large property, we could have some level of security and privacy, Jo. But sooner or later someone will discover us."

They entered the dining room and headed for the empty table. Noise emitted from the kitchen; coffee stood waiting on the buffet.

"JJ, do you want to start with a cup of coffee, and then we can get a mimosa with breakfast?" He started to move past her. "I'll grab it. You have a seat. I'll be right back."

Jo turned with brimming cups and headed his way.

"It's weird not seeing Lily yet," JJ said.

"I'm right here," Lily announced, causing Jo to nearly fumble the cups. "Are you two ready to order?" she added after Jo sat.

"You walk like a cat, Lily," Jo chuckled.

"And you served that coffee like an experienced waitress. Want a job while you're in town? With your smile, I bet the tips would be fantastic."

Jo shook her head, still tittering. "I'd like a mimosa, scrambled eggs, and berries—any kind, please."

"I'm in for the mimosa and three eggs over easy with any sort of fried potatoes, sausage, and fruit, please."

"No problem. You want the drinks first?"

They nodded, and Lily rushed toward the kitchen.

"I am looking forward to the spa. Lily raves about the place." Jo picked up the glass Lily delivered. "JJ, I guess I forgot to mention, we are getting a couples massage." Her big brown eyes focused on his.

"I'll drink to that, love."

"Hi, you two," Joyce blurted then clapped her hand over her mouth as her face turned red. "I'm sorry. Did I mess up a moment? I can come back."

JJ stood and pulled out a chair. "Please, Joyce. Join us. Right, Jo?"

"Yes. We're just having breakfast before heading to the spa. I was able to schedule us in this morning for the works. Would you like breakfast?"

Joyce took the seat and appeared to collect herself. "I just dropped Jason at day camp this morning. He enjoys the activities, and it keeps him outside most of the day. I wanted him to meet some kids before school starts. He's at that shy age and doesn't make friends easily."

"That seems like a good plan. Perhaps we can meet him while we're here." Jo smiled, sensing by Joyce's fidgeting that she had a different agenda. "Did you have something for us?"

Joyce's face blossomed into a grin. "I did. I found the cutest places…"

"Hi there, Joyce," Lily interrupted. "Did you want to order a mimosa and breakfast too?"

Joyce looked over. "Hi, Lily. No mimosa, but a plate of your French toast and sausage would be nice with a cup of coffee." She returned her face toward Jo. "It's not often I get the treat of breakfast at Flower. Though I do try to bring Jason once in a while."

Lily set breakfast for Jo and JJ, then returned with coffee for Joyce. "Back soon, enjoy."

"Thank you," Jo and JJ said.

"Joyce," JJ asked, "do you mind if we start?"

"Please, go ahead."

"You were saying you…" Jo inclined her head as she loaded up a forkful of food.

"Yes, well, I found three properties I think you'll like. Negotiable prices and financing available. The properties are well maintained—no upgrades needed. Established neighbors and sidewalks, if you like to stroll after a long day like I do."

"Wow, thanks." Jo felt a reality check to the gut. "I hadn't thought you'd have success this fast."

JJ leaned over and kissed her cheek while his hand patted her thigh. A surge of reassurance raced through her. "We'd love to take a look."

Relief crossed Joyce's face. "Oh, good. That's actually why I came by early. We can see them all this afternoon starting around one."

Jo chewed slowly while calculating the timing. "We should be finished with our spa appointment by then."

Lily slid Joyce's plate across in front of her, and extra mimosas for Jo and JJ. She winked at Jo and grinned. "Enjoy your day, you two."

"Yummy," Joyce voiced after the first bite. "Lily's cooking is always good. I'll meet you here at one and be your chauffer."

Jo smiled as she took a fresh sip of her beverage.

"Thank you, Joyce," added JJ.

JJ looked around, instantly comfortable with the quiet décor of the spa. Soft music floated in the air along with the scent of lavender. He squeezed Jo's hand. "This looks interesting."

She patted his flank and giggled. "It'll be fun. With any luck, we might get another glass of champagne. I have a nice mellow glow."

"Good morning."

JJ noted the man displayed distinctively Nordic features, framed by sandy, blond hair, long on top but with shaved sides. His intense blue-grey eyes took an inventory of each of them.

"I believe you must be Mr. and Mrs. Rodreguiz, here for your ten o'clock appointment, right?"

Jo extended her hand. "Hi, I'm Jo. This is my husband, JJ. You must be Stefan."

He shook her hand and then turned it to look at her nails. "You indicated a manicure, but your nails look perfect."

"Thank you. But I like to keep them that way. I'm hoping for a color change."

A woman's voice interjected. "Hi, I'm Marta. I'll handle the mani-pedi for you. Did you want a wax, too?"

JJ turned toward the voice and noticed a generous smile on a tanned face, with purple and turquoise hair caught up in a ponytail. The colors suited her complexion and blended with her silken robe. Her hair bounced from her constant movement that jiggled from head to toes, like a kid on too much sugar.

"Yes, please. JJ is going to try a pedicure and maybe a nail buff, too."

"Stefan," Marta said, "they also signed up for the salt cave and a couples massage." She looped her arm around Jo's elbow and guided her toward the nail station. "We've only opened this

57

location recently. Stefan and I started this concept in Florida. It was such a success we decided on our own franchise, expanding to Texas first. The Texas Hill Country is lovely, and we've done well since opening."

"Awesome. We found out about this location when we booked our reservation at Flower B&B. Lily recommended you. We're celebrating our anniversary."

"Splendid. This is a perfect venue to share with your honey." Leaning closer, Marta added, "We enjoy the salt cave at least once a week after we close."

A door marked *Women's Locker-room* opened. JJ recognized Ms. Duncan from the evening before at Flower. He nodded, but before he spoke, her eyes flashed in recognition then looked away as she hurried out the door. He shook his head confused.

Marta indicated JJ needed to take the seat to the right of Jo. She filled the tubs by their feet with warm water containing effervescing salts.

Jo kicked off her sandals then slid her feet into the water. "Ah." She sighed and closed her eyes.

JJ followed suit. "Jo this feels relaxing."

"Yes. It gets better, I promise."

Two and half hours of pampering felt like minutes. They walked hand-in-hand back to Flower.

"Jo, I have to admit, Marta and Stefan know how to remove tension. I've had massages before, but Stefan hit the tight muscles in all the right pressure points. You do great massages, sweetheart, but his strong hands demanded even the toughest areas yield. How about you?"

"One of the best massages ever. I'm glad you gave them a good tip. I've heard other models talk about the benefits of halotherapy, but I never had time. I feel invigorated."

"We may need to return for another session before we leave town."

Lily greeted them. "How was it? Did you leave your stress behind?"

Jo hugged Lily. "Wonderful. The salt cave made my skin so soft. Here, feel." She extended her cheek and Lily touched it with her fingertips.

"Wow, very soft. If it removes wrinkles too, I'd go every week." Lily inclined her head toward the dining room. "Joyce arrived a few minutes ago. Did you want sandwiches to eat while you tour the houses? I can pack y'all a picnic in minutes. I'm excited you're looking at homes here. Joyce said she picked the best little places available."

"We'd enjoy sandwiches to go, Lily. But we'd like to run up and change. Let Joyce know we'll be right back." JJ pulled Jo toward the stairs, and they dashed up, almost racing. At the top, he paused and looked back. "Maybe a couple of those cookies I smell…chocolate chip I bet."

"Right away." Lily laughed and JJ heard her feet retreat as they hurried to their room.

He opened the door and pulled Jo into a quick nuzzle.

"Honey, let's get changed. We don't want to keep Joyce waiting," she whispered.

JJ opened his drawer to grab fresh shorts. "Honey, did you move Hank's plat map? I wanted to look at it again later after Joyce's options."

"No. But, why did you leave your laptop on the floor by the bed? I don't recall you trying to sneak in work this morning." She held it up.

JJ felt annoyed. "Thank you. I'll lock it away." He mentally recounted the activities from the night before and was certain he hadn't moved the laptop.

Jo got on her knees where the computer had been. She peeked into the open space and pulled the paper roll from under the

59

bed. "JJ, here's the map." She handed it to him. "It must have been pushed there after dessert, and we didn't notice it this morning."

"Thanks. It's in the drawer for later." He glanced around and realized the room hadn't been made up yet, which made sense that Lily would do it in the afternoon since she had other guests.

"JJ!" Jo tugged on his arm, nose-to-nose with an odd expression. "Are you okay?"

He laughed, not wanting to worry her. "You bet. I was thinking of all the fun we had last night. I was too distracted to put things away. You do that to me."

Her expression appeared less than convinced, but she was ready. She ran her fingers through his hair. "You look perfect. Let's do this. Today is starting so nice."

Joyce met the couple in the foyer as Lily brought out a bag. "Joyce, I packed a sandwich for you as well and bottles of water. Have fun."

"Thank you." Jo plucked the bag from Lily.

"My car is right outside. Any of the three houses I think will work for what you said you needed, Jo."

CHAPTER 13

# This, Not That

After the third and final house, JJ noticed Jo seemed pensive. Joyce tried to generate a discussion, citing different considerations for each of the properties. Jo nodded or weakly smiled but added no comments.

Parked at the front of Flower, JJ commented, "Joyce, thank you. You've given us much to consider. We'd like to discuss the possibilities over dinner. How 'bout we call you tomorrow or the day after?" He opened the door for Jo, who stood and put on her practiced smile.

JJ saw the disappointment flicker across Joyce's eyes, then she straightened her shoulders, a pitcher who missed the strike zone but had another throw. "I understand. You two discuss and…oops. It's later than I thought. I need to pick up Jason. Call me tomorrow and let me know your thoughts." With a quick wiggle of her fingers, Joyce took off.

JJ held Jo's hand. They silently ambled to Flower's entrance. Before Jo marshaled her thoughts, the door burst open.

Lily stood, tapping her foot. "Come on, you two. We've tried to keep the food warm. Renata is leaving shortly, and I don't wanna do the dishes alone."

JJ brightened at the distraction. "Lily, if she needs to go, I'll help you with the dishes."

Jo nodded but offered no comment.

JJ pushed in her seat and sat across from her. He took her hand, running his thumb over her soft skin. "Honey, you've hardly said anything. And you look so sad. Talk to me."

"Sweetheart, those houses aren't what I had in mind. It was a bad idea to look. I'm sorry."

JJ noticed emotions struggling to surface. "Okay, tell me more."

"I don't want a quaint little one-story with small…everything. I don't want neighbors so close you can hear them chew. I'm not interested in a white picket fence, or small sidewalk around the neighborhood. Each of the properties made me feel claustrophobic."

"You could tell her."

Jo nodded. "I could, but she was so excited. I do hate disappointing people."

"I know, but your feelings count."

"I am under a microscope when I work. I need to live where I see someone by mutual invitation. Or get on a horse and ride to meet them."

He held both her hands and stared into her beautiful eyes. "My love, I believe it's important to shop other options. And you proved it by identifying what you don't want. I have to agree they appear less private. I've lived on large properties with lots of space around, too. If your heart is set on the property complete with ramshackle house and decaying barn, then okay. If we want to look at another place in Brazil when we return, I won't object. What would you like?"

Jo beamed between sniffled threatening tears. "Seriously. You aren't mad?"

JJ shook his head and kept his eyes locked on hers. "How can I get angry when you're speaking your heart? That's what our marriage is all about. Let's reach out to Hank and Ann to ask for their advice on next steps with the bank. I'll start some research so we get a better perspective. I'd like a smile back on your pretty face, honey."

Jo's eyes brightened, and she pulled at his hand and kissed it. "Thank you."

Calvin pulled the car into a space behind the B&B. He turned off the vehicle and huffed, "What an odd duck. I thought we bonded over the discussion on my short football career. When I pivoted to talk about the desire for our financial group to invest, he stopped listening. I felt he shut down, and we had no common ground. Stacie, you were there. What's your perspective on his cordial but uninvolved response?"

Stacie, lost in her own thoughts, didn't respond. Calvin reached his hand in front of her face and snapped his fingers. "Stacie? Are you in there? I said, what was your take on Gunter Fight?"

Jarred back to the present, Stacie fretted. "Calvin, you came on a little too strong. One minute you are doing an end run around to get the needed yardage, the next minute you want to buy the bank so Gunter can retire to the home and wife. What if that's the last thing he wants? One conversation, as you know, doesn't build a relationship with anyone. He's never met you before. Yes, he's in Texas. Of course, he likes football. But you don't come with a local stamp of approval or recommendation."

Annoyed at the stark observation, Calvin pulled the keys from the ignition and angled toward her. "Fine, Duncan, how would you have played it?"

Stacie bristled at the comment, meeting the prolonged icy stare with one of her own. She turned away with a shrug. "It's been a long day, Mr. Montgomery. I'm ready to go in for dinner. We'll go at it again tomorrow with a new plan."

"Fine." He exited and slammed the door with a decided movement that felt good, like a tackle once did.

Stacie coolly got out, shaking her head at his lack of maturity. They walked in through the front door and wiped their feet on the rug.

Lily spotted them. "All y'all hungry? We're feeding my other guests, and I've got plenty."

Not seeing many open seats, they plopped down at a table adjacent to Jo and JJ. Calvin felt pissed at the day's outcome and Stacie's snotty commentary. He and JJ acknowledged one another with mutual nods.

"Good evening, folks," JJ said. "Lily created a terrific menu for this evening. I don't think you'll go wrong with anything on it. I chose the steak because the last time I had it here with the loaded potato, I savored every mouthful."

Calvin, surprised by JJ's friendly attitude, jested, "Thanks for being the food testers for us." He reached across to shake hands. "Name's Calvin and this is my auditor, Stacie Duncan."

"Hi there. I'm JJ and this is my bride Jo, celebrating in Magnolia Bluff."

"Nice to meet you both." Calvin grinned and they joked. "Young man, I hope your day went better than ours. We're here on business, and today I bombed. Are you celebrating a honeymoon or simply a vacation?"

JJ smirked. "Yes. We are on vacation for our first anniversary. We got bit by the home buying bug. We spent the afternoon seeing what we don't really want."

Jo beamed. "Some wonderful friends, Hank and Ann Franklin, told us of a nice vacant property we might have a chance at, next door to them south of town. We rode horses over to check it out. We took lots of pictures. We've been studying the plat maps of the area. We want land for privacy."

Calvin sized up the young couple. "Pardon me for stating it, but a large parcel of land won't be cheap here in the Texas Hill Country. Could be tough for a young couple's resources."

"We've reasonably good jobs. Plus, the property's been vacant for twenty-five years. From a distance, it looks like we'd need to bulldoze the existing structures. That works as Jo is already imagining possible designs. We heard from locals that it once had lovely gardens which we'd enjoy as well."

Stacie leaned forward, intently listening.

"It's an unhappy history around the original owners." Jo added. "It's made us sad."

Stacie toyed with her wineglass, running her finger around the rim to listen to the low hum. "What kind of sad history? Do you know?"

"The story was about a young couple, the Stevens, who began wonderfully but fate dealt them a tough blow. Enough of that sad story. Tomorrow we are off to the bank to identify the options we might have."

Stacie nervously fidgeted with her glass. "Perhaps you'll bring happiness to the property and make it the home of your dreams." She abruptly stood. "Apologies. I don't feel hungry," she mumbled and turned to leave. "Calvin, please tell Ms. Lily I'm sorry I'll miss dinner."

They exchanged puzzled looks as Stacie departed the area.

## CHAPTER 14

# Peeling Back the Onion

Due to the conversation with Calvin and Stacie, they returned to their room a little later than planned. An interesting pair that JJ felt needed a closer look.

He placed his laptop on the table. "What's our itinerary for tomorrow, Jo?"

"No appointments, if that's what you mean. I thought we'd walk around the Green. Maybe visit the shops. Then do whatever strikes us."

"Sounds good. If you don't mind, I'd like to start the due diligence part from our side and see what's in the public records on the property. Since he owns property here, I want to talk to Hank and Ann about the process."

Jo did a little dance. "Perfect. Let me know what I can do to help." She added, "I'd like to know more about the sad couple who owned it before. What a shame to be young, in love, then separated by cancer. I feel sad for both of them."

"I don't want you to feel neglected this evening."

She hugged him from behind as he sat. "This is for us. I'll work on update notes to Lara and Carlos on our trip so far."

JJ heard the click of her fingers on the screen and smiled, because she knew him so well.

"Honey, we might want to go to the library or newspaper office to do more research tomorrow, if that'll help."

"Good idea, Jo."

JJ's fingers flew across the keyboard, researching the property records. He was surprised at the ease of accessing public information. He learned about the city and county alignments to the tax rolls. Several incidents cited property lines getting redrawn to make the taxes better for a given city. He tapped into his office supercomputer ICABOD for the analysis routines and to start research on Thomas and Marissa Stevens. JJ retrieved Thomas's employment records from the bank, indicating his university degree. He wanted ICABOD to take that thread to uncover the history of birth, and hopefully where he and Marissa connected. Satisfied at the progress, he gave ICABOD a few other assignments as time raced toward dawn. He shut down his machine, securing it in the closet.

He took a quick shower and snuggled up to his lovely bride, asleep in moments.

Sounds and singing from the bathroom roused JJ. He ran a hand over his face, noticing the sun sitting close to mid-morning and then retrieved his laptop. He plumped up the pillows, leaned back, and logged in. Nanoseconds later, ICABOD started a conversation.

"Good morning, JJ, I doubt you had enough sleep, but the answers to some of your queries, I think you'll find interesting. Do you have a preference on the information you want to receive first?"

"No, ICABOD. You deliver it how you see fit."

"First, someone did try to access your laptop and tried passwords like Jo, your anniversary date, and the driver's license number off your rental car agreement."

JJ raised his eyebrows but just watched the screen.

"Your anniversary is noted in the reservation with Flowers, and I suspect you aren't locking your vehicle in small-town Texas. I was not able to get the entire fingerprint from your keyboard, but I'm working with the partial to find something."

"Thanks, ICABOD. I'll clean the keyboard when I shut down, in case the visitor wishes to try again. Please go on."

"Thomas Stevens grew up near Springfield, Illinois. His parents are buried in the small town of his birth. His only sibling, Dwayne, died as a child to SIDS. His mother had repeated issues and illnesses with prescriptions for depression, anxiety, and insomnia.

"Thomas graduated from Ohio State University with honors in finance, and returned home in time for Marissa's graduation at his former high school. An incident occurred, as reported in a local newspaper, at the ceremony attended by Thomas along with his parents, after Marissa Branson received her diploma. During family photos, Thomas asked for Marissa's hand in marriage. Mrs. Stevens attacked the young girl, calling her many things including a gold-digger. The police were called in to break up the fight. Mrs. Stevens was hospitalized for mental evaluation. Mr. Stevens told his son to leave town and be happy in his life. His father refused to let Thomas take any responsibility for the care of his mother, though I found evidence of checks sent from his job at the Magnolia Bluff bank but never cashed.

"Within three years of his marriage to Marissa Thomas received death benefits from both his parents. It appears he paid for the property with the inheritances."

"Jo will cry over this story, ICABOD. What a tragic situation."

"I think, in today's vernacular, it's a hot mess."

"True that, ICABOD. Please continue."

"Yes, sir. Marissa's parents are also deceased. She had one sister named Anastasia who seems to have disappeared two decades ago and a brother. I am still working on that search."

"Okay. What about Calvin Montgomery?"

"Calvin Montgomery played football, and was in high demand until he blew out a knee. He went on to complete his degree in finance with honors at Alabama, and was selected into a mentoring program with a renowned financial investor. He's single and pays his mother's bills in Alabama, seeing her several times a year. He seeks good investments in the industry and has built a solid portfolio of assets. He met Stacie Duncan and hired her a couple of years ago. Her auditing capabilities are highly recommended by a former employer and her college professors."

"She does appear capable." JJ shifted in his chair. "And the value of the property if I can overcome the tax and permitting issues?"

"In 2020, the cost per acre rose twenty-five-percent. It appears to be a good investment. Likely less than five-thousand dollars per acre in the Hill Country will secure your purchase if the bank can cut through the red tape."

"Thank you, ICABOD. Unless there is something else, I'm shutting down."

"There is a thread I'm working on Ms. Stacie Duncan. I found her masters study and graduation with honors at the University of Chicago ten years ago. Her work record is good to the point of being hired by Mr. Montgomery. But I also located a sealed court record I am still working to access regarding a name change. It could be she married and changed her name to hide from a former husband. Or, gave testimony and needed protection. Do you want me to pursue this avenue to open the record?"

JJ thought back to the weird non-acknowledgement by Stacie at the spa. "Yes, if it is easy. If it gets too hard to find it, pass it by. Thank you, ICABOD." He wiped the keyboard after the device shut down.

JJ's attention got pulled to his right. He saw Jo standing with arms folded and an almost-smirk on her face. "I knew you'd never sleep in, honey. How much sleep did you get?"

"Enough to drag you back to bed for hours of enjoyment." He grinned mischievously with open arms.

"I'm hungry, so let's play later."

"Fine, spoilsport." He rose and tucked the laptop in the closet. "I'll take a quick shower. We can go over some of the details I uncovered over breakfast." He kissed her sweetly, inhaling her fresh scent, totally wishing she'd taken him up on the offer. He continued toward the open steamy door. "Would you please grab me some clothes?"

"Oh, good. You can start with the highlights."

CHAPTER 15

# Small Town Insights

Jo danced down the stairs ahead of JJ, pausing at the landing to see if he was close.

He closed the distance, lifting her into an embrace. He nuzzled her neck. "I'd follow you anywhere, darling."

Jo pressed her hands against his chest, breaking loose from his grip. "Good." She waltzed into the dining room, selecting their preferred table with a window. "JJ, the flowers look happy this morning. I wonder if it rained last night."

Lily appeared right behind JJ just as he moved to help Jo with her chair. "Nope, but I did run the sprinklers. It's getting warm, and they appreciate the evening drink to soak it all in. You have the place all to yourselves this morning 'cos Mr. Montgomery and Ms. Duncan went to Harry's for coffee and his special this morning. What can I get ya?"

Jo placed a hand on her chin and tapped her finger against her cheek. "Lily, you can surprise me, though a little sweet would be good."

Lily rolled her eyes. "That's helpful. And you, young man. Do have something more specific?"

"I'd like an omelet with the works, side of toast with honey, berries, coffee, and skillet potatoes if you have them." He grinned at her stunned expression. "Oh, and tabasco sauce on the side. I'll grab us coffee from the buffet area."

Jo laughed. "That helped. Lily, I'll take a small stack of pancakes and sample from his plate."

JJ stared at her then chuckled. "All's fair, love."

Lily clapped her hands. "I'll get this in a jiffy, then I want to hear about your plans. I did overhear a little of your discussion at dinner last night. But I want the latest details."

"Of course." JJ rose and followed Lily's retreat, stopping for coffee. "Hey, Lily," he called. "Did you want coffee with that conversation, too?" He heard her snarky reply, '*Of course.*'

"Thank you, honey. The coffee smells wonderful. Maybe we should stop by Harry's and do a compare."

"We can. We'll be in town." He sipped and sighed. "I found a few things out about the Stevens couple. Lots of sadness in their background. They did get married after Marissa graduated high school. They came to Texas to start married life. She went to a specialist to find out why they weren't getting pregnant. The results of several tests indicated cancer was the culprit."

JJ heard Lily shout from behind the kitchen door. "Louder, JJ, with the frying noises, I'm not catching all you're saying. Or wait a minute, I'm nearly finished."

They looked at one another, chuckling. Jo commented, "My, what big ears you have."

Lily exited the kitchen butt first, plates in-hand. "Damn straight, Jo. How else would I know about things if I didn't listen in?" She set down the plates and napkins with silverware, then rushed back for the extras on an additional plate, and a carafe of coffee. Then she sat across the table. "Go on, JJ."

"Lily, you've been in this town for years. Did you know Marissa Stevens and her husband Thomas?"

"Sure. Marissa had a green thumb and an enviable garden on their spread. In fact, it was her that got me so interested in flowers. In many ways, Marissa felt like a daughter or a younger sister, all full of ideas for her future with Thomas, and a family. She even helped me design the flow of the gardens. What a tragedy she died so young." Lily paused. "Thomas came for lunch now and again, usually with co-workers or customers. Folks boasted that his investment advice was rock solid." She took another sip then freshened their cups from the container. Her eyes misted a bit, JJ noticed, as she continued. "My husband, Cody, was alive then. We were trying to launch this place. He was building out the addition and doing the overall maintenance, while I worked on my cooking repertoire. During those days we only had weekends open for food or overnight guests. The town mourned her passing. It was like a candle blown out." Lily placed her elbow on the table, cocked her head, and leaned her chin on her fist. "Never understood why Thomas left, or why he never sent anyone a message. He knew we all cared and would-a helped him."

JJ nodded and patted her other hand, lying flat on the table. "Thank you, Lily. We are sorry for your loss of Cody."

"It was a long time ago. I've grown used to it."

"Do you recall a girl named Annie who helped Thomas with Marissa? Ann or Hank mentioned her when we discussed the Stevens' vacant property. Which, by the way, is where we'd like a vacation home, but let's not tell everyone yet," Jo said with a smile. "JJ is looking at details to see if we can swing it."

Lily raised her eyebrows and appeared pleased. "Annie Flagstone is who you mean. Sure, she worked part time for me. She was a bit forgetful, shy, and young. Younger than Marissa, that's for sure. I paid her in cash to help do cleaning after weekend guests, so she never had a work record per se. When Thomas put out the word, he needed help taking care of Marissa after she started treatments—which did no good—I recommended Annie as she wanted full time employment. I'm not certain where that girl laid her head before she worked for Thomas and Marissa.

I suspect she often slept in the park. The reason she wanted to be here was the meals were free as one of the perks for working for me. She was a thin thing with the softest Southern twang."

"She disappeared too, right?" JJ asked.

"Not really. She stopped in here a few weeks or a month or so after Marissa's funeral and said she'd saved enough to try to earn her degree. She'd found a room near a small university with a lady who wanted housekeeping help. Annie said she wanted an education."

"Did you ever hear any more?"

"No." Lily scrunched her nose. "I'm sure she got her degree and even found a husband in school. I haven't thought about her in years."

"I think we've occupied up enough of Lily's time. We need to walk around town like you suggested. I think we could go to the library and newspaper office for the rest of our research. If we find what we need, then I want us to make an appointment at the bank."

Jo jumped from her chair bubbling with excitement. "Lily, don't tell a soul about our desire for the property. Not yet, but you'll be the first to know if we go forward."

Lily gave her a big hug. "My lips are sealed. Nothing would make me happier, sweet pea."

Sunshine and a slight breeze convinced JJ and Jo to walk to all their planned stops this morning. Their hands were gently clasped as they walked toward town.

"Where do you want to start, Jo?"

"If any of the shop windows look interesting, we can take a look inside. Otherwise let's head to the newspaper office. You wanted to review back issues, which could take some time."

Nine in the morning and the streets were quiet. JJ suspected most folks were at home sleeping in or doing chores. He spotted the coffee shop. "Jo, do you want to grab a latte now or later?"

"Later. I'm still full." She pointed. "Look, there's the newspaper office."

JJ moved his hand to the small of her back and guided her across the street. He noticed movement inside. "It appears someone is working. By the size of the man, I bet he is Graham Huston. That's who Lily said we should speak with first." The door was unlocked, so JJ opened it.

The man looked toward them. He appeared to be just over forty, with jade green eyes that moved as if assessing them both. "Hi, there, how can I help you?"

"Are you Graham Huston?"

"The very same."

"I'm JJ Rodreguiz and this is my wife, Jo. We're staying at Flower. Lily suggested we ask you if we can review back issues of the paper."

Graham looked at them, his eyes growing wider. "Aren't you the pair who assisted the podcast mavens resolve their transmission issues last year? You exposed the human trafficking operation by Mateo, too."

"We are. And we did, but we're here for our anniversary vacation and are looking at a piece of property to buy."

"For investment or to join the community?"

Jo nearly burst with her excitement. "We're hoping to build a vacation place to come and get away. We like the people here."

"I do too, young lady." He scratched his head. "Not to be rude, however your face is striking, ma'am. We've not met before?"

Jo walked closer and shook his hand. "We have now. May I call you Graham?"

"Sure. Young man, what years did you want to see? And do you have a specific subject of interested?"

"We're interested in a piece of property near Hank and Ann Franklin's spread. It's been vacant for decades. Someone stopped paying the taxes, so we might have a shot at getting it. The couple who owned it were Thomas and Marissa Stevens. She died too young and ended up in Magnolia Bluff's cemetery. He left town, probably couldn't deal with the memories. We'd like to see if we can find him before we do the investment in remaking the property."

"I've spent considerable time in the graveyard." Graham raised a hand and tapped his cheek. "I sort of remember her name on a headstone. I seem to recollect she was twenty-three or twenty-four when she died. You're right, that's way too young. I wasn't working here then. The original editor of this paper passed away, so that won't help you. There might be some older birds who knew them." His hand stroked his chin in thought. "I suppose you spoke to Hank and Ann Franklin. They have a ranch outside of town." He jerked his chin up with a nod. "Oh, Flower is owned and operated by Lily Greenly, too. They've been around long enough to perhaps recall them."

Jo nodded. "Yes, we have some insights to the couple. We're hoping to find articles about some of the events they hosted on the property. Thomas worked for the bank. Maybe the obituary had details of the funeral or photos."

Graham agreed. "Folks, I only keep five years of back issues here. I simply don't have the room for more. Forty years of back issues got taken to our library to film. It's stored as microfiche to preserve our Magnolia Bluff history for researchers. I'm glad, I guess, that someone will get value out of those efforts. I'm not certain how familiar you are with microfiche, but there's no search engine optimization or SEO, as you likely know it, for that material. As I recall, we have a bit of an indexing schema with date, section of the paper, article title, byline, and the content. Last time I spoke to Caroline, she said four of her microfiche readers were operational. The high school kids often review old magazines to learn fashions for some of the school plays."

Jo laughed. "I can see that being a walk down memory lane. Styles do come back around."

JJ inclined his head and grinned. "Thanks for the information, Graham. We'll go check with Caroline, whom Lily also suggested we visit."

They shook hands, and JJ guided Jo outdoors. They paused outside, trying to determine the direction to take when JJ noticed Graham staring through the window.

"JJ," Jo questioned, "do you think he recognized me? I can't see him reading fashion magazines, but one never knows. Heck, Lily does, which surprised me."

JJ patted her back. "For some reason, I think it's okay. I'll keep an eye on you."

He looked at the map and decided a left turn would take them to the library. The air had warmed during the short time they chatted with Graham. "If you're not hungry or thirsty, let's head to the library and start our research. It could take a while."

Jo shook her head. "No, let's visit the cemetery and get the information off her headstone first. We can pay our respects."

JJ checked the map and mentally changed their route.

CHAPTER 16

# Where Did You Want to Eat?

Calvin glanced around at the interior, comparing it to Flower. "I don't know why we came here," he grumbled. "Lily's coffee and food seemed fine to me. This place is noisy, and we waited to get a seat."

"There's two landmark restaurants in this small town," Stacie conveyed with contorted expressions. "We're staying at the first, Flower B&B. Harry's Really Good Wood-Fired Coffee shop is the other. At Flower, Lily serves upscale food for the more discerning patron. There are choices for calorie-conscious folks, and silverware with cloth napkins. Her coffee is arabica and blended with other coffees for a refined, upscale flavor."

Calvin sensed she talked down to him and found it rude. Still, he always listened.

"Harry has a valued reputation for his coffee making. Outside of Flower, this is the best destination in town for breakfast. During the week, Harry closes most afternoons by two. People who don't want that foo-foo style of coffee come here for his strong, secret blend. His coffee is reported to be just short of an illegal stimulant. The only person to drink five 12-ounce cups in one sitting claimed to see the future."

Stacie smirked. "The food served boasts traditional breakfast dishes created by his chef, Miguel. People who patronize Harry's like the spices of the chilaquiles, a Mexican dish consisting of strips or pieces of corn tortillas that are fried, then sautéed with green or red salsa, and topped with cheese, crema, and onion. At times, he also serves chilaquiles verdes, which uses the tortilla chips and fresh avocados. Look around." She gestured giving a swipe of her hand, palm up. "With the summer tourists and new marketing efforts, Harry's seen an uptick for a month now. It's crowded with the line out the door. Folks often opt for seconds to go. It could be less crowded when school starts back up."

Calvin tried to figure out if he should laugh or shake his head at her detailed monolog. "You've explained the *what*, now tell me *why*."

Suppressing a grin, Stacie motioned with her chin to the doorway where Gunter stood in line to get seated.

Calvin looked then turned to face her. "How did you know he'd come for breakfast?"

Stacie innocently fluttered her lashes. "Boss, it looks pretty crowded. Ask him to join us so he doesn't have to stand in line."

Calvin moved near Gunter and gained his attention. Gunter dabbed his brow like a man who'd gotten rescued from a burning building. "Mighty nice of you, Calvin, to share your table. I waited twenty minutes for a spot yesterday."

"No problem." Calvin waved the waitress over, indicating the additional person.

"What's your pleasure today, Gunter?" the waitress asked while she filled the coffee cups.

"I'll have the special this morning, and a pair of breakfast tacos. Always a good choice. Thanks, hon." Gunter looked between his table companions. "I'm kinda sorry Harry's using the newfangled marketing plan that brings in the tourists. I'm hoping it goes back to the quiet spot to eat during the week."

After her breakfast description, Calvin shifted his eyes between Gunter and Stacie.

Gunter sipped his coffee. "Thanks again, Calvin, for a seat at your table. I planned to arrive sooner, but my wife had the honey-do list pinned to the door."

"I understand. Glad we had an extra chair."

Gunter squirreled his expression as if searching Calvin for an answer. "Our discussion yesterday wasn't what you wanted. I'm surprised at the invitation."

Stacie took a sip of coffee. "We were lamenting the conversation when Calvin spotted you. You seemed so resistant to our investment discussion that it doesn't sound like a good use of our time or yours. We heard you're not interested in selling to the investment group, or even allowing us to buy seats on the board of directors. Calvin mentioned, because this area is thriving, perhaps a second bank would be as prosperous."

Calvin nodded. "Likely more so with newer technology and state-of-the-art customer experiences. A broad portfolio of banking, investments, and loans for the anytime-any-mode consumer. With the right marketing we can bring in some light manufacturing affiliates associated with our group. We'd naturally encourage those new employees to bank with us."

Gunter's meal arrived. The aroma and appearance resulted in an appreciative sigh by the banker.

"Ma'am," Calvin asked, "may I also have an order of those breakfast tacos?"

She nodded and left.

Calvin played on Gunter's reaction to a new bank. "The second bank was only a topic of conjecture. Our first plan in your quaint city involved a partnership, Gunter. We both know the regulatory permits, the site location, the…well, building a bank from the ground up would take time, and we believe the time is ripe to expand the small business in this region. I'm sure you can appreciate the time-to-money value of buy versus build. Right?"

Gunter studied the meal in front of him a moment, appearing deep in thought. The tortilla was filled and soft. He took the knife and fork to cut up bite-sized forkfuls before tasting. Gunter swallowed a few bites and asked, "What's your schedule like this afternoon?"

"We planned some reconnaissance of possible site locations within a five-mile radius. But if you have some time for us to chat in private, I'm sure we can rearrange our schedule to accommodate."

Gunter, half finished with his meal, pushed it to the center of the table before he stood to leave. He snapped his napkin to the side of his plate. "Be at my offices when the bank closes at three. We'll talk."

Calvin smiled and signaled the waitress as Gunter disappeared. "Miss, please put Mr. Fight's meal on our tab. He had to dash."

CHAPTER 17

# Moments of Reflection

JJ and Jo strolled to the cemetery on the neatly trimmed sidewalks. They smiled and nodded to the few folks who passed. JJ noted the gate into the graveyard opened easily—no squeak. The grounds appeared well maintained.

"Finding her grave might take a while, Jo."

"True, but if we stay on the paths, we will see all the headstones. The bright bouquets scattered about indicates someone still thinks about these people. I wonder if they talk with them."

JJ picked up her hand and pressed his lips to it. "I imagine some do. The dates are late 1890s. It might be the newer graves are to the back?" JJ looked out across the area. "I wonder how many folks are buried here."

"Here, JJ." Jo stopped. "I think you're right as I'm seeing dates of the 1940s and flags on the headstones. I bet this man fought in World War II."

JJ scanned the headstones for dates, then glanced at names. "Some of these headstones are so ornate, with the etchings and elaborate angels." They turned a corner onto another row with a big oak tree. He scanned the headstones under the shade.

"My theory is a little off. This group is from the early 1900s, but they have the same last names. Maybe the family bought plots in advance."

They walked on, still seeing bouquets and interspersed newer earthen mounds. "JJ, these dates are all over the place. I wonder why."

JJ shrugged his shoulders. "No idea. I don't know about you, honey, but I wished we'd thought to bring water."

Jo chuckled, "I'm prepared. I've got two bottles in my sling purse." She reached in and handed him one, while she opened the other.

JJ took a long drink and held it in his mouth while he scanned the rows ahead, trying to decide whether to stop for now or continue. "Maybe… Come on, Jo." He started at a short jog two rows up on the corner. "I did read it right." He drove his fist into the air.

Jo sighed as she reached the bright white marble headstone. "My dearest love, Marissa Daniels Stevens. Wife of Thomas. Born August 19, 1974. Peacefully died October 10, 1997. That is so sweet, and final at the same time."

JJ agreed, wrapping his arms around Jo from behind. "Nearly twenty-five years ago. But now we have a date to look for articles and obituaries. We might want to check out the social pages, or local events too. Plus, we have a new conundrum."

"What's that, honey?"

"Who left the pretty bouquet of daisies?"

"Oh, you're right. Someone in this town remembers her."

JJ and Jo stopped at Harry's, surprised there was no one inside. They each ordered a sandwich and a cup of coffee to-go. Jo added two bottles of water to her satchel. A short walk took them to the library. JJ noticed a few tables on the side and folks reading on blankets.

"Let's sit and eat before we tackle the microfiche."

"I've never seen any. Can you explain it to me?" Jo asked as they sat.

"Microfiche is a film strip made up of individual pictures. Depending on who converted these from paper and the processes at the time, they are organized and indexed by origin, such as the name of the newspaper, and dates. The film is inserted into the reader." He took another bite of the sandwich and swallowed. "Sometimes a wheel is used to advance through the images. There is also a way to enlarge to make the print more readable. It's tedious, but, if Graham is correct, at least they have a record. When our eyes get tired, we stop." He crumpled the paper and stuffed their trash into the bag. "I'm sure Caroline McCluskey will remember and help us."

"Yes, I recall she was nice last time we were here. I wonder if she's found a companion yet."

No sooner had they cleared the door when Caroline rushed to them from behind the counter. "Jo, JJ, I knew you were here; Lily told everyone. I couldn't make it to your welcome party. How are you? I heard you got married, of course. Let's see the ring."

Jo grinned and held up her hand. "We are married and celebrating our anniversary in one of our favorite places."

Caroline rolled her eyes. "Seriously, don't you live in Brazil? Now there's a place I'd like to go."

"We do, and we love it. We realized we like the friendly people here. We're doing research regarding some property. Graham at the newspaper said you have microfiche of the paper five years and older."

"I do. Come on. I'll show you." Caroline led them to the back area. It contained cabinets with multiple drawers and four similar looking machines on an adjacent work surface. "These are older technology but were well done. The subjects or origins are alphabetized in the drawers. She pulled open M and fingered through to the start of the newspaper files. "What dates did you want?"

"We'd like to start at December 1997, and go back a few years," JJ said. "If we have time, we can go forward later."

Caroline set each of them up on a machine and showed them how to read and select images if they needed them printed. "Anything you print will be up at the welcome desk. I'll check you out when you finish. Any questions?"

They eagerly began their task. Half an hour later, JJ retrieved another roll, loaded it, and continued.

"JJ, how are you reading so fast?"

"I read the headline and a sentence or two. If it's not relevant I move on. Are you reading the entire article?"

Jo sheepishly nodded. "It's interesting."

"Enjoy, honey." He returned to his process.

Three or so hours later, Jo reached her arms up and stretched. "I need a break."

JJ admired her profile. "Definitely time for a break and walk-around. Good that you found the obit and some of the garden party photos and sent them to print. I located a couple of random announcements about a promotion for Thomas, and a customer thank-you party at their home. I noted where we stopped. Let's grab our copies and see if we can identify any of the people in the pictures."

"Sounds good. I'd like to return to Flower and snatch a short nap."

They paid Caroline for the copies and exited into the afternoon sun. They twisted to get the kinks out from sitting and started toward Flower, seeing more folks on the street. "Let's head toward the B & B and look in windows on this side of the street on the way back."

Jo spotted a couple of items in the gift shop's window and pulled JJ to a stop, pointing. "That puzzle of flowers might be a lot of fun to put together. It has a booklet showing the native Texas bloomers too."

"We can get it if you want. I bet Lily would like to have it in the sitting area for the guests to construct."

Jo, excited, looped her arm in JJ's and pulled him along. She rushed through the door in such a hurry they almost took out Joyce, who was on her way out.

"Hi, you two. I was planning to call you in a while. Serendipity, I guess. Did you decide on a place, or should I continue hunting?" Joyce asked, with an arched eyebrow and hopeful expression.

"Jo, I'll grab the puzzle while you explain our plans to Joyce."

She nodded, and JJ rushed to purchase the puzzle. There were two other folks in line, so it took a moment. He turned with his bag and headed toward the door, noticing Jo and Joyce were gone. He stepped outside and located them on the bench, chatting like friends.

Jo looked up at his approach. "I explained our plans for property to Joyce, honey."

"She did." Joyce beamed. "I'd like to see if I can help you get your dream. There are title forms and more that need completing for any piece of property. My title company is fast if the deal is done correctly. We discussed me going with you to Hank and Ann's later when you return the plat map."

"Sounds like a good idea," JJ acknowledged.

"I'd like to bring Jason and see if we can arrange riding lessons. His camp is ending this week, and he mentioned wanting to learn."

Jo and JJ giggled. "I imagine Camila would be thrilled to have a student."

Joyce's eyes darted between them. "We'll talk more later. I need to grab Jason. We'll eat and meet you at Flower in an hour and a half. Is that enough time for your nap, Jo?"

"Perfect."

## CHAPTER 18

# Country Fun

**JJ** and Jo felt refreshed after their nap. They sat in the dining room finishing up some fruit and iced tea, waiting for Joyce. Lily handed them a sack of fresh cookies to eat on the way, and added a plate for Ann.

Joyce entered, accompanied by what JJ immediately suspected to be a future baseball star. The kid easily topped his mom's height that Jo said was close to five foot six inches. He had lanky limbs, a tanned face with no hint of facial hair, and styled dark hair. He seemed shy, looking at his feet. JJ noticed, Joyce's animation blossomed, like being with her son made her complete.

Jo and JJ advanced with their goodies toward the foyer.

"Jo, JJ, this is my son, Jason. Jason, this is Mr. and Mrs. Rodreguiz."

Jason looked each of them in the eye as he shook their hands. "Nice to meet you, ma'am, sir."

Jo's laughter sounded like mellow notes on a piano. "Hi, Jason, call me Jo. None of the formal stuff between friends."

The young man's grey eyes danced with being included. "Glad you're going along." JJ called, "Bye, Lily. We'll call you if we won't make dinner." They started down the steps. JJ asked, "Joyce, do you want to ride with us or take two cars?"

"I'm happy for you to drive. I get to look around that way."

"Let's you and I sit in back. I'll fill you in on some of what JJ and I have in mind so far. Jason, do you mind riding up front?" Jo smiled sweetly.

Jason held open the door for his mom while she slid into the backseat. JJ copied the gesture for Jo on the other side. He started the car and glanced at the girls through the rearview mirror. They maintained a steady stream of chatter with intermittent giggles. Joyce made notes of items she intended to follow up on.

JJ pulled onto the road to the ranch. "Jason, your mom says you're enjoying the activities at the camp. Do you enjoy any sports outside of camp?"

"I like baseball. I get to try out next week to see if I can secure a spot on the school team."

"Nice. What position?"

"First or third base is what I want. Last year I was stuck in the outfield. Boring."

"I understand," JJ said, with a nod and grin. "The team needs all the players to win."

"I know."

JJ glanced at the kid and noticed he looked a bit sad. "Do you like horses?"

"I do. My parents wanted to let me ride, but never had the time. They argued a lot before they split up."

JJ nodded. "We're headed to Hank and Ann's place. They have horses. Jo and I've ridden. One of their adopted daughters, Camila, is a friend of ours. She's about your age and loves to ride. She also takes care of the horses."

"I saw her at school at the end of last year. She's pretty. Too pretty for me."

JJ rocked his shoulders, looking for the right words. "I think she's shy like you because she had a tough go before her adoption. That's her story to tell, but I suspect you both have some common ground. You seem like a nice, polite guy. She'd be a good friend if she trusts you."

"Maybe."

"I'll introduce you, then you decide."

JJ maneuvered the vehicle through the gate to the front of the house before he parked. Hank and Ann waved from the porch table when they exited the car.

JJ watched Jo's exuberance as she bounded up the steps. She greeted Ann with a hug, then clasped Hank's hand. "Great to see you both!"

"Hank, Ann," JJ said, with a grin. "We brought Joyce, the realtor we met at Lily's, and her son Jason."

They exchanged handshakes taking seats and enjoying the slight breeze.

"Can I offer you some sweet tea?" Ann asked.

Jo slapped the side of her head, jumped up, and took off to the car. JJ saw everyone's eyes following her. She retrieved the cookie plate and bag, then rushed back to the group. "Only if I can give you the cookies Lily sent." JJ leaned in to brush his lips across her skin, causing a slight blush.

"Good move, Jo," he laughed.

Camila called from the paddock and waved, grabbing everyone's attention. "Hi, you two." She raised her hand above her brow as if to see better. "I'll be right there. I didn't know you brought people with you."

Camila vanished through an opening into the attached barn and ambled toward them, fingering her hair, looking apprehensive.

JJ met her part way and gave her a hug. "Hey, Joyce's son, Jason, is here. He loves horses." He leaned and whispered in her ear. "He's kind-a shy."

She nodded, and mumbled, "Me too. Some kids at school still laugh at my accent. Ann tells me they're jealous of me and Renata for speaking two languages."

JJ laughed. "Ann's right, you know. You are both adapting perfectly."

Greeting Jo with a hug, Camila paused for introductions to Joyce and Jason. JJ watched the teens eye each other before reaching some silent agreement.

"Would you like me to show you the horses, Jason?"

"I would. Mom, is it okay with you?"

"Of course. Thank you, Camila."

Camila nodded. "Hank, Ann, can I?"

After a nod of ascent, the kids headed off.

Ann commented, "He seems like a polite young man."

"He's a good kid. His dad and I divorced, and he misses his friends from Austin. His dad wants him to live here while he plays house with his mistress." She gritted her teeth and turned bright pink. "Sorry, TMI. Clearly, I'm not bitter."

They laughed and found seats. Ann filled glasses and everyone grabbed cookies.

"Hank, Jo and I did some research and found a few things." JJ shared what they'd learned.

"Oh my!" the couple exclaimed.

"I only found a little information on Marissa. She had a younger brother and sister. Her sister had trouble in junior high and her records are sealed. It appeared her single mom sent her to a reform camp, but which one and for how long is unknown. The brother joined the army and was killed in action in 1995. That same year, her mom got into a multicar pile up on the interstate and died at the scene."

Ann tapped the table with her fingers. "Marissa never mentioned any family. She cared for her flowers and treated everyone here in Magnolia Bluff like family. What hardship they overcame. I wonder if she ever connected with her sister."

"Unknown," JJ indicated. "Still doing a bit of hunting, even for her name. The birth name was Anastasia Daniels, but with her juvenile record, a name change might have occurred."

"What a story. We never knew," admitted Hank. "With all the history, do you still want to pursue the property?"

Jo squealed, "We do. Joyce indicated she'd start on the formal title research."

"Hank, I'm hoping you and I can go to the bank and sit with Gunter. You mentioned he knew you wanted the parcel. I think if we go together, that conversation could go smoother."

"I agree, young man. I'm all for you getting the piece if that's what you want."

"Are you thinking of moving here, Jo?" Ann asked.

"Not full time," Jo admitted, "but we'd like to make it a vacation home as a start. We love the peace and quiet."

Ann lit up at the idea. "That would be great. The girls would love it."

"Hank, if you can help me work the deal with Gunter, I am hoping Joyce can get a survey team out and maybe we can even demo the structures. Jo wants to salvage the weathered wood for artists if they want it. She's also working options for the structures."

"We hoped for a couple of horses, but if we aren't living here full time, we need to work out their care," Jo said. "Lots of details but securing the property and starting the cleanup is first."

"I'll call Gunter right now." Hank rose and disappeared into the house.

Ann refilled the glasses as they waited for the outcome. JJ looked toward the corral and noticed the teens each brushing a horse. He admitted to himself that was a great conversation activity. They already looked to JJ like fast friends.

Hank made it outside, looking like his walking had eased some.

"JJ, we're on for nine in the morning. That work for you?"

"Yes, sir."

"Ann, Camila, and I will meet you for breakfast at Lily's around eight, then you and I will talk to him. I gave him a heads-up on the details, so he may have some information for us."

"Outstanding. Thank you, Hank," said JJ. "Jo, Joyce, are you ready to get out of their hair?"

Ann slapped both palms on the table. "Don't you dare. We're fixing dinner and you're all staying."

Everyone looked at each other. "Yes, ma'am." JJ pulled out his cell and sent a text.

> Lily, we're eating with Hank and Ann tonight. They'll join us in the morning for breakfast.

## CHAPTER 19

# We Had a Deal

**JJ** and Jo arrived in the dining room shortly after seven. Sounds and smells from the kitchen alerted them Lily started preparations for breakfast. JJ rubbed his hands together imagining the possibilities.

"Jo, you look especially pretty this morning." JJ pushed in her chair and affectionately rubbed her shoulders. "Would you like coffee and juice to start?"

Jo nodded. JJ went to the buffet and poured coffee. He selected two juice glasses and filled them. Like an efficient waiter, he carefully returned with all the items in-hand and deposited them in the correct places.

Jo chuckled. "You're way too good at that, honey. Did you spend time as a waiter?"

"Nope. Just big hands." He ran his fingers down her tanned arm.

Hank and Ann arrived a short time later with the girls in tow. Following greetings, Renata rushed to the kitchen to help Lily while Camila took a seat. The girl's eyes sparkled with what JJ suspected was a hidden secret. "Mama Ann said I could have breakfast and stay the morning. Are Joyce and Jason coming for breakfast, too?"

"Joyce is," JJ advised, wondering just how smitten Camila was. "I'm not certain about Jason. I think he has a couple of days of camp left. Jo, do you recall?"

"I don't." She reached across and patted Camila's arm. "He seemed to like the horses. It looked like you were giving some basic instructions on the currying aspects."

The teen beamed. "He did. He wanted to go riding last night but it was too dark, so he's going to ask his mom when she might bring him back. Mama Ann told me I get to teach him to ride, if his mom approves." Camila shot Ann a sweet smile.

Lily and Renata delivered platters of breakfast food family-style. Dishes offered steaming fluffy eggs, bacon, sausage, and warm croissants with sides of butter and jam for each guest.

"Renata made the raspberry jam. Y'all must try it," Lily declared. "JJ, Hank, do you boys want pancakes too?"

Hank looked up. "If they're made, Lily, sure. Otherwise, don't go to any trouble."

Joyce and Jason arrived. Jason helped add a table to extend the arrangement allowing everyone to sit together. JJ and Jason moved chairs. Renata brought out two extra plates and silverware. JJ didn't miss the smirk or sideways glances toward Jason between the girls.

Lily rushed through the swinging door with extra cups and glasses. JJ noticed her confused expression when she stopped.

"Lily, I promise we'll put the table and chairs back when we're finished." He shrugged. "It just happened."

The group chatted and laughed. The sounds of forks and knives on the ceramic plates reinforced the positive comments on the delicious food from the group.

Hank held up his hands in protest as Lily set another plate of pancakes next to him. "Woman, I'm full. Ann was over-the-top last night for supper. It seems you're trying to outdo her for breakfast. Is there a competition between you two? I'll need to skip eating for this week and next, so I don't get fatter than a forty-pound robin."

JJ joined in with Hank's statement. "Lily, you win. I'm stuffed. Hank and I will have to waddle around the square a couple of times before heading to the bank to talk to Gunter."

JJ noticed a look of concern flash across Jo's face.

"You mean we aren't both going with Hank? I'd rather be included, but I won't interrupt your negotiations."

Hank leaned in conspiratorially. "Buddy, you're lucky she wants to stay informed. If I didn't include Ann, she'd reach for her broom to sweep me into line—after hitting me with it."

"My apologies, honey. For some reason I thought you'd rather stay here and review the designs."

Lily and Joyce grinned. "I knew you were smart, JJ," Lily added with a chuckle.

Jo studied JJ and smiled. She knew he was thinking about her ability to wield a frying pan as a way to convince him. Jo smiled and leaned over to kiss him lightly on the cheek "Thank you, honey. We can work on designs later if we close the deal."

JJ, Jo, and Hank strolled into the bank at nine by the chime of the courthouse clocktower. Gunter stepped from a doorway to greet the group. They shook hands. Before he escorted them to his private office, he offered coffee, which they declined.

JJ spotted rows of classic novels with gold embossed lettering on the spines carefully arranged in two of the built-in wooden bookshelves. Gunter's modest collection of sports memorabilia was interspersed with books and family photos going back decades. The quiet ticking of the grandfather clock, coupled with the leather chairs, rounded out the eclectic small-town banker's domain. The setting gave JJ a sense of conservative, community values making him feel comfortable with Hank taking the lead for the opening of the discussion.

Pleasantries were exchanged as the old friends checked on family, property, and upcoming football games. Hank cleared his throat. "Gunter, the main reason I brought JJ and his lovely bride, Jo, is to assure you I want this couple to purchase the Stevens' property rather than Ann and me."

Gunter listened intently then shook his head. "No can do, Hank."

JJ felt like he'd been gut punched. Jo visibly flinched but kept her features in check. Hank stared incredulously at his banker and friend for nearly twenty-five years. He bristled, barely concealing his annoyance. "I'd like to understand why. You and I've talked about this off and on ever since the property was abandoned. You even alerted me that the taxes were no longer being paid. You let me think the bank could quietly let me have it as a quick transfer if the taxes got paid, avoiding a courthouse bidding frenzy." His eyes narrowed and he leaned forward. "What's changed?"

Gunter opened his hands and rested them on the table. "Hank, if it was anyone else but you, I'd say it's on a need-to-know basis. These two don't need to know. Because you suggest a quitclaim transaction, I'm gonna tell you a bank investor and his accountant are looking to join the bank board. They requested all transactions get frozen pending their audit. I'm obligated to hold off on selling the property, Hank."

JJ noticed Jo's eyes filling with tears and reached over to hold her hand.

Hank sneered. "I've never known you to back away from a deal so dishonorably, Gunter. These fine folks want to buy and build on the property. Me and Ann want them as neighbors. It's not just them but us too."

JJ saw Gunter's resolve falter.

"Hank, as soon as they do an audit, we…"

The door burst open, and Mary Lou rolled her wheelchair as if she'd pushed a gas pedal. "Gunter, how long are you gonna keep me waiting? You know I always want to get to Noonan's on Wednesday, when he puts out the savory salami and cheese croissants at ten thirty. I need to beat the lunch crowd."

Before Gunter's administrator Gladys quietly shut the door, she held up both hands palm out, pointed toward Mary Lou, shaking her head.

"Dear," Gunter said with a sweep of his arm, "I'm meeting with these folks. Can you give me…"

Mary Lou appeared to swallow hard as her eyes rested on JJ and Jo. She maneuvered the chair closer. "I'm sorry to have busted up the meeting. JJ, Jo, I heard you were in town but didn't get a chance to…Jo, why are you crying?"

Jo sniffled. "I'm sorry, Mary Lou, we're trying to work with your husband on buying property next to Hank's. We decided we'd like a vacation home at the least in this town…"

"Gunter! Why's this a problem?" Mary Lou snapped. "These two defeated the human trafficking scum—" she pointed toward JJ— "and he saved my life."

Hank saw the tsunami Mary Lou got started and joined the ride up. "Mary Lou, I'm trying to get Gunter to honor his commitment to sell that property at a discount so this wonderful couple, who selflessly helped our community, can buy it. Gunter said he ain't having none of it."

JJ felt sorry for Gunter. He watched the man age from the verbal onslaught. Gunter closed his eyes, likely previewing the dressing down he'd get from his long-term wife. It was clear who wore the pants in that family.

JJ placated, "Gunter, can you move the non-performing asset off the books before the audit? The investor won't need to know. If they discover it, they'll be pleased you were smart enough to groom the bank's portfolio for a smooth transaction prior to investment in a seat on the board."

Mary Lou steeled her stare in Gunter's direction while patting Jo's shoulder.

Gunter paled. He grabbed his phone and punched a button. "I need a quitclaim deed for the Thomas and Marissa Stevens property. Now, Gladys."

While they waited for the document, Gunter commented, "JJ, I sure hope you have a handsome checking account so we can close this transaction. I need to take Mary Lou to the bakery and then to lunch."

JJ shook his head. "Gunter, I don't have a checking account."

Gunter visibly blanched.

"If you give me the bank routing numbers here, I'll do a wire transfer immediately from my financial institution in *Zürich*. If we do that then it won't have to go through the standard ACH clearing house. I hope that will be satisfactory."

Gunter relaxed, and the corners of his mouth upturned.

JJ pulled out his cell and pressed a number. "Gunter, if you'll write down the delivery number here and the selling price, we can complete this transaction in a few minutes."

CHAPTER 20

# Needs a Little Work

Gunter completed the transaction before his hurried departure. Hank, JJ, and Jo leisurely walked out of the bank. JJ felt satisfied with the results of their plan yet realized the work just started.

Jo winked at JJ in mutual admiration.

JJ pumped Hank's hand. "Thank you, sir, for your help securing the goal."

Hank snorted. "Ha! It t'weren't me. It's Jo with her tears and sniffles that helped clinch the deal."

Jo flashed a bemused happy expression. "Gentlemen, I'd maintain Mary Lou took out the goalie, for the score. Hee, hee, hee!"

A police vehicle pulled to the curb and came to a stop next to them. The passenger window rolled down. The grinning officer leaned over and hollered, "What, you two again?"

Jo beamed and waved.

JJ shouted, "Chief Jager! We planned to stop in. Jo and I have a bet that you wouldn't remember us. Or, at least didn't want to remember us."

"Y'all still too formal. Doesn't bother me like it used to. What brings you back to our Magnolia Bluff?"

"Chief Tommy, they bought the ten-acre plot next door to mine," Hank said. "The bank sold it this morning. They're waiting for the title change once the survey is filed. They're planning to build a vacation home where the Stevens couple once lived."

Tommy's face clouded at the mention of the young couple. He moaned, "Their story was heartbreaking. Nothing worked out for those two."

JJ leaned into the window. "Chief, we have a quitclaim deed for the property. The survey is in the works, which is what the title company needs to complete the formal transfer of ownership."

"Sounds good, son."

"We'd like to get onto the property to evaluate it. No Trespassing signs are everywhere along the fence line. Can we remove them?"

"Not until the title transfer." Tommy parked and got out of the car, leaning on top to continue the discussion. "When do you want to look at it?"

Hank and Jo joined JJ at the car.

"As soon as possible. There's a sizable padlock on the gate. Am I entitled to use a hacksaw to gain entrance? I don't want to break any laws."

Tommy smiled slyly and rubbed his hand across his chin. "There might be some eyebrows raised, or you might get shot at, on your own. Let me see those papers."

JJ handed them over and watched as the chief scanned the documents, pointing at the signatures.

"If Chief Tommy was doing the cutting, no one would challenge me." He jerked his thumb to his own chest to emphasize his confidence.

"I've got a few free minutes. How 'bout I meet you there in twenty minutes?"

The three high-fived. "Thanks, Tommy," they said in unison.

Tommy laughed. He got back into his car and drove off at the speed limit.

They gathered around the gate. The aging padlock was no match for Tommy's bolt cutters. Hank and JJ pulled open the gate which squeaked and groaned in protest. Jo rushed in and pulled JJ's arm, bouncing along side, pausing to take pictures. "Stay on the path, honey," suggested JJ. "We aren't wearing boots or long pants. I don't want you scratched everywhere."

"I just want to get close enough to get some shots of the weathered wood."

JJ turned when he heard Tommy laughing.

"JJ," he called, "did you think to bring a new padlock for the gate?"

JJ grinned, holding up a small sack. "Hardware store on our way here."

Hank saluted the couple then turned to leave. Tommy laughed aloud, returning to his cruiser with a wave and thumbs-up. JJ watched his car until it disappeared in a cloud of dust.

They stayed on the rutted path toward the house. Jo bumped JJ with her hip. "We should have asked Tommy to stay a little longer so he could get us into the house."

"Let's try the door anyway. It might yield. I'd like to look inside."

Jo looked around as they walked. She pointed. "Are you seeing these, JJ? It looks like random holes, here and there. Wonder why."

"I don't know if it was made by an animal or something else. We need to get some of this scrub brush removed to see what we have. I'll ask Hank. He might have an idea."

They spotted several holes on the way to the sagging porch. The corner post was broken. "I'm gonna try the door. Please, wait here. The porch deck might be unstable."

Jo frowned. "Okay."

The wood creaked and groaned from his weight. One board cracked where he stepped. It sagged in the middle.

"Careful. I see what you mean."

JJ tested the handle and found it locked. He studied the frame, took a step back, and lunged at the door with a powerful sidekick. "Bang!" The sound echoed into the vacant interior as the door disintegrated in a shower of splinters. He leaned over and laughed, covering his nose with his handkerchief. "Honey, I found a way in."

Jo clucked her tongue and muttered, "My husband, the human battering ram."

"Thanks, sweetheart. I have so many talents left to show you."

"I bet this was cute when it was set up. The rooms are small but functional."

JJ smacked his lips. "It has that musty, uncared-for smell, but I agree the layout is nice. I'm surprised at the furniture remaining in the living room."

They continued their photo survey of the interior of the house.

"Jo, I see some men's clothes in the closet."

"Yep. I spotted linens and blankets. Maybe someone in town would like the donation. The appliances might be useful, though they need a thorough cleaning."

"Agreed. I don't think this space is what you had in mind, even with the stone fireplace."

"You're right. I'm surprised there isn't more than a little trash and cobwebs in the corners."

"As in no critters?" He laughed.

She nodded.

JJ opened the back door and headed to the barn.

Jo cautioned, "Sweetheart, please don't open the barn door the same way you did the house. I'd be afraid it will collapse on you."

Chuckling, JJ replied, "Yes, dear. I don't think people lock the barns like their houses, but I'll be careful."

They snapped photos in all directions outside around the building then stopped at the front of the barn door.

"Honey, this could require both our efforts. I wish we'd brought gloves."

JJ lifted the lever and pulled, but nothing happened. Jo leaned into the side to add more weight to their efforts. The rollers holding the door groaned in protest, but relented to their united pressure. Light exposed the dark cave allowing them to peer into the structure. They walked around the space looking in the corners. It was empty except for an oversized top-load freezer sporting a heavy padlock.

JJ clucked his tongue in annoyance and moaned, "These people must have been real security conscious. Padlocks on the front gate and now this freezer. No trespassing signs everywhere."

"JJ, this is a utility barn. I like the area which might have been used for her gardening. There're no stalls for horses, but it could hold a car."

"It's a big storage area, we could use it for a new riding mower or an ATV."

Noticing the sun setting. Jo observed, "JJ, it's getting late. We've got a lot done today, as well as a lot to think about. Let's head back for supper with Lily. We need to establish a plan of attack."

He nodded, placed a light kiss on her forehead, and agreed. "Back to the car and put on the new padlock. I'll check with Hank to see if he has some bolt cutters to open this freezer. But you're right. We have a lot to arrange and limited time during this trip."

Jo sighed. "It's ours."

JJ groaned. "Needs work."

CHAPTER 21

# Connecting the Missing Pieces

JJ needed quiet to do additional research into Thomas and Marissa's families. Jo left their room and wandered into the sitting area, picking at the jigsaw puzzle she'd given to Lily. Someone had turned it out onto the card table, and connected a few pieces. She had her notebook in hand in case any more ideas occurred. After the discussions with Joyce and Lily the night before, she and JJ had talked about their ideas. She'd tried to capture them all and then started to classify them between 'must have' or 'nice to get'. The overall plan felt doable. They were worried about the permits and title transfer. These were required to make plans for the demolition crews, including the crew to start on short notice.

Lily walked in startling her. Jo jerked her head up. "Jo, why are you chewing on your thumb nail?" Looking around to make certain no one was near, she added, "Don't you have a modeling assignment when your holiday is over? You'll want your hands looking nice, I suspect."

Jo's eyes went wide. "Lily! Shhhhh. Don't let anyone hear you. They'll just get nosey."

Lily chuckled. "No one's around. The other guests are gone. Renata's singing and doing the dishes. She loves country music. Where's JJ?"

"He's upstairs doing some research. I didn't want to disturb him. The puzzle looks fun."

"Thank you for getting it. Guest will enjoy it. Come, let's sit." They chose the comfortable tall-backed chairs with a view toward the front. "Now, what's the matter?"

Jo wrung her hands. "Tommy said while we were with him taking photos of the property, we couldn't start demoing or even be there alone until the title change. The title change is waiting for a survey, and then there are permits too. Joyce stressed the timing because we are leaving at the end of the month."

"Oh, dear, Jo, I wish you'd told me sooner. That's easy. Joyce is new to the community, so things aren't as greased for her, as when we old timers get involved." Lily shot Jo a look. "I wasn't referring to age either, sweetie."

"I never thought that for a second, Lily," Jo promised with a chuckle.

Lily pulled her cell out of her apron pocket and searched for the right contacts. She grinned and pressed the button. Her eyes rested on Jo while the call connected.

"Hi, David. Hey, it's Lily. Can I bother you for a favor… Thanks, I need you to take a crew over to the old Steven's property adjacent to Hank and Ann's and complete a survey today… It's important. JJ and Jo need to finalize it so they can start renovation…I know, right?" Lily grinned at Jo. "It's going to be fun to have them here at least part-time…Yes, I can fix you and your pretty bride prime rib on Saturday…" Her smile grew wider. "I forgot it was her birthday. I'll fix her favorite cherry cheese cake… Six sharp, got it. My treat, David…Your team can get started this afternoon?" Lily shot Jo a thumbs-up. "Great. I'll call Mildred for the permit and have it faxed over. Thanks. See you Saturday…Of course, candles. Bye now."

Lily reached over and fist bumped with Jo. "Let me call Mildred at the town offices and Phyllis at the title company, then I'll be ready for a cup of tea."

"Me, too! I like the way you cut through the red tape in Magnolia Bluff, Lily."

Lily brought tea into the sitting room to share. Together they reviewed the list of things Jo and JJ planned to complete before they returned to work.

"Here we go. Whatcha got?"

"Lily, if we can get the demolition completed, can you help round up artists to pick up the materials if they want them?"

"Is this a giveaway thing?"

"Yes, of course. I'd rather artists put the wood to good use."

"I'll make a note to get the information out. Also, we have an art teacher who likes to have weekend classes in art. Do you mind if I let her know as well?"

"Fine by me. I wouldn't mind taking an art session if they offer one next time we're here."

Lily tittered and clapped her hands. "We'll have a ladies' night, with wine and snacks next time. What fun."

"JJ said last night if I can pick out the house design I want, we can get contractors to bid on it." Jo opened her phone and thumbed through the photos. Finding the right starting point, she turned it toward Lily and suggested, "The gate opens to a dirt and gravel driveway. It would be resurfaced at some point, but I thought the front door of the house might face the entrance even if set back further from the current buildings."

"Makes sense. You can see folks drive in. You'll have security cameras and a code to enter, right?"

"Security is a big deal. JJ will use all sorts of cameras, sensors, keyless entrances. He mentioned voice biometrics for access too."

"You are important to him, sweetie!"

Jo felt pleased and twisted her wedding ring for reassurance. "I can't believe we will have a home to enjoy when we come here. But I still want to eat here sometimes. It'll be nice to invite you over for a meal and maybe card games. I love cards. Do you think—"

Jo's question got interrupted by Lily's inbound call song that played the start of "Let Me In". Lily seized it from her pocket and pressed accept.

"Hi, Mildred, what's up?...It's okay...I can't come over right now I need to prep for lunch...David doesn't understand that fax machines break now and again..." Lily covered the mouth piece and whispered, "Jo, if I give you directions, can you go pick up the permit at the courthouse and take it to David's office?"

"Sure."

"Mildred, Jo's gonna head your way in a few minutes and grab it...Well, she's tall with dark hair, thin, pretty face, early twenties...Har, har, har. No, it's not a guy, and she's married. We need to find you a man, Mildred. Thank you."

Lily ended the call. "Jo, let me have your tablet."

Jo handed it to Lily who feverishly drew a map and directions to both destinations. Then she turned it around and walked her through it.

"Easy, Lily. I got this. If JJ comes down, let him know I'll be right back. This is so cool."

Jo performed a little dance toward the hallway and opened the door, nearly colliding with Stacie Duncan. "Hi, Miss Duncan. Sorry. I got carried away, but only because I'm so excited. My dreams are coming true." She delivered a quick hug, then dashed down the stairs calling out, "I gotta run."

"What in heavens name is wrong with that girl?" Stacie asked.

Lily laughed. "Not a thing. She and her husband, JJ, who you and your boss spoke with at dinner the other night, are buying property. They are starting demolition in the next few days. They had no idea how we Texans can get things moving when the need arises."

"I never realized. What place did they decide on?"

Lily waved her hands. "The old Stevens place. Oh, you wouldn't know. It's a piece of property abandoned by the owners some time ago."

Stacie sagged, groping for the corner of a small table. Lily reached and steadied the woman. "Stacie, are you all right, hon? Do you have medication in your purse you need?"

Stacie swatted Lily's hand away. "I'm fine. The heat overcame me. I'll go upstairs and lay down." Stacie hung onto the handrail like a life raft and stomped upstairs.

Lily watched her ascend and muttered, "She doesn't look well. Perhaps I should call Doc." She turned and headed toward the kitchen. "Or mind my own business."

CHAPTER 22

# Bragging at Breakfast

**JJ** and Jo discussed the additional information he uncovered with regard to Marissa's family, admitting some gaps remained. He submitted requests with two attorneys he knew, but it would take time. Nothing that would prevent their moving forward. Gunter had called late the day before indicating they could plan for the demolition while they waited for the final survey. Nothing could actually be changed until the title company completed their package with a formal signing.

JJ inhaled and caught the odor of bacon. "Do you smell that? I think it's almost time for breakfast. After we eat, we'll head over to Hank's."

"I want to talk with Ann about options for having the property routinely checked. Especially if we add horses at some point."

"I'm glad you're planning ahead, but it could be months before we add animals."

"I know, but I don't want it forgotten. I also need to chat with Lily on the native plants to make certain where to invest time and effort. We really won't get any planting done until next spring for flowers."

JJ tugged her into his arms. "I'm so glad you're enjoying this," he murmured into her neck.

She returned the affection. "Thank you, sweetheart, for indulging me."

They dressed and skipped downstairs toward the aroma of coffee and bacon. They secured their favorite table near the window. Jo retrieved the coffee and JJ grabbed the juice.

At the sound of footsteps, JJ looked toward the doorway. Stacie Duncan peeked into the area, shrugged, and walked toward an open table next to theirs.

"Good morning, Ms. Duncan," JJ said with a smile as he raised his coffee cup. "The coffee is great again this morning."

"Good morning to you two. Please, call me Stacie," she said with a forced brightness. JJ realized the smile from her lips never touched her eyes, nor could she look at his. "Jo, did you meet the deadline you were focused on when you rushed out yesterday?" she asked.

Jo's hands became animated with her words. "I did. I had no problems getting the papers and delivering them on time. It's so exciting. Have you ever owned property, Stacie?"

She appeared surprised at the question. "I haven't. When I was very young, I lived in my parents' home, but that was long ago."

JJ stood and pulled a chair over to their table. "Stacie, join us. We don't need to do a long-distance conversation. If Calvin comes down, he can sit with us as well."

Stacie picked up her cup and accepted his invitation.

JJ sat. "Where did you grow up, Stacie? I'm not hearing much of an accent."

She laughed for a little too long from JJ's perspective, as if trying to decide what to say. "I, um…had an interesting childhood. My parents decided I was gifted and sent me to a girls' school in Florida. I learned so much and applied to get a business degree. I was good with numbers. I received a small scholarship and financial aid."

Jo applauded. "I admire those who finish schooling. Well done."

"Hmm, thank you. So, what property are you getting, and what are your plans? You mentioned the other night you were on vacation here for a month. Has that changed?"

Jo shook her head. "No, we both need to return to work. We bought a piece of abandoned property. We want to create a vacation home. We'll be back and forth overseeing the construction."

"Sounds like a full-time job by itself. It'll take time to get things rolling, I expect."

"Not as long as one might imagine," interjected JJ.

Lily appeared at the table. "Sorry for the delay. What may I get you all for breakfast? Good to see you, Ms. Duncan. You appear to be right as rain this morning."

JJ arched his eyebrows and looked at the woman.

"Ms. Lily, I'm fine. I hadn't eaten yesterday. I snacked in my room and slept great. I believe I'll have the waffles and eggs with sausage on the side. I'll grab some tomato juice." She ambled to the buffet and poured herself a juice, while JJ and Jo placed their order. Lily disappeared to fulfill the requests.

Stacie returned with her pasted smile. "When do you plan to return?"

"Probably within three months, depending upon work and Jo deciding on the house plans."

"Yes, I am headed to Ann's this morning after breakfast to show her some ideas. Plus, she has some contractor connections she wants to share. JJ, did I mention she wants us to get three bids no matter who gets recommended to us?"

"Good idea. Ann will guide you well."

The food arrived and they dug in. The oohs and aahs suggested the hunger pains would vanish.

Stacie wiped her mouth and set down the napkin. "A terrific breakfast. I need to head out. I have an appointment at the bank."

"We do as well. I need to get with Hank to map out the demo strategy before it gets too hot. Then I'm hoping we can take a ride. They have a couple of horses we enjoy."

Stacie stiffened, cocked her head. "Did you say demo strategy? For what?"

"If we can access our new property, we need to decide what goes and what stays."

A panicked look crossed Stacie's face, and the rosy cheeks vanished to a white pallor. "How could you close on the deal so fast? It sounds shady to me. Are you sure it's legal?"

Jo laughed. "Apparently, in Texas, with the right contacts, things can get done in a hurry."

Stacie trudged away, clearly distracted.

JJ reached across the table with his napkin and grabbed Stacie's empty glass by the rim. "Sweetheart, may I borrow your cosmetics? I need that terrific blush case, the one with the delicate brush, for a moment."

Jo shot him a strange look, as if questioning his sanity, but produced the items. "JJ, I don't—"

"Now hold the napkin at the bottom of the glass while I dust it. Ah, excellent. A perfect fingerprint set. Now for a quick photo." JJ caught the Cheshire grin emerging on Jo's face as he snapped a couple of pics. "There. All done, honey." JJ uploaded the photo. "Did I ever tell you I loved you, babe?"

Lily burst through the door. "JJ, are you bussing tables now?"

He chuckled. "Lily, I was going for more juice. It seemed polite to bring the glass to the bin to save you the effort."

Lily rolled her eyes. "Fine. Don't tell me what you're doing. But you two are up to something."

"Not us," JJ added with a sly grin. "But we do seem to get caught up in odd situations when we're in Magnolia Bluff."

Stacie and Calvin entered Gunter's office. Calvin stated in low tones, "Let me do the talking. I know you're upset. I can work this out and get into the bank as a director."

Gunter, sitting behind his desk, indicated the chairs with a hand gesture. Stacie and Calvin took seats in front of the desk. Gunter played with his pen, not making eye contact.

Calvin cleared his throat. "I thought we had an understanding, Gunter," he rebuked. "We agreed NO transactions outside of transactional deposits and withdrawals by customers until my auditor reviewed the books."

Gunter continued to stare at the blank notepad.

"This young couple at Flower B&B bragged they secured a defaulted property yesterday. If this is how the Bank and Trust works, then you should drop the word, *Trust*."

Stacie, unable to contain herself, said, "You did a quitclaim deed for a property with no research or due diligence?"

Calvin noticed her face turning crimson. He reached and patted her arm, which she shook off and then delivered him a glare.

"What if that property is worth more than you sold it for?" She took in a gulp of air and promised, "I've a good mind to report you to the FBI, FTC, and IRS, Mr. Fight. If this institution is an under-the-table/backroom deal organization, a second bank would thrive here."

Calvin snapped his gaze toward Stacie, knowing the damage was done. He closed his eyes, sending up a useless prayer.

The silence became deafening. Gunter stared at Calvin, dismissing the shrew. "I don't believe we could share a good working relationship. Your heavy-handed tactics, disrespectful attitudes, and vile threats have caused me to reconsider associating with you or your AUDITOR. You don't get to come in here and let your junkyard dog tell me who reports who. This meeting is recorded. A copy automatically shared with my attorney. I may be small-town Texas, but you, son, associated with the wrong auditor to do business in this state. This meeting is over. Get out."

Calvin practically pushed Stacie outside to avoid any further fury. In the car, he bellowed, "I'm so mad at you for running off at the mouth! You're this close to being backhanded. We're done." He took a deep breath to reel in his anger. "I'll take you to Flower. Pack your shit and check out. Find a ride share. I don't care. You're fired."

Stacie rocked her head back and clenched her fists. "Nobody fires me from a relationship I helped build. You're nothing without my help, so don't screw it up. We've got other bank candidates in this region to work."

Calvin shook his head with a sense of disgust. "I'm going to replace you. I can assure you the next auditor won't be stingy with the sex."

"So, you'll look at young boys too?" Stacie snapped.

Calvin felt his whole being shimmer with rage, preventing his response. He started the car and drove to the B&B. After shutting off the engine, he slammed out of the car and stormed through the front entrance.

Stacie got out, kicked the door shut, and muttered, "You shouldn't have done that, asshole."

CHAPTER 23

# An Unexpected Adventure

JJ slung his arm over Jo's shoulders during the short walk to their car. "Sweetheart, I brought the spare laptop in case you and Ann want to search for additional ideas for our new home away from home. Hank and I are going to run the perimeter of the property on his ATV and outline the demolition plans." He opened her door and she slid in, looking excited. JJ walked around and got inside, buckling his belt before turning on the vehicle.

"Great. I want to get the local art folks in to scavenge the weathered wood if they want." She bit her lip and turned toward him with her big eyes. "We aren't going to have to charge them for the wood, are we?"

"No. Let them have what they can reuse. Maybe you can wangle an art class and learn to create some rustic pictures for our walls. You've a creative streak."

"Good idea. After you guys' finish, should we take a ride on our property?"

"We could. I would rather save that for after we sign the papers." He clasped her hand and raised it, placing a gentle kiss on her knuckles. "Then we can get this show on the road."

They headed toward Hank's ranch with shared comments about the fall wildflowers along the roadway, and blue skies dotted with cotton balls pretending to be clouds. JJ parked next to the ATV. The well-maintained Polaris Sportsman supported two riders. JJ's blood pumped as he was hoping he could talk Hank into letting him drive.

"So, you like Mabel? That's her name."

Hank's greeting pulled him from his daydream. JJ ran his hand over the shiny red paint. "When you told me it could ride two, I was surprised, but she's a beaut."

Hank laughed. "Yep, you can drive her. I'll ride behind. It's a lot of fun and an easy way to get around that property." He gave Jo a quick hug in greeting. "Ann's inside with Camila, trying to figure out the best way to do riding lessons for Jason. She is expecting him tomorrow. Maybe you can shed additional insights with the girl. I think she's smitten."

"I'm happy to help. She is a teen, after all. There was a chance she might look at boys at some point." She kissed JJ. "I'll be here when you get back."

He handed her the car keys. "Take these in case you need to go somewhere."

Jo grabbed her things from the vehicle, handed JJ his notebook, then turned to leave. His gaze lingered in her direction until she disappeared inside. He looked at Hank and flipped his head. "Jo's a beauty, too."

Hank clapped JJ on the back. "You, son, are a lucky man. I have water and a few snacks in the back. Today is going to get warmer." He pointed. "Do you think you can drive Mabel without instructions?"

JJ nodded. He helped Hank in the backseat and climbed on, wiggling to get seated and properly balanced. He knew riding the vehicle was also a bit of a workout. The engine roared to life ready to take on the world They plopped on helmets, lowered the visors, and started out the gate. JJ guided the vehicle along the uneven dirt road to the entrance of his property. He loved driving this ATV that responded with the lightest of touches. He stopped, leaving the engine idling, and hopped to the ground. He gave Hank a thumbs-up when he undid the lock and swung the gate open.

"Hank, I think we circle the edge of the perimeter first, then measure off the buildings."

Hank nodded.

JJ drove to the left where the fence line was closest. They bumped along the edge, dodging trees and scrub, taking a right at the corner. JJ paused.

Hank shouted. "The fence line for this side looks good, but we need to cut back some of the mesquite. The thorns are nasty and livestock avoid it. The grasses and alfalfa growing out of control might be tempting to a few of my cows, if you want them to graze it down. Your choice."

JJ nodded, took out his phone for some photos in each direction, and continued down the back side, bypassing brush and big rocks that he mentally noted he'd mention to Jo to move for her garden. Reaching the corner, he spotted the tractor and paused. "Did you know the Stevens' had a tractor?" JJ bellowed.

"Now that I see it, I do. I thought it might be in the barn, but out here it's going to have rust. Might not be salvageable."

"I don't want to check now, but it's good to know where it is." JJ shifted his gaze to the right and pointed. "It seems I do have a couple of sections of fence down." He maneuvered the ATV to the area, assessing the damage and taking more photos. "Hank, does this appear like weather caused it?"

"Nope, but the tractor could have easily done that. Thankfully it is only two sections, easily fixed. Let's continue down the line."

JJ followed the property boundary, mentally noting additional huge rocks. He chuckled at a few lizards sunbathing atop one huge rock. They returned to the starting point with no further damage to record. He turned the four-wheeled vehicle and parked between the two structures in the shade.

The men got off the Polaris and shook out their legs, Hank grabbing his cane for stability. "JJ, the tractor and downed fence might explain the random squatters we've suspected over the years. I wouldn't be surprised if we find residue of parties with cans and trash in the house."

JJ nodded. "I found some trash in the house, but it was amazingly intact, like he just walked away. If Thomas left, he didn't pack up to do it."

Hank rubbed his chin. "That's odd. Let's start there."

"Just take care on the porch, some of the wood is rotted."

The men entered the dusty house and surveyed the rooms with JJ snapped pics as Hank pointed out specifics he and Jo hadn't considered. Dishes in the cabinets, furniture and a refrigerator, fortunately with no science experiments inside. The bedrooms were the same. JJ wasn't surprised to see only men's clothing, as he suspected Thomas donated much of his wife's things when she died. Hank pointed out a few holes in the walls in every room. They suspected vandals caused them, especially with the candy wrappers and chip bags near each hole. The fireplace bore the residue of cinders and ash.

"Lucky no one got hurt in here. I'm surprised none of the windows are broken."

"It's like he just walked away. We probably should go through the drawers at some point before it's bulldozed," mentioned Hank, shaking his head.

"Good idea. We need to bring back some garbage bags."

JJ drew out the rough floor plan on his note pad. He added details of the furniture, dishes, and clothing that might be salvageable. The two men measured the outside of the house before they stopped for a short rest. Hank offered the water and snacks.

JJ took a generous drink. "I don't think there is anything I've spotted that can't be fixed."

"Agreed. I can contact some of the needed resources when you're ready, JJ. It'll get you a chance to meet some folks you might not know. Ann said folks are talking about how nice it'll be to have you around some." He bit off the granola bar and chewed. "It's a shame to realize that Thomas got fed up and left. I hope he found a way to start fresh."

"I can only imagine the grief he felt. I know I'd be devasted."

"Me too, son." Hank carefully added the empty bottle and wrapper to the small trash bag affixed to the side of the ATV.

JJ followed suit. "Let's get to the barn. Maybe there are tools we can use to fill in some of the holes. I wouldn't want anyone turning a foot if they attend the demolition party, as Jo likes to think of it. Maybe the holes were made by animals digging out dirt to find a cool spot to lay during summer."

Hank shook his head. "An animal wouldn't-a done that. More like a shovel, but the locations we've seen and driven over make no sense, particularly around the back of the house."

JJ reached the sliding barn doors. Each one slid open allowing light to pour into the space. As they entered, the men were greeted by dust motes swirling in the air, along with a mustiness comprised of old hay, dirt, and a hint of fertilizer. JJ kicked himself that he and Jo hadn't noticed the bags of compost on the floor, and the workbench laden with garden implements, gloves and pots.

"That's the stuff Marissa used to work in her garden. I can almost picture her happy smile when she showed Ann and me her garden that first year. Her mud boots are there on the side," Hank indicated. "Ann's gonna cry if she sees this."

JJ moved to the left behind a wooden half-wall. "Hey, Hank. Did you know they had a freezer out here? Jo and I found it yesterday. It's huge."

Hank ambled to it and ran his hand over the dusty top. "Yep, this must be nearly twenty cubic feet. Perfect for storing a side-a meat. I have one nearly this size but could always use another if it still works."

JJ looked behind and reached for the cord, unplugging it from the wall. "The cord looks in good shape, no rodent chewing. It might be good, depending on when the power was shut off down here. I didn't think to check that before, but I bet we can find that out from the city, right?"

"Yes, you can. They would have all those records. Funny, we knew the taxes were paid but didn't think about the utilities. We also didn't check the post box for mail. We can do that on our way out to the road."

"Hank, I think I can break the lock on here without damaging the freezer if you want to haul it back to your place. Or we can just scrap it."

"Give it a try, if you think you can aim." Hank chuckled.

JJ returned to the ATV and grabbed the hammer included with the modest supply of tools in the back. Three swings later the mechanism broke off and fell on the dirt.

JJ gave it two perfect hits before the padlock split. "Good, I didn't have to call Tommy for his bolt cutters." He picked off the remnants of the lock and flipped the latch.

Hank helped lift the lid from one side, while JJ took the other.

"Oh, crap! Hank, tell me this isn't what I think it is."

"I can't. This is about a million dead blow flies atop a decomposed body."

"How…why?"

"Someone committed the crime and left the lid up until the flies infested the scene. Closing the top on the living beasts would give them time to do their worst."

"Hank, we gotta phone Tommy. He's never going to let us back in town."

"Come on, JJ. Let's contact him from outside, and I'll let Ann know we'll be later than we thought."

CHAPTER 24

# How Did We Get Here?

Tommy's cruiser halted next to the ATV. He pulled out his latex gloves and slid them on as he strode toward Hank and JJ standing in front of the barn. The humidity made the air feel heavy as the sun indicated it was close to noon. Tommy scanned the grey clouds to the east, suspicious of a light rain coming before evening.

Tommy turned upon hearing another car door slam announcing the arrival of Jake the weekend coroner. He waited until Jake reached him. "Thanks for heading over so fast. JJ said it's in the barn. They left it open about," he glanced at his watch, "forty-two minutes ago now."

"Not a problem, Tommy. Doing this kept me from having to finish my honey-do list and eat the wife's leftovers. Maybe now I can stop when I get back to town for some good food."

Tommy laughed. "You should do the cooking."

"I do most times, but she likes to use the leftovers and has a knack for messing them up."

Tommy studied Hank and JJ, while Jake headed inside with his bag in hand.

Tommy leaned on the barn door shaking his head. "If your leisure moments are covered up in crime scenes, what's your regular day job like, JJ?"

"Actually, my day job isn't much different, except I do it from a computer keyboard. I haven't worked out how to break this to

Jo yet. Honestly, Tommy, we came to Magnolia Bluff to vacation, not to bring you problems."

"Hank, you keep still while I ask JJ here some questions, then I'll get your side."

Hank agreed with a grunt.

"Tell me all the events leading up to finding a body in a locked freezer."

JJ went through their arrival and activities before they ever got to the barn.

Hank interjected, "When we got to the barn, we found this locked freezer. JJ said it was huge and didn't see any use for it in his future so asked if I wanted it. I figured I could use it for storing deer meat when the season opens up."

Tommy frowned. "Hank, I asked you to wait."

"I know."

Tommy rubbed his hands together, a bit frustrated. He heard Jake holler, "You folks have something to hold the lid open while I process this body?"

Hank replied to Tommy. "Off to the side of the barn, there's a good sized two by four that will help, I suspect."

"You two made a pretty thorough inventory before I arrived."

"Like I said, Tommy," clarified JJ, "we saved the barn for last."

"I helped Thomas locate the freezer when they were building out the ranch," Hank added. "I'd forgotten all about it until we found it. Ann and I liked the Stevenses. Was there anything else on your mind, Chief Jager?"

After a few moments of silence, Hank added, "But if you're thinking I had something to do with putting a body in the freezer, ask yourself why I'd be stupid enough to help cut off the lock and look inside before moving it."

"Hank, we were both shocked to our core when we opened it. Tommy's not going to blame you for anything at this point.

Relax." JJ continued, "Chief, let's get the chunk of wood to the coroner, and I'll go through the other details we discovered before we opened the barn."

"I wasn't accusing you, Hank, just looking at this from all angles." Tommy grabbed the wood and entered the barn with JJ and Hank in tow. "Here you go, Jake. How can we help?"

"Ready when you are, Tommy. Let me shoot pictures, then we can start moving the remains onto my body bag. Those blowflies cleaned off everything before they died from a lack of oxygen. Someone left the top open for at least six hours to get them started. Then the little boogers did the rest."

JJ and Hank watched Tommy string out the crime scene tape to cordon off the area inside the barn.

Hank leaned in and commented, "This isn't gonna be good for your compressed timeline, JJ. As I recall, once that yellow crime scene tape is up, you can't disturb the area. I suspect he'll widen the tape line to the front of the barn. We won't be able to git anyone in here to even start grabbing the wood Ann mentioned Jo wanted."

JJ pulled out his phone and keyed a request to his favorite reference librarian. Minutes later he smiled at the response. "Chief, when are you going to move the freezer and its contents so we can go back to work here?"

"JJ," Tommy huffed. "You're to stand down from any activity until I release it. This is now a crime scene. Having a bunch of folks come in here to start work on your dream home is gonna have to wait. I don't want any crime scene evidence ruined."

"But Chief, this isn't a standard crime scene. All of your evidence is in the freezer with the body. There are no body fluids, no tire tracks, no evidence of a struggle, and too many seasons have passed to find trace evidence. We can pack up the contents of the house, if that'll help. The best protocol left is to take the freezer with its contents to a forensic laboratory to examine the bones. All your evidence is in the freezer, so if you take the unit and body then there is no real need to mark the property as a restricted crime scene."

Jake looked up from his camera and added, "Technically, he's right, Tommy. I need to find out who this is, and a cause of death."

CHAPTER 25

# Check it Out

Lily gently rapped on Calvin's door. "Breakfast is ready and available 'til ten. The other guests have already eaten and left for the morning." Hearing nothing, she muttered under her breath. "Perhaps the separate rooms were a ruse." She walked upstairs to the third floor and knocked at Ms. Duncan's door. She reached to knock but noticed the door wasn't closed, so she eased it open.

Lily was stunned. The sheets were wadded and half on the floor. The closet was open and empty. A quick look in the bathroom presented towels on the floor, no water in the tub, and trash strewn not even close to the basket. She ground her teeth. "Ah, hell. Looks like someone packed up and left in a hurry. She didn't bother to mention anything or leave a note. Didn't care for her much, something off about her." Lily stomped her foot and rushed to the window that looked out over the guest parking. "No rental car. I wonder if Calvin's room tells the same story as this one."

Lily secured the room, then trudged back down to Calvin's room, unlocked it and went in. It was in a similar condition, and he was definitely gone. She swore under her breath at seeing the broken lamp. "I liked that lamp; it was an antique." Lily assessed the time it would take to right both rooms, then locked the door as she left. "Thank goodness I have their charge cards on file. A few lines for damages will be added before I process. Like I need extra work."

She made notes in the journal at the front desk and verified no one else was booked into those rooms for the remainder of the week. Lily looked up as JJ and Jo reached the ground floor from their room.

"Hi again, you two. Did you want any leftover breakfast to take along for a snack?"

"Yes, please, and a few bottles of water, if you have them," JJ said.

Lily rushed to the kitchen, returning in under ten minutes with a bag in hand. She handed the bag over the top of the desk then scratched another note on her journal. She didn't look at Jo.

Jo squinted toward Lily. "Are you all right? We heard you on the stairs, which surprised us."

"Calvin and Stacie, whom you visited with in the dining room a couple of times, apparently decided to trash each of their rooms as they snuck out. No note or thank you or kiss my…um, never mind. The antique lamp in Calvin's room is shattered." She sighed. "I knew they weren't staying together which is why they were on different floors, but I'd swear there was a fight. Did y'all hear any shouting?"

"Not a sound," JJ replied but added with a sheepish grin, "We had music on, and well…" JJ shifted one foot to the other. "Don't you take credit card information up front and test a charge? You did for our room."

"Of course," Lily said. "But, it really chaps my…uh, frosts my cookies when folks bolt like that." The tears welled in her eyes. "I treat folks like family. I sort of liked Calvin. He teased sweetly sometimes. Not terribly fond of that Ms. Duncan. She seemed a bit too big for her britches, if you know what I mean. Now I have unnecessary work I don't deserve."

Jo engulfed Lily in a brief hug. "Lily, I can stay if you need extra hands."

"Me too!" JJ added, rubbing his hands together. "Tell me what you need." Lily grinned and wiped the moisture from her eyes. "Renata will help me. And I can practice my swearing in Spanish. I bet she won't need to correct me." She waved both her hands to indicate the door was behind them. "Never you mind, I'll be fine. Go have a great day on your property. Fill me in on all the details later."

"Do you think it's still necessary to alert Hank and Ann before we show up?"

Lily chuckled. "Nah, you'll be fine." She reached under the counter and pulled out a red and black bullhorn. "Take this and announce your arrival."

JJ accepted the device and uneasily looked it over. As his gaze met Lily's, she broke out giggling. "Made you look."

He passed it back to her, laughing riotously.

They made the short drive to the ranch with the wind blowing in their hair. "Jo, we're almost to the final signing. Are you excited?"

"I'm glad we found a fun place."

With the freezer gone and the poor body still being identified, I think we're lucky we get to start the next phase toward cleaning up the area."

"I bet it's Thomas like you do. So sad."

"On a brighter subject, what's our next step?"

"Ann said she'd forward the two-story design we settled on to the three contractors for bids and estimated timing, start to completion."

"She didn't want to give you a single recommendation?"

"Nope. Ann said she trusted them all to be fair. Whoever wins the bid will likely sub some aspects to the others. It'll give us the best results."

"All right. We will determine how to verify different phases. Jo, one or both of us may have to return for a weekend here and there to ensure certain tasks stay on schedule."

"I know. We'll make it work." Jo reached over and stroked his leg.

JJ looked at her briefly before he turned into the open gate. "Good. They expected us." He parked next to the house. "Ann, Hank, we're here."

Oddly enough there was no response, even though JJ could see through the screen door as he opened the car door for Jo. They walked onto the porch where Camila rushed to greet them. She unlocked the door, motioning them inside.

Ann stood with the princess wall phone in her hand and a serious expression in the kitchen. It appeared that she was near the end of the call. Hank leaned back in his easy chair with his leg up. His face reflected pain and discomfort. He opened his eyes and raised a hand, acknowledging them. Camila replaced the ice pack on his foot and kissed his cheek. "Sorry if that hurt."

Ann gave Jo and JJ quick welcoming hugs. "The doctor will see us in an hour. They'll meet us at the emergency entrance. JJ, I need help getting this old stubborn fool in the pickup."

"Ann, would you rather take my car? It might be easier than lifting him up into the truck."

"I don't care. Mr. Obstinate needs x-rays. The foot and his attitude are equally bad. I'm not waiting for it to get any worse."

Hank growled. "She accused me of shirking my chores and making Camila cover for me. I was trying to get an idea of what was going on over on your property last night. I heard noises as if them squatters were back. She saw lights flickering. I hobbled over to get on the Polaris to have a look-see and stepped on a stone, twisting my foot. I yelped, and they both helped me to bed. I didn't get a wink of sleep last night."

"JJ?" Jo looked at him with concern. "Why don't you take Hank and Ann to the hospital. I'll stay with Camila to keep her safe. Ann, where's your cast iron skillet in case we need protection?"

Ann howled. "That's right. I've heard them say you're the frying pan queen. Which reminds me, Lily called and said her out-of-town bank people skipped out. You know Gunter met with them yesterday and tossed them to the street. Haven't learned why yet."

"We heard they left in something of a hurry and left no message that they were leaving early. Hadn't heard about any bank issue yesterday though."

Ann shook her head. "Some people. Come on, JJ, help me move this old man into the truck so I can git him to town."

Hank appeared stricken. "What? You take my truck and mess up all the mirrors and move the seat forward for your dwarf legs? Argh! No, I'll drive and..."

"Do you want me to drop a frying pan on your other foot? We're leaving now and I'm in charge."

"Ann, you can take the Mustang."

"Oh, no. My dwarf legs can't wait to mess with the pickup seats and adjust the mirrors. Plus, I know how to hit all the potholes. Camila, I need you to stay in the house until I get back. I'll call you with updates."

Jo handed Camila her phone. "You can use mine in case we go to the new property. Call if you need help." She showed her the fast link to get hold of JJ."

"Thank you, Ms. Jo."

JJ leaned over to help lift Hank and whispered, "I believe you've lost this argument. Cooperate now and plan your revenge for later."

JJ looked up at Ann and winked as Hank chuckled.

Once he was secured, JJ asked, "May I borrow your Polaris to check the property? I'd like to see if there's any evidence of squatters."

Ann fished the keys from Hank's pocket and pitched them. He nodded agreement.

Through his mischievous grin, JJ said, "Thanks, Dad, I'll be back before midnight."

CHAPTER 26

# Start of a New Chapter of Life

JJ grabbed his laptop backpack and headed to the door. As Jo exited, she delivered parting instructions. "We're headed over to the property for a few hours. If you get nervous, call JJ's phone and we'll come right back."

JJ heard Camila's response. "I'm fine, Ms. Jo. I'll get the house chores finished so when Ann and Hank return, she can spoil him. I'll crank up the radio and sing along while I work."

Jo nodded and laughed as JJ reached around her and nuzzled her neck. "Come on, sweetheart. I get to drive the ATV again."

Jo snagged her scarf and Lily's supply bag from the Mustang. She skipped to JJ's side, and they walked toward the corral where the ATV was parked. JJ checked the tools in the back and added the snacks into the shaded nook. He extended his hand so Jo could climb into the seat. He mounted and turned on the machine. "You're gonna love this, honey."

She hugged him from behind. JJ maneuvered out the gate and toward the property. They bounced along singing Home on the Range all the way to their gate. JJ climbed down to unlock the gate then returned to the driver's seat, expertly bringing the machine into the area. He took the same route he had with Hank and pointed out the first big rock he'd found.

"That's a good one. If we can get it moved, I can make it work. What else?"

They traveled the path. He pointed out the downed fence area. "Jo, there appears to be fresh breaks on some of those plants."

"You could be right. Maybe kids were in here last night."

"Maybe. Fence repair just jumped to the top of the fix list." He drove them from that area through more of the middle of the spread, where Jo pointed out several more rocks to add to their garden.

"These rocks will make an interesting back drop for the plants Lily told me were native to the region. She said she'd help me select the right types for low maintenance, drought resistance, and as much color as possible. She said we must see the spring wildflowers in the area with their riotous colors."

"Sounds good." JJ drove to where Tommy had the guys park the tractor after they transferred the freezer to a trailer to have it processed. They'd mounted the loader attachment onto the tractor. JJ decided he might start moving the rocks closer. He became concerned when he spotted newly churned earth near the house.

"Jo, someone used the tractor after we locked up. I know we left the key in it in case we needed to use it." He jumped down taking pictures of the freshly mounded dirt. Jo, right behind him, accompanied him around the house pointing out the new mounds she saw.

"You're right, honey, this is fresh. Looks like someone digging a moat to me."

He saw the glow on her skin, signaling to him she was getting overheated. JJ considered who might have moved the tractor, wondering if Hank tried to help after JJ left the other day. He clenched his gut, worried that something more was going on. "I'll move a few of the rocks closer. Why don't you take a look in the barn at the garden work bench. I'll join you shortly. Maybe take our snacks into the shade. It's cooler in there than outside." He handed her the key to the ATV.

Jo mischievously grinned and headed toward the ATV. JJ shrugged at the thought she might take it for a spin. She certainly could if she wanted to. He started up the tractor and methodically moved ten of the big rocks before deciding he might impede the demo efforts if he continued. He parked the tractor and pocketed the key, heading toward the barn.

Jo was singing softly and cleaning off the gardening workbench.

"I'm back."

Jo spun around. "JJ, this is perfect. She must have enjoyed herself here. I found some flowerpots, extra gloves, bulb planter tools. The boots fit perfectly." She raised each foot and turned to emphasize the fit. "No matter how much manure I spread, I can walk around without tracking it inside. All the bags," she pointed, "are in great shape and usable. That'll save us a lot."

JJ grabbed a water and twisted the top, drinking almost all of the bottle before stopping. "I moved the rocks closer, but once you figure out the garden design, we can place them to their final position." He found a nail at her workbench and hung up the tractor key. "We'll store the tractor in here since I got a new padlock for the barn door."

"At some point I want to learn to drive both machines."

"No problem."

She waved her arms around the building. "If we can restore this place, I know we're going to keep the gardening area in here. It's perfect with the bright, natural lighting and—" she whirled in a circle— "look at the amount of space!"

"I think the framing is sturdy. All we need to do is replace the outer wood and decide how to paint it. Red like a traditional southern barn or whatever works to blend with our house."

"Do we want to buy a couple of horses?"

JJ walked around the area considering the possibilities. "Keeping horses when we're not here isn't smart. A few cows in the pasture might not be bad, or loan the pasture to Hank for a portion of his herd. We could add a couple of paddocks to hold horses when we are in town. If we contributed to the upkeep for our faves at Hank's, maybe he would reserve them for us." JJ jumped up and started playing an air game of basketball. "This place just begs to be finished as a half-basketball court." He jumped, twisted, dribbled, and took a shot toward an imaginary hoop mounted to the side where Tommy and his team had removed the half wall. He landed with a hollow Thump! and stopped.

Jo's grin vanished. "Are you okay?"

"I'm fine. Did you hear the change in sound?"

"What change?" She shook her head.

JJ jumped around the area again, listening for the sound as he landed.

"There and there." Jo pointed. "Maybe hollow. Let me mark it while you jump again." Jo grabbed the hoe and made marks while JJ hopped around the area.

"Thanks. Hand me the hoe. Please grab a shovel, and let's see what's down here."

Jo pushed open the door as wide as possible, then rushed for the narrow plant shovel. She returned to the spot to remove dirt while JJ broke up the area with the hoe.

He stopped when he reached the color change, maybe two inches below the surface. Seeing something green peeking up from the dark dirt, he knelt. "We've got something, honey. Let's see if we can find the edges."

They carefully worked the dirt up and out of the way. It wasn't long before a bundle of green fatigue fabric, tied with thick rope, was revealed. "It looks like a box of some sort, six or so feet long by nearly two feet wide. Let me borrow the shovel and see if I can mark a border on this side."

JJ scraped a gulley around the item and found the bottom around fifteen inches or so below the top. He wiped his brow and took another bottle of water, drinking deeply. "I'm not sure how heavy it is. We have a slope to the bottom shaped like a wedge. We might slide it to ground level."

"No problem." She raised her arm, flexing her plex. "I have great muscle tone."

JJ chuckled. "You sure do, sweetheart. I'll rock it, then we'll try to move it together."

She nodded. Several minutes later, with collaborative actions, the box rested on the level dirt of the barn floor. JJ lifted one end. "I'm guessing it's less than sixty pounds but too bulky to carry before we discover the contents." He stood and reached into his pocket, extracting a pocketknife. He knelt again and cut the strings. The far side of the fabric edge became visible, and he pulled it back.

"It looks like old army fatigues." Jo took a few photos.

"Agreed." He released the fabric from the top and laid it down on all sides, discovering it was a footlocker with a lock. He frowned. "Should we open it?"

Trying to cover her feminine curiosity, she offered, "Why not?"

He went for a hammer and chisel in the ATV and returned to attack the lock. Repeated hits finally made the metal yield and fall to the ground. He carefully picked up the box lever and raised the lid.

They were stunned for several moments.

"Honey, it's time to call Tommy again, right?"

He stared at the green and white stacks of Andrew Jacksons, feeling another delay in their future plans. "Take my phone to make the call, Jo. As soon as you get him on the way, I want to take a more pics, and then we step outside to wait for him to arrive."

Jo nodded and placed the call.

CHAPTER 27

# Déjà vu

**G**ravel and rocks hitting metal announced Tommy's car siding up next to the ATV. The slamming of the door announced his imminent approach. They heard the crunch of his boots as he navigated around the obstacles toward the barn. JJ pulled Jo a bit closer for reassurance.

"Hi, Tommy. Glad you could find time for us."

Tommy pulled off his Stetson and bounced it off his leg. "JJ, what the heck are you two up to now? What Jo said on the phone made no sense, which usually means a new problem."

"Come inside. We'll explain what we can."

Tommy tromped in next to JJ. They stopped as he gazed into the open footlocker. "Where in tarnation did that come from?"

"The best news I have, Tommy, it was under the freezer on the left side. See those broader indentations we didn't disturb at the back, where the freezer rested."

Tommy nodded raking his hair with his fingers.

"We removed the dirt around until JJ spotted the green, then he created the slope in the front to move it out. We were together the whole time." Using her hand, Jo crossed her heart with her eyes focused on Tommy. "Honest."

JJ's heart swelled with appreciation for his bride standing up for them.

Tommy walked around the box, gauging it from each angle. "Tell me the steps you took in detail while I think of what we're going to do next."

"I was jumping around playing air hoop basketball. When I took a shot and landed, I heard a sound change. I jumped several more times until I decided to find out what was below. Seriously, I thought maybe it was an access point to a root cellar." JJ took a breath. "We worked the dirt loose. The tarp was tied on. The string holding it is underneath now. I cut it and peeled back the tarp. I didn't have gloves on, Tommy so my prints will be all over it."

Tommy frowned. "Who would have a root cellar that would need regular access, put a freezer on top of it, needing a crane to move it? No matter, fingerprints wouldn't be on the fabric anyway. Go on."

JJ recounted the preceding events in detail until he took a breath.

"That's when I called you, Tommy," Jo said.

"We stepped away and waited for you," confirmed JJ.

"You never touched anything inside, correct? The stacks look federally banded but not bank-specific."

"There could be other presidents in there."

Tommy shook his head. "Oh, brother." He put his hat back on and handed Jo his keys with one in particular sticking out. "Can you open my trunk? JJ, let's drape the cover over this and we'll take it back to my office. No one else is on duty today."

JJ watched Jo scamper off to the police car before turning his attention back to the task at hand.

The men hoisted the box. "It weighs less than sixty pounds," Tommy commented. "Just awkward."

They secured the item into the police cruiser. JJ did a short explanation about Hank and Ann going to the hospital. "Great," he replied. JJ secured the gate on their property, then Tommy followed them back to the ranch behind the ATV.

JJ parked the ATV, grabbed his backpack, and walked to where Tommy stood. "Jo, have Camila lock up here and drive her to Flower. She can help Renata with dinner. Call Ann and let her know to pick up the girls when they return home. Don't say anything about the findings," Tommy emphasized. "Just say you and JJ need to come talk with me about the freezer. Do you understand?"

"Yes, sir."

JJ provided the keys to Jo and rode with Tommy behind Jo and Camila.

The silence inside the squad car was nearly deafening. JJ was relieved sitting in the front as opposed to behind the plexiglass. Tommy smacked the top of the steering wheel, his lips in a thin line. JJ swallowed the lump that had lodged in his throat.

"Let's hear the rest of it, JJ."

"You know, sir, I didn't start any of this situation, nor did I last time. I really don't want us at odds. It started because my wife wanted a slice of Magnolia Bluff to visit regularly. I like answers when I see problems I can fix."

"Last time, I discounted you and Jo's determination, which turned out incorrect and resulted in my eating crow. This time I'm mad, but I'm not discounting you. I figure you're knee-deep in this hot mess, and it's about time you spring new material on me. Let's get all of it out on the table."

JJ laughed, feeling relief course through him. Perhaps Tommy was an ally. "Fair enough, sir."

Tommy pulled the car to a stop. "I can pull the officer of the law card. You can dole out pieces of information like tortilla chips in a Mexican restaurant. Or we can work together, and you can call me Tommy!"

JJ swallowed again, to make sure the lump was gone and his voice would come out loud and clear. "The property Jo and I wanted; well, you know that history."

Tommy nodded.

"A lot going on since we've arrived. Their story seemed so sad with a man setting up a trust to pay taxes for twenty-five years, yet he vanished from a town that rallied around him. A part-time caretaker for the same man's wife made a scene at the wife's funeral, had friends in town, but also left town for greener fields. A lady at Flower recently made my skin prickle for no identifiable reason, so I captured her fingerprints. I'm waiting on feedback to see if she has a record. A financial investor comes to town to invest in the bank, yet had some sort of disagreement with Gunter Fight. A body gets found on the property I invested in. And now buried money. I've been digging around every loose thread. I've some documentation I'm happy to give you."

JJ ran his fingers through his hair then moved the vent pouring out the cool air so that it was pointing toward his face. "I'm stuck at unsealing court records of a sister to Marissa Stevens which might open other threads to pull. My, uh…resources are unable to access them. We've tried every angle. Oh, and our room at Flower was visited by an unknown someone looking for something, messed with my laptop, and who forgot to put stuff back. That's the worst because I will do anything to protect my wife. A hint of her being at risk in this town sends me into total protect mode."

Tommy looked out the window in the distance for a moment, which JJ hoped was a positive thing. Then he turned back to JJ. "If I were married to the acclaimed model Jo W, I'd be careful too. Now the court records issue…that I can help with. I am a peace officer with contacts."

JJ tried to contain his surprise and concern that Jo was not safe. Fury welled in him. If Tommy knew, others likely did too. This wasn't a haven. She'd be heartbroken. "When we get to Flower, I'll tell Jo I changed my mind about the property. With all this mess, we can leave tomorrow, and she can write letters and call her friends to keep up with the changes. I don't know how you found out, but if everyone knows, then this is not the refuge she hoped it might be. We wanted to be a part of this town, but now…" JJ pulled out his phone to put some flights in motion out of Austin. He stopped feeling Tommy's hand on his arm.

"JJ, wait. Everyone doesn't know. Lily does, of course, because she and Jo spoke about it. Lily enjoys her gossip but loves Jo like a daughter. She is thrilled you might be here part-time. I found out when you were here before. Dare I repeat myself, I'm a darned good peace officer. Lily folded like a cheap lawn chair after she was attacked, and Jo wielded her frying pan. She begged me to keep it quiet. Heck, I agreed. Y'all are nice people." Tommy put the vehicle into drive, moving at the speed limit. "Whose fingerprints?"

"I get irritable when someone tries to break into my laptop, so I asked my reference librarian if they could, uh…shed some light for me. Stacie Duncan is not who she pretends to be. She and Calvin, who were not a couple, according to Lily, left with no explanation."

"They pissed off Gunter with some heavy-handed tactics, and he threw them out of his bank." Tommy laughed. "He's a Texan who can spot a con even when it's called a friend. He told me yesterday when he filled me in that he has no evidence. As a banker, character assessment is something he does quite well."

"Before we leave town, I'll give you my research on Stacie for your investigation. We have nearly three weeks left on our vacation; I'll find another place to relax."

"Son, I suspect neither you nor Jo know the meaning of the word. You folks found a body no one was looking for, and a footlocker of cash that everyone's gonna want. Now you're going to vanish. With all the clues you keep turning up, you can't say you don't want to know the answers. Heck, if you stay, will you at least let me be your deputy when they elect you Chief of Police?"

"I don't know. How good are you at getting coffee?"

Tommy laughed aloud. "At Flower I'm great, and the price is right, but don't push your luck." He positioned the vehicle close to the station's door behind the building. JJ and Tommy wrestled the footlocker into his conference room.

Tommy clapped JJ on the back. "You're safe in Magnolia Bluff. We're fond of stories, and you keep uncovering some dandy fodder."

JJ sent a text telling Jo to let him know when she arrived. He debated how much he'd share of his conversation with Tommy. "Let me figure out how to tell Jo, okay?"

"Of course."

## CHAPTER 28

# The King in His Castle

Tommy moved the chairs to one side of the conference room. The table was bare except for the parcel they deposited. Tommy and JJ put on rubber gloves. Tommy slid the footlocker to one side of the table and unwrapped it, careful about capturing possible trace evidence.

"JJ, hold open this bag and I'll add the tarp."

Tommy felt this case could change history in Magnolia Bluff.

"Okay. I can hold bags and mark them if you want."

"I'll send anything we collect for Jake to look at, or on to Austin if necessary."

He dusted the footlocker for fingerprints and directed JJ to take pictures. His gut clenched from worry that he'd miss something. "You're sure neither you or Jo touched the box or the latch?"

"I'm positive I flipped the latch with the edge of the chisel."

"Then we have two partials. The best one is on the underside." He laid out lines of fresh butcher paper off a roll he grabbed from the corner. "Now, I want to dust the outside of each stack of money for prints. Since it was new money when it was put into the box, the number of prints should be limited. We might get lucky."

Tommy stopped and retrieved a badge from his desk. "Hold up your right hand. I'll swear you in as my deputy for now, but I do the direction."

JJ nodded and raised his right hand. "Yes, sir."

"It's going to be tedious, but with both of us we can make it like an assembly line. As a standard, there are a hundred bills per banded group. For Jackson then, that is two thousand dollars per stack."

"Tommy, since it is new, do you think the numbers might be consecutive in the stacks?"

"It's possible, and a good call. It would make it easier to count that way. Banks band by the hundred so counting is easier if the recipient doesn't have a machine. Band colors are denominations, like the violet we see here is twenties."

JJ's phone lit up with an incoming text. "Jo's here. I'm going to let her in."

"Fine, just lock the door afterward. She'll get sworn in too."

Tommy heard them talking before he spotted them. Jo carried a bag and appeared to have changed into cleaner clothing. He wondered if she'd brought JJ clothes. They were such a cute couple.

"Hi, again." Jo grinned. "I decided we might all need food, so I had Lily prepare lunch. I hope it's okay." He swore her eyes twinkled when she set the bag on the empty table.

"I like a girl who thinks on her feet. You timed it well, Jo." Tommy went and retrieved another badge. "I need you to swear to uphold the law and do as I direct."

Jo raised her hand, appearing serious. "Yes, sir. I do."

He handed her the badge. "I was giving your husband some ground rules for handling this cash while we count it. Would you mind writing down some serial numbers if we find them in order? It may help for counting."

"Sure. Where do I find a pad and pencil?"

Tommy pointed through the glass windows toward a cabinet. "Second drawer for a notepad in the grey cabinet, and pencils on any desk. My deputy is on vacation until next Monday."

Tommy kept an eye on Jo while she fetched the materials and returned. He was comfortable trusting these two, and that was an odd sensation for him.

Once the photographs were captured, they dusted the stacks and laid them in rows on the table.

"Whoa. Hamilton made an appearance under the latest stack I pulled. Jo, we've been reading numbers to you. Do they match up?"

"Not to one another. A few of the number sequences equate to the one hundred bills you mentioned, but the others are not in order. They look like the same height though."

"Feds have used counting machines for decades and the color bands as well. How many stacks so far?" Tommy asked.

"I have one hundred and twenty so far."

"We have five more stacks on top of the ten-dollar denominations," JJ announced. "That would equal two-hundred and fifty thousand."

Tommy looked up and caught Jo's eyes as wide as saucers.

"That's a bunch of money." He scratched his ear with a gloved finger. "I have no unsolved robberies in the area for that amount, or more, based on the next layer we've got. And they aren't in total consecutive order. This is weird; something doesn't add up." Tommy eyed JJ.

"Don't look at me. I'm out of ideas for now."

"Let's grab some food. Thank you, Jo, for bringing it. Then we can attack the next denomination. Makes me wonder if Lincoln is below Hamilton, if these were stacked low to high bills."

They sat in chairs, staring at the stacks of money. "Tommy, why would someone put a freezer on top of a stash of money?"

Tommy chewed and swallowed. "I got a better question. Why would anyone dispose of a body on top of a cash stash in a barn for years?"

"Drug monies stashed here since no one is living here but the property is vacant?" JJ mused. "If no one comes prowling around like we did, the money was safe."

"If that's true," Tommy reasoned, "putting the freezer on top of the money meant they weren't coming back anytime soon. It looks like the area hasn't been touched in years. Your theory doesn't seem to add up."

"Perhaps the dealer or trafficker got interrupted and couldn't return. Perhaps the body in the freezer was an isolated event, and the two are not connected."

JJ stared toward the invisible horizon. "In light of the digging occurring around the property, someone must know enough to come to look for buried money."

"Let's think of other ideas. Anything is possible, it seems," suggested Tommy.

Jo daintily dabbed at the mayo on her lips. "What if the body turns out to be Thomas Stevens? Then it might be no one knew where, if he hid it."

"Jo, you are not only a champ at swinging a pan, but you have a point. I'm waiting for Jake to update me. Just before I rushed to your place," he eyed JJ, "Jake said he found some teeth in the freezer that might match dental records. I asked him to check within a forty-mile radius first, maybe pull a few favors with long-time practices first. The scavenger flies cleaned up everything before they expired, so no fingerprints. Using county support, Jake dusted inside and out of the freezer for prints and sent them in for checking. That could take a few days or more without getting the feds involved."

JJ rounded up the trash and placed it in the receptacle inside the conference room. "Tommy, can I go wash up before we start again?"

"Yep, no phone with you when you walk out. I'll do the same when you get back. And, just so you know, I am trying to keep us above board in case we need to testify."

JJ nodded and washed up, returning so Jo could take a turn, then Tommy.

With the production line in place, they started on the ten-dollar bills. Again, some stacks were sequential, but not all of them.

"Tommy," Jo said, stretching. "I looked for the dates based on the serial numbers like JJ suggested. None of the bills so far are newer than 1973. Based on the sounds you guys are making when you finger them, these are new bills."

"No new monies were added since it was buried," stated JJ. "We must stay within the time capsule for the crime."

"JJ, can you use your source and upload a few of those fingerprint photos to see if we have any identified?"

"I can, but I think we only have a few more to go. Jo, how many stacks of tens do we have so far?"

"Our count is at two-forty. Tommy, that is nearly half a million dollars, right?"

"Yes, ma'am. And I am counting ten in here before we hit a plastic wrapped bundle. Looks like an old Comet Cleaners garment bag. We had that company in town before Quik Clean bought it out. Let's count these bills. I want to see what is on the bottom."

They pushed through the last ten for a total of two hundred and fifty stacks of Hamilton bills. Tommy lifted the bundle, and JJ moved the empty footlocker to the side. They scooted the stacks to one end of the table. Tommy used the open space to loosen the plastic. JJ picked up the plastic and added it to a new evidence bag.

Tommy leafed through some pictures, circa seventies and before, based on the clothes and hairstyles. There were baby clothes neatly folded, along with a baby-sized spoon and matching fork, stamped sterling silver. Then he located an envelope between the clothing. It was unsealed with a handwritten letter inside. Tommy opened and read the letter silently. With a shaky hand he handed it to JJ, then wiped his tears.

"Are you all right?" JJ asked as he held the letter.

Tommy waved his hand that suggested he needed a minute. JJ held it while he and Jo read it together. Halfway through, Jo clasped her hand over her mouth. Her eyes filled with tears while she continued to read. JJ turned the page over and they finished.

"Oh, my goodness," Jo started, with tears trailing down her cheeks. "Marissa's sister Anastasia was actually our Annie Flagstone. I wonder how she discovered her sister was ill. A kindness to take care of her sister, but the price. Poor Thomas."

Tommy punched his right fist into his open hand. "I need a picture of the letter, and I need to talk to Gunter."

"Tommy, I found the sister, Anastasia. Those are the court records I couldn't get unsealed," reminded JJ.

"Good. You two go back to Flower. Make certain the girls and Lily are safe. I'll call you after I speak to Gunter. And again, keep this a secret, deputies." He shook his head. "What a mess."

CHAPTER 29

# Meetings Within Meetings

Tommy marched into the quiet bank. There were no customers inside, and folks behind the counters were chatting, looking bored. He approached the first window and cleared his throat to get service. "I need to speak with Gunter. Let him know I'm here."

"Chief, Mr. Fight is in a meeting with some high-profile clients," the teller announced. "Can this wait?"

Tommy flexed his jaw muscles. Holding in his temper, he leaned forward and lowered his voice. "With the extra time on my hands, perhaps I should rework the warning ticket I gave you last week into a misdemeanor for drunk driving. Your thoughts?"

The man's face turned scarlet, and he raised his eyebrows, looking left to right hoping no one overheard. "Chief, I'm sure Mr. Fight would be grateful to know his current meeting ended early. Give me a minute, please." He picked up a phone, turning away as he spoke.

Less than a minute later, Fight's office door opened and two businessmen, appearing confused, shook hands with Gunter as he escorted them out the entrance. When Gunter turned, Tommy noted his sour face and clenched teeth, emphasized with a hand gesture for the chief to follow him. Tommy entered and heard the door shut behind him.

Both men took a seat. "What the heck, Tommy, you come in here without an appointment? I do run a business. I don't mind you scheduling a meeting." Gunter sighed and set both hands atop his neat desk. "You wanna tell me what this is about?"

Tommy set his jaw and stared at Gunter. "What happened at your bank in 1973? One minute Johnny Laughlin ran this place, then you took over. I was fairly new and not paying attention to local politics, but the rumor mill was cranking at full steam. Why did you take over?"

Gunter shifted in his chair then gazed toward the open window. "You mean, how did a guy like me with no formal training become a bank president?"

Tommy watched every nuance from the man. "Yes."

"I started out as a crazy wildcatter in both Texas and Oklahoma. My new in-laws invited me to buy in on a speculation hole. We hit right where the geologist said, but it was mostly natural gas. The back pressure ejected the drilling pipes. Before the pipes landed, the lead partner offered to buy me out for twice my investment." He smiled. "Needless to say, I got hooked. I hit four of the next five wellbores, and money poured in. I shoved my speculation winnings into the bank. First National Bank of Magnolia Bluff, to be precise."

Tommy frowned. "I don't need the whole story of how the West was won. What I want is—"

Gunter banged his fist on the desk. "If you're gonna barge in and interrupt my day, then you listen to the whole story, Tommy, or git."

Tommy snorted and his nostrils flared.

Gunter blinked. "Playing it safe, I cashed out as quickly as I could. I worried the oil high was too good to last. I was right. The following year, oil and gas prices went to hell in a handbasket. I laughed all the way to the bank as I was free and clear. Six months after the industry shift, it cost more to pump and transport the stuff than the selling price. I felt smug about my market timing."

Tommy looked at his watch, his impatience growing.

Gunter delivered a stink-eye. "Yes, there's a point. Keep still. I felt like king of the hill until Laughlin contacted me to talk." Gunter's face turned a bit red with anger. "Laughlin was there wringing his hands, while the FDIC auditor lectured. The man stated, 'You called us in because you can't find half a million. Insolvency means ruined careers. If this is embezzlement, someone's doing jail time. What do you suggest, Johnny?' I interrupted asking Laughlin what they meant. 'I had all my money in here, but now I'm broke?' The auditor replied, 'Mr. Fight, we asked you to come in since you are the largest depositor. We thought you should be part of the proceedings. In situations like this, we seize the bank and look for a buyer to quietly take it over. If that fails, we shop the crippled bank to other regional banks. The process is designed to be stealthy and quiet so people don't panic and create a run on the funds. We're here to prevent a repeat of the nineteen thirties financial collapse.'"

Gunter shook his head and refocused on Tommy, looking him in the eye.

"My options were simple. Either I take over the bank as president using my existing deposits as equity, or risk another bank coming in to settle with me for pennies on the dollar. Times being what they were, I took the job."

Tommy chuckled. "Ah, federal coercion with good intentions. What about the money? Where did the trail lead?"

Gunter practically spat. "That clown Laughlin had no business running a lemonade stand, much less a bank. We ran down every lead, every clue, looking for a culprit and the missing funds. Nothing. Nothing except the lead teller at the time disappeared shortly thereafter. Following exhaustive reviews, we found accounting rounding errors on the books. A sleight of hand. Ten dollars here, twenty dollars there, skimmed from transactions for a year. No one wanted to believe Thomas Stevens could take the money, especially when his wife died and he disappeared."

Gunter took a sip of water. "After Thomas buried his wife, he worked harder than before, like he was trying to drown his sorrow, with work, not with a bottle. He took off a few days at a time, calling in to say this or that document needed handling. I was burning through cash with outside accountants looking for a culprit when the investigator said to drop it. Even Mary Lou chided me for throwing good money after bad. I took stock in what we had and moved on."

Tommy cocked his head to one side. "How much again?"

"Half a million. In cash."

After a few moments, Tommy's lips rose. "Want it back?"

Tommy leaned patiently against the kitchen prep table, watching and listening as Lily burned up the airwaves with her mobile phone in hand.

"Hi, Connie, have you heard? The lost bank money from 1973 was found! Woo-hoo! Let me let you go so I can tell someone else the good news. Bye, hon."

Lily lowered the phone and stared at him with guilt written on her face "Like that?"

Tommy smiled. "Yep."

He turned, dusted his pant leg with his Stetson, and left Lily to her phone tree. He whistled and did a jig until he reached his cruiser. He got in and started it up. "Ah, making people happy. First, the Bank of Ebenezer Scrooge, then the all-time gossip champion of the Texas Hill Country. I think I'll try out for the Santa Claus role in the Christmas parade this year. See if I can't bring more cheer to others. Har! Har!"

## CHAPTER 30

# Patience is a Virtue

JJ sensed Jo was awake, so he wrapped his arms around her. "The appointment with the title company is at nine," he whispered. "Before we head over there, I need to tell you something."

"That you want breakfast and you love me. Maybe not in that order," she softly giggled.

"Those items go without saying. No, this is something else. I want to make certain, before we sign these papers, you absolutely want to do this. It's provided some trials and tribulations already. We could go someplace else for the rest of our…"

Jo bounced out of bed and glared at him. "Are you admitting this isn't a good idea, and you don't like it? After I get all excited about building a house, creating a garden, and having a place to just be us, you decide to bail?" Jo stamped her feet and balled up her fists to the point JJ feared she'd breathe fire.

He reached for her hand, but she evaded his grasp.

"Don't you dare try to sweet talk me, Mr. Change-your-mind. Grrrrr, you. I'm going to take a shower." She gathered up clothes for the day and turned toward him with her hand extended. "You can talk to the hand because I'm not listening."

JJ shook his head as he watched Jo enter the bathroom and decidedly close the door. "How did my conversation go so wrong?" he muttered. "I wanted to tell her about Tommy knowing my fears for her safety, but wow, everything came out wrong." He closed his eyes and patted his forehead, trying to get the pieces to fall into the right order to fix it. "I forgot how fast she moves, especially when her temper is up. Usually, she waits until I finish, even when she disagrees. I still think she needs to know…"

"Know what?" she asked.

JJ opened his eyes and saw her next to the bed wrapped in a plush bath sheet. Not wishing a repeat performance, he scooted away from her and patted the side of the bed for her to sit.

She sat and watched him with those big brown eyes he always got lost in.

"I'm sorry, Jo. I was trying to figure out the right order to explain, and messed up yet again."

"I'm listening again, since I overreacted. I'll wait 'til you finish. I'm sorry too."

"Yesterday, when I rode back with Tommy, he and I had a couple of discussions. One was about the evidence he figured I gathered, and the other was about you. I told him our suspicions and some of what we learned during our searches. I told him I wanted to keep you safe."

"I know that, JJ."

He looked at her as she ran her fingers across her mouth and made a movement like locking her lips shut.

He laughed. "You're too cute. He said he would be worried too if he were married to such a well-known model who is drop-dead gorgeous."

Jo appeared stunned with her eyes wide. She covered her mouth with a hand as a groan escaped from her lips. "Oh, dear. Does everyone in town know? You're right. This is a problem I hadn't even considered. Everyone has been…"

"Tommy said he believes only he and Lily know. When he questioned her after the attack last year, Lily inadvertently gave him a clue. She'd feel awful if you knew she'd spilled the beans. He also suggested this town likes us and is glad we returned for a visit. He thinks we should stay if we can get over the mess we found."

Jo scooted under the covers next to JJ. He pulled her closer. "You aren't opposed to fixing up the property?"

"No, honey. I'm only against you being fearful that someone will rip your sleeve or shove a microphone into your face. We both need the peace and quiet. I think I can set up the necessary security to keep out the riffraff in a fairly discreet manner. Having Tommy aware of who you are actually works to our favor. You were with him yesterday with no hint that he was treating you any differently."

"True. I like Tommy because he's genuine."

"So are you."

JJ kissed her and she kissed back. "Go take that shower and dress. I need to eat before we sign the papers. We'll finish a lot before we leave town to go back to work."

Jo danced to the shower, pulling off the bath sheet at the last second before she closed the door. JJ smiled wistfully at the delightful sight.

They scurried downstairs for breakfast. Lily had the buffet filled with eggs, sausage, biscuits, and coffee. "Lily, again you've out done yourself," JJ commented between bites.

"This is a basic good breakfast that should last until you return from the signing. Renata is working on the trays you asked for. We'll keep them in my walk-in cooler until you head out. Did you need her to go and help you?"

"No, I think we'll be fine. Did you get the rooms that were messed up ready for your next guests?" asked Jo.

Lily nodded. "I even found a new old lamp at the antique store on sale. I also billed their credit cards." She snorted. "I took pictures of everything in case they try to make a case of not paying."

"Good." JJ checked his watch. "Honey, we need to get going to avoid being late. I have no idea how long this will take."

"I'm finished." Jo wiped her mouth on her napkin. She stood and hugged Lily. "Wish us luck."

All the papers were assembled when JJ and Jo walked into the title company. The bank's representative reviewed each of the documents before they signed, and the papers were notarized. The thick stack of papers provided the details for the title transfer, homestead exemption, rules for claiming, animal for farm tax deduction claims, taxes for the current year and other taxes in the county they would be liable to pay. Thirty minutes later, they shook hands.

"I'm taking the files to the courthouse now," explained the representative. "Congratulations on securing a nice piece of property at a great price. You can proceed with whatever activities you wish on your new property."

"Thank you," they chorused.

They held hands as they walked outside into the mid-morning sun. "Let's go back and stash the papers in Lily's safe at Flower and let her know it's a done deal," JJ suggested.

"Yep, then we need to go to Hank and Ann's to get the ATV so we can open up for the art people who're due around noon. Lily is providing several trays of food and beverages. Maybe we can get Camila to help set up for that."

"That works. I'm glad Hank is back home, taking it easy. He doesn't get to put any stress on that foot for at least six weeks, Ann said."

Jo counted the items off her fingers as she listed them. "I notified the artists and school art teachers to bring string to bundle the wood, their own hammers, and cars. Bill Anderson, the owner of the demolition team Joyce secured, is coming to help remove anything we want to keep. He will also inspect the area to begin with his team as early as tomorrow. He's bringing the contract he emailed last night, for us to read and sign." She paused for a breath then continued. "Three, did we want to ask Joyce if Jason could help too?"

"Sure. The more the merrier. Let's get back to Lily's and start the list before you add any more things."

JJ realized a load got lifted from his shoulders. Jo sat in the passenger seat, animatedly pointing at this flower or that cloud. "Jo, I'm glad we can start moving this project forward."

Her smile brightened as she rubbed her hands together. "We're going to have so much fun meeting people today. It's the opposite of a community barn raising, Ann explained to me."

"It'll help us verify the structure is intact. Remind me to go inside and level the hole we made in the barn."

"I'll ask if we can borrow a shovel or two from Hank so I can also help. He's supposed to stay home and rest so he won't need them."

They pulled into the gate, surprised to see Joyce's car. JJ parked next to it and pointed out the two teens at the paddock. They got out and joined the adults on the porch.

"Hi, everyone," said JJ. "Looks like the kids are saddling up their mounts."

"Camila wanted to go help with your artist group, and Jason was hoping for a short ride," offered Joyce.

"A perfect way to get used to the feel of a horse. The shorter ride then walking around might minimize him feeling saddle sore." Jo grinned. "We can use their help."

"Hank, I'd like to borrow a couple of shovels and a couple pairs of your heavy gloves." JJ asked. "I'll load them into the ATV if you tell me where to find them. I'd like to get set up before folks start arriving."

"The shovels are inside the barn; Camila can show you. Gloves too. I wish I could come help, but Doc here—" he shot a thumb toward Ann— "said if I'd stay here, she'd make me an apple crumb. I do love her pies, especially with ice cream."

Ann reached over and patted his arm. "I picked up the homemade vanilla on the way home, just for you. His foot was broken, but with the cast, in a handful or so of weeks he'll be dancing to the lake with me in no time."

Hank reached over to squeeze her hand.

JJ walked to the barn and interrupted the verbal lesson. "Hi, kids. Jason, Camila knows her horses so pay attention. Camila, I need a couple of shovels and some work gloves, please."

"Sure, JJ, come with me." She led the way into the barn, finding the shovels and passing them to JJ. She opened a rough-out closet with a slide latch door. JJ noticed it held neat rows of horse grooming supplies, buckets, a workbench, and several pairs of gloves. She picked up four pairs of varying sizes and handed them to JJ.

"I think this will do it. Ann said there use to be a gardening bench inside your barn. Is it still there?"

"It is. Why do you ask?"

"I was thinking Jason and I might ride over to help you set up. That might be the best place for folks to grab a snack or drink."

"Great idea. I'm driving the ATV there, and Jo is bringing the Mustang. Give us thirty minutes or so, then we'll be ready for you. Jo wants to share a little us-time in our place, since we signed the papers this morning. We're both thrilled."

Camila got animated and threw herself into a quick embrace with JJ. When she let go, she bounced. "You two are staying here? I told Renata I thought that might be the case."

JJ laughed. "Not full time, but we'll come often, I suspect."

The teens followed on his heels to the ATV. He secured the items. "Jo," he called, "let's get going. We need to get things ready for our first wave of visitors."

Jo waved and he swung up on the ATV, starting the engine. They drove to their property where he unlocked the gate and pulled between the house and the barn. He breathed a sigh of relief, seeing the tractor as he'd left it last time. With tools and gloves in-hand, he opened the barn door in time for Jo to bring in the first case of drinks.

"Honey, I could unload. Just give me a second."

"JJ, I can too. We wanted to fill in the hole in the barn before anyone got here. I just thought I'd carry this in on the way."

JJ handed her a pair of gloves, took one for himself, and set the others on the workbench in case someone needed them later today. They each took a shovel and evened the area disrupted from the discovery of the footlocker, scraping dirt from the edges of the walls to the opening. JJ went outside to the loosened dirt and carried in a dozen shovelfuls before the area looked level. Jo spread some older dried grasses and jumped until the area blended.

"I don't think anyone will roam to this area inside, but if they do at least they won't fall."

"Ann gave me a couple of tables I stuck in the car. We could arrange those in this open area and stack the food bins for easy access. Things stay cooler in the shade. If we get the expected crowd, it will be comfortable." She looked at him with those innocent brown eyes and sly smile.

"Woman, you have a devious streak."

"Only when protecting my family." She leaned into him, wrapping one arm around his back. "Thank you for making this ours."

He kissed her cheek. "It will take a while, but I feel we will make our mark." JJ turned slightly. "Nice timing. I hear the sound of horse steps. I think our first guests just arrived."

Camila and Jason pulled up close to the barn wearing happy expressions. Jason hopped down and helped Camila. JJ thought it was cute.

"Hey, kids, not certain where to tie these beasts up, but they need shade and water," recommended JJ.

"There are several containers of water in the back of the ATV under the tarp," said Camila. "I guess you missed 'em 'cause they were covered."

Jason pulled the portable feeders and water bucket from his horse. "Camila said we might find a place to nail up the container near to where we secure them. I like riding, and she," he pointed toward his riding buddy, "says I'm a natural."

Camila's laugh sounded like happy musical notes. "He did well. We might go ride the property, Ms. Jo, later after the crowd leaves." She glanced at her watch. "We have thirty minutes before your advertised start time. Jason, let's secure the horses and help get stuff ready."

Fifteen minutes or so later, JJ took the kids around the outside of the house and barn, pointing out the target wood. "Jo or I will be in the barn in case you have questions."

"I also have two groups from the local churches who will be removing clothes or furniture from inside the house to give to their members to use or resell," Jo explained. "They were delighted to help out and make certain folks who need stuff get first choice."

The emblazoned letters on the side of the pickup announced the arrival of Anderson's Demolition. He pulled his vehicle behind the barn. He appeared around six feet, with a plaid shirt tucked into worn jeans, scuffed boots, and dusty black Stetson atop longish greying hair. He approached Jo and JJ with a friendly expression.

"Hi," he said, extending his callused hand to each in turn. "Nice to meet you both. Please call me Bill. Looks like I arrived before the townsfolk. I had several calls from friends saying they were looking forward to meeting you and helping out. You two have quite a fan base, it seems."

"Nice to meet you, Bill. Please call me JJ," echoed JJ after Jo. "Did you bring your contract? I want to make certain I can read and sign it."

Bill chuckled, hauling out the two-page letter. "I like simple things and to the point. This states in straight talk everything we will do. I do want to take a look at the barn, only to make certain the frame is solid, though at first glance I agree with you. A couple of my guys will be here shortly to help folks load up the used wood. I figure we'll start in the morning, unless folks pick it clean in seconds."

"Sounds like vultures."

"Guess you've never seen a swarm of bargain seekers. Get your cameras ready for the fun."

JJ looked around, spotting Jo working with the teens, both of whom had their gloves on. "No photos needed. Meet and greet to help new acquaintances."

Bill clapped JJ on the back. "Just kidding, son. No time for that anyway, the first wave is inbound."

"Let's take the contract into the barn," JJ said, leading the way. "I can read and sign it while everyone gets situated."

Relieved reading the straightforward agreement, JJ signed both copies, as did Bill. The price was less than what JJ estimated. There seemed like an advantage to smaller town connections.

Jo sashayed in as Bill left. "Honey, is the contract signed?"

"It is. Let's see how much we can donate to the community."

JJ kept Jo in sight most of the day. They each shook hands and met people from the extended community. No one brought unruly kids, which made JJ relax from his worry of injury, especially as people worked in the house.

Bill brought JJ a clear bag of papers. "Found these personal documents in a drawer inside. Thought you should give them to the police. Maybe they can trace the owner."

"Thanks, Bill. I recall spotting these, but forgot."

"The inside of the house is mostly empty." He pointed at a couple of men moving out the last bedframe. "Your wife and Camila are helping get the weathered wood for the art folks."

JJ laughed. "Yes, and my wife will get art classes for free if she wants them. She was over the top."

"Pretty lady. Nice heart."

"She is that, Bill. I'm a lucky man."

Camila and Jason finished the last bit of asks by Jo, before mounting up and riding back to the ranch. Camila told JJ she was too tired to ride much more today, but asked if they could come tomorrow.

Jo entered the barn with a broad smile and a dance in her step.

"How can you look like you just hopped out of bed ready for the day, when I want to take a shower and curl up with a glass of wine?"

She engulfed him in a hug. "I'm so ready for the glass of wine and a soak in the marvelous tub. We did good today. It came together better than I imagined."

"I'll lock up here. We'll drop the ATV off then head to Flower." JJ secured the barn, making certain the key for the tractor hung on the hook. Tomorrow was an early start, he thought, as he walked to the ATV. He started it up and headed toward the gate. After Jo passed, headed toward the ranch, he swung the gate closed. From the corner of his eye, he spotted the same car he recalled Calvin driving, parked along the side of the road. When JJ jumped on the ATV and started in that direction, the car took off leaving a slight cloud of dust.

## CHAPTER 31

# A Truce – No way

Closing the front door of Flower behind them, JJ looked up the daunting stairs and rethought his plan. "Sweetheart, I had every intention of swooping you off your feet to carry you upstairs ready to celebrate. We worked so hard today. The artsy folks seemed happy."

Jo appeared pleased with the comment. "Yes, and I get an art class whenever I want. I met Blue Bonet today." Jo snickered. "She studied art in Paris and promised anytime I wanted a couple of hours of instruction to call. Her property is on the lake." Jo covered a yawn.

"Jason and Camila were a big help all day."

"They were, and I think we need to pay them for their time. I would be more exhausted if they hadn't lent a hand."

Hearing noise to his left, JJ turned and spotted Lily with her arms crossed leaning against the doorjamb. She raised an eye at JJ.

"You two going to go upstairs and shower, then have dinner, or keep staring thinking I added stairs while you were gone. The number of steps hasn't changed for years, let alone today. You can carry her or not, but standing in my foyer is getting you nowhere fast."

JJ felt sheepish. "It was a long day. Are we too late for dinner?"

Lily walked toward the pair with arms wide and fingers wiggling encouragement. "Hold hands and walk upstairs, then take a quick shower. I'll have your places set up and candles glowing. I need to hear all about the day and the next steps."

JJ reached for Jo's hand, and she clasped it, straightening her shoulders. She joined him in lock-step, suppressing giggles. Their exaggerated cross steps got Lily good naturedly laughing, too. "All right, you comics, I'll have your steaks, potatoes, and fresh salads ready to serve. Don't dawdle now."

JJ called over his shoulder, "For a steak, maybe with some wine, we'll be back in a flash."

They rushed up the last three steps, sounding like a herd of elephants.

JJ unlocked the door and stood stock-still, easing Jo behind him. Their clothes were strewn over the bed with drawers ajar. Faint light from the window added dark shadows to the room. The breeze from the open window seemed to make the drapes move excessively and obscured a full view.

"JJ, what the—"

He held up a finger to shush her and flipped the switch on the wall by the door. Nothing happened.

A sudden flash of bright light from the window caused temporary blindness. JJ heard the sounds of movement outside the sill. Jo screeched and grabbed him close. He blinked several times, focusing in time to see a shadow drop outside. JJ slowly moved forward, but Jo hung tight, delaying him. Finally, he spotted the dark figure running for cover.

Jo whimpered, "JJ, do you think they found me?"

"I don't think it was reporters. Sit on the bed while I find out why the lights didn't switch on."

JJ went to the bathroom and successfully switched on the light. He then discovered the cords to the floor lamps laying on the carpet unplugged. Once he replaced them, light was restored. The place got tossed, no doubt. Both of their laptops were still inside their backpacks. The only thing askew were their travel documents lying on the floor as if thrown. JJ took some photos.

"Honey, the bathroom wasn't touched. Go take a shower. Dress in something clean and handy. I'll be there in a minute. I want to phone Tommy. Then we'll go down and tell Lily."

"Okay, but I'm leaving the door open."

"I may come join you, and I'll call Tommy afterward," JJ said with a grin. "Whoever it was is gone." He closed and locked the window then wished he'd considered intruder-prints.

Jo nodded and grabbed a dress off a hanger along with fresh undergarments. She selected a few items for him. "Come on, you can wash my hair faster than I can. You're right, we'll feel better clean."

The shower was fast and efficient. He watched Jo comb out her beautiful hair. He wanted to straighten up the room, but Tommy said to wait until he arrived. He phoned Lily to alert her to the situation. Under protest, she promised to wait until Tommy arrived to assess the mess. JJ was angry but grateful they were safe. He hated the idea that Jo might have been hurt if she'd come to the room alone.

JJ heard pounding on the door. "JJ, Jo, it's Tommy. I have Lily right behind me."

JJ opened the door. "It's a mess. Lily, I don't think anything is broken. It seems like the guy was hunting for something specific."

Tommy assessed the scene and nodded. "I'd agree, JJ. It looks like a rushed need to find something. At least they didn't take your passports. Where were they, do you recall?"

Jo piped up. "Both were in my small carry-on in the closet." She pointed to the case on the floor, opened at an odd angle.

Tommy moved toward it and reached out a pencil to turn it over. "I might have fingerprints here. Not on the clothes though.

Lily, can you get me a couple of large boxes. Anything that might have a print, I'll take with me."

"I can," Lily said. "What a mess, kids. I'm sorry. I left for an hour or so for some extra items I needed for dinner. I actually got back just as you two arrived. Jo, come help me, sweetie. We'll let JJ and Tommy talk. Then we'll have supper." She looped her arm around Jo's, patting it as they started out the door.

"When I opened the door, air was coming in moving the drapes. I saw a dark blob at the window. You know, it's at the odd time of early evening with the sun on the other side of the building. Shadows were long. It felt like someone was here, but the lights weren't working because they'd been unplugged. We saw a flash like a camera or a powerful flashlight. It startled us and caused temporary blindness. It sounded like someone climbing out the window. By the time I looked, it was the tail end of a runner. That's it. I closed the window, not considering there may have been prints."

"Climbing down the trellis would be fast, especially if they cased the place in advance. Did it sound like a heavy person or a light one? Breathing noises or unfamiliar smells that you can recall?"

"Not really. I felt the presence. I heard nothing but noticed the drapes erratically moving. The soft hallway light showed the clothing everywhere. Reaching for the switch, nothing happened. Let's ask Jo about the smells, she may have noticed something.

JJ and Tommy arrived downstairs as Lily fussed with the table. JJ failed to spot Jo immediately and felt his stomach clench for a moment until she walked to the table with two glasses of wine. JJ rushed to pull out her chair to seat her, and whispered in her ear, "Honey, are you okay staying here tonight?"

She reached up and patted him. "I'm fine. You'll protect me."

"Tommy, you sit down too, and join us," insisted Lily. "I've fixed steak and all the trimmings. No one else is here. I secured the outside doors. I want to figure out what happened and how to avoid reoccurrence."

"Yes, ma'am, thank you." Tommy pulled out her chair.

She swatted his hand. "You sit. I'll be right back with the rest of the food. If you want wine, I put a couple of bottles on the buffet. Help yourself."

JJ watched Lily disappear, secured his wine and sat, then turned toward Tommy "We seem to have a combination of things here. Maybe if we list everything, we can find a thread to tie things together."

Lily, hearing the end of the comment, rushed to bring the steaming plates. She took a chair at the table with Tommy. "Did I miss anything?"

JJ grinned. "Not at all." He listed the events. "We came to town and found a piece of what turns out to be controversial property. We found the body of a man in a locked freezer; then…"

Tommy swallowed and interrupted. "Based on a dental match with a local dentist, the man in the freezer is definitely Thomas Stevens. When I spoke to Gunter—Lily, this part is not for your phone tree—he said the embezzlement took place over a period of unknown time, but Thomas could have been involved. His disappearance was unexpected. He had set up a trust with the bank to pay taxes on the property for twenty-five years when his wife was getting expensive treatments. I suspect he wanted to protect the property from bill collectors."

JJ thought about the possibilities. "That confirms the apology letter Thomas wrote to his wife that we found buried under the money. It was written after she died, and—"

Lily coughed and nearly spit out her mouthful. "Letter, what letter? No one told me about a letter?" She eyed the three of them and folded her arms, looking hurt. She sniffed then added a pout. "Some friends."

"Lily," Tommy said. "I told them both not to say anything about it. It was in the barn under the freezer. We don't want that part to get out either. Gunter and I reviewed the details and he locked up the cash. I'm asking you to wind up the gossip mill to flush out who else might be involved."

"We found part of the fence down on our property," added JJ. "Not certain when that occurred. Hank and Ann mentioned seeing lights now and again, plus holes in odd places. We discovered the tractor recently moved. And someone was in our room upstairs before the incident tonight, looking for something. I thought that might have been Ms. Duncan, but she's gone, along with Calvin. Tonight, might have been the same person, so not them."

"Lily, do you have different keys for each room?" Tommy asked.

"Yes, each guest key is unique. I do have a master that overrides each lock for cleaning and such. Why? I have three keys for each suite. If one gets lost, I make another. I keep two master keys in the drawer at the registration desk in the foyer, and one is in my pocket." Lily pulled out the one from her pocket to prove it.

"I don't think the person in the room climbed up the trellis, but at the same time, I'm not certain how they got past you or got inside the suite."

"I left for a while to get some supplies. I never lock the front door when I have guests," she said, with her hand up indicating the couple.

"Are you short any keys?" JJ asked.

"Nope. Even Calvin and Stacie left theirs in their respective rooms. I found them when I cleaned up their messes." She wiped her lips. "I inventoried the keys when I put those two back. Nothing missing."

"JJ, didn't the letter also say that Marissa's sister wouldn't get a dime of the money, even though she pestered him?" Jo asked.

He and Tommy nodded.

Lily scrunched up her face with confusion. "What sister? I never knew she had a sister. She never mentioned it to me."

JJ grinned. "The letter indicated Annie, who helped take care of her while Thomas worked, was her sister. Marissa didn't want anyone to know because her younger sibling had gotten into trouble and was shipped off to a reformatory. As much as they both appreciated her help, it sounded in the letter like they were ashamed of her."

"Annie!" Lily screeched. "She worked for me before Marissa turned up ill. She seemed fine. Eager to work, willing to take on any task I gave her. She did the cleaning for all the rooms, decorated some, and even worked in the garden. I was glad she could assist the Stevens, but I missed her when she went to take advantage of the advanced education. She never mentioned a word, other than how sad she was Marissa was so sick."

"Tommy, did you ever receive feedback on unsealing the court records on the minor?" JJ asked. "We might not need it now, but if we know the details, we might find another piece to the puzzle."

"Not yet, but I'll follow up in the morning. I want to check outside during the daylight to see if anything shows up from your visitor." Tommy stood. "Lily, your cooking is still some of the best I've ever eaten. If you are all good, lock up here. I'm heading out."

"I think we can handle it." JJ extended his hand to Tommy. "Thanks again for coming so quickly."

Tommy looked toward Jo. "Jo, keep this husband of yours outta trouble."

She shrugged with a grin.

CHAPTER 32

# Morning Revelation

Jo tossed and turned to the point that, near dawn, she finally slipped from bed. She curled into the cozy chair under the soft, flower-patterned fleece throw. Following the intruder, they'd cleaned, taking down a load of laundry. Jo was restless despite the inviting appearance of suite. JJ asked multiple times if she was okay. Her response was yes, but something unidentified kept nagging.

Hoping for distraction from the replay loop, she propped the book about plants Lily had lent her against her knees. She had enough light streaming through the window to enjoy the colors and read descriptions. One plant caught her eye, a small purple flower with a sweet lavender scent. It reminded her of the Destiny Fashions' eau de parfum that smelled like lavender mixed with oranges. The scent was light, designed for women over forty.

She flew out of the chair. "Yesssss!" Jo launched onto the bed and pushed on JJ's shoulder repeatedly. "JJ, I figured out what I smelled last night when we were putting things away. It reminded me of Destiny Fashions mature ladies' scent."

He rubbed his eyes. "Sweetheart, if your bottle of perfume got wasted in the free-for-all, we'll get more."

She snuggled next to him. "No, honey. You don't get it. I don't wear older lady scents. I wear fresh fragrances. It couldn't have been mine. I think our intruder was Stacie—both times."

JJ pulled into a sitting position and rubbed his eyes. "Perfume is particular?"

"It is. I would have recognized it under different circumstances, but the mess distracted me."

It felt marvelous when JJ wrapped his arms around her. "We'll go with the theory until it's disproven. You are the fashion expert, not me. Though I definitely like how you look, in and out of, anything."

Jo laughed. "Let's get ready to go watch the demo guys. I'll change the laundry before we leave. We can fold it later."

"Fair enough. I'd like to take a look around the grounds for footprints." JJ stretched. "I'll call Tommy and let him know what you discovered."

The aroma of fresh coffee and breakfast rolls greeted them as they approached the dining room. JJ touched Jo's hand then slipped outside.

Jo stopped Lily. "I'll pick up our clean clothes later."

"Child, your clothes are drying now. They'll be on your bed when you get back. Joyce will be by shortly; she wants to ask a favor. Go get your breakfast done and load up on coffee. You have roughly forty-five minutes until Bill and his crew arrive. I have a large tote with snacks, sandwiches, and Cokes, along with waters, for you to take to feed the troops."

"Lily, you need to stop feeding the people coming to the property. It's not fair for you to do extra work, or expense, though your food is delicious. We need to pay you."

Lily patted Jo's cheek. "It's on your bill, sweetheart. JJ already told me the ground rules. No worries. Y'all would never take advantage of me."

"You're the best, Lily."

JJ squeezed Jo's hand as he started the car. "Jo, I looked around. The ground was hard so no prints, only smashed grass. That led me to a rocky area where a car could have parked."

JJ drove to Hank and Ann's per Joyce's request to drop off Jason. Jason and Camila planned to ride the horses to their place. They offered to lend a hand wherever needed. Hank and Ann were on the porch and waved when JJ pulled up the car. Hank, seated with his leg on the cushion of another chair, bounced his rubber-tipped cane.

Ann dashed down the steps and leaned in JJ's window. "Thanks again for helping with Hank, JJ. He feels more rested—at least not so grumpy."

"Glad to hear it. Jo and I were happy to help."

Ann patted JJ's arm resting on the open window. "He's pleased as punch you closed on the property and that you figured a way to get your project moving. I want him to get a little stronger before I drive him to take a look. We are thrilled to have you as even part-time neighbors."

Camila ran up to Jason when he got out of the passenger side. She beamed, like a kid at Christmas. "Jason, I'm glad you made it. Let's get the horses ready and head over. I think we can go around the fence line of Jo and JJ's property. No racing, but a chance for you to get the feel of the motion of the horse. I like walking or galloping because they feel smoother."

Jason turned toward Jo and bent down. "Thank you for driving me here. I hope we can discuss more about my keeping an eye on your place when you aren't here."

JJ and Jo grinned in agreement and drove away.

Pausing at the entrance, JJ exited to unlock the gate. He shoved it open and eased the car through. Bill and his team arrived, tailgating onto the property. JJ parked by the barn to unload the supplies. Bill helped Jo carry the tote inside.

"Good morning, Bill," JJ said. "Thanks for the help. We brought snacks for your team to grab as needed."

"Much appreciated. I want to take one more walk, starting from the house to the back fence, to verify our approach toward the demo."

JJ turned and found Jo organizing the snacks on the potting table. "Honey, let's walk with Bill. I want to make certain we are pointing out everything we agreed to."

Jo bounded to the car and grabbed her notebook and JJ's backpack from the backseat. "Bill, this is so exciting. I brought my list. It may not be in order but it has what JJ and I discussed." Jo pressed the backpack toward JJ. "Can you please carry this? I didn't think you wanted it left in the car."

JJ slung the straps over his shoulders. "Great idea." He grabbed hold of Jo's hand. "Bill, let's start at the back of the barn, then we'll head toward the house. Can we level the holes and troughs? I'm not certain if we have critters wanting to hollow out cool spots, or if it's erosion."

Bill extracted his plan and scratched notes in the areas. "Kids, these aren't critters, these are man-made holes." He pointed to a wide swath of dirt mound. "This looks like a tractor rather than a shovel, though I see shovel efforts too. Some appear impacted by the weather. My guys can level them, no problem."

JJ noted no holes had emerged in the last couple of days. He didn't think any more would appear on their property. The security cameras he'd ordered would capture any intruders after he installed them.

"Bill, I plan to have two gardens between the barn and the house. The one closer to the house will have flowers and shrubs." Jo provided him a sketch around their planned foundation.

"And you want the rocks in those shaded spots? If so, then I'll get the crew to move them together until after the foundation gets poured. Have you folks decided who gets that contract so I can coordinate with them?"

Jo grinned. "We decided on your friend Stan as the prime contractor. He said he wanted to use local talent like your team, Handy, and some others. He said you do more than demo and excavation work. Using local small businesses, we think, will give us the best results."

JJ admired Jo's enthusiasm as her hands periodically skipped steps, highlighted by her excited voice.

"Jo's right. Stan seemed like a good central contact for us, especially when we are away. Gus, at the hardware store, has an account set up and Stan can order most things." JJ pulled up their joined hands and passed a fast kiss. "We trust the folks here."

Bill looked pleased. "Good to know. We'll do a good job for a fair price."

"Once you get the house down, can you verify if the foundation is worth saving?"

"Ma'am, can you show me your picture again?"

Jo handed him her drawings.

"I'll look at it, but my guess is, it can't be reused for the house you have in mind. With the water, sewer, and electrical line positioning, it's better to start it right. We might save part of the foundation for a gazebo if you have one in mind, or an outdoor grilling area. Though you might shift the house location. I don't see a pool planned. Will there be one?"

JJ chuckled. "When we have the reservoir so close, we decided it would be easier to use, and no maintenance. I do, however, like your thoughts on a portion of the foundation. Perhaps a hot tub and grilling area. We'll look again after things get cleared."

Bill called one of his men to get them started on the area behind the barn, leveling the house, covering the main water shut off, and identifying the location of the septic tank.

"I think we'll need to replace the septic tank to get it up to current code, but Stan can verify. The two dumpsters arrived, positioned for us to fill and replace later this afternoon as needed."

They walked the area. Bill suggested a few dead stumps get pulled while the equipment was on-site. One of his workers also did fences, so JJ agreed to use him for the repairs. Less than an hour later, they returned to the barn with the noisy activity in full swing.

Camila and Jason strode in, each pulling a horse behind them. Camila waved them over. "We figured you two might like a ride with us."

Jo looked at JJ with hopeful eyes. "Let me store this bag in the trunk and lock the car. Jo, can you grab a couple of waters for us?"

Jo nodded and returned in time for JJ to help her mount.

Camila led everyone toward the reservoir. She pointed out some of the family camp spots. A few had mobile home hook-ups. Tourists could rent them by the day or week.

JJ admired the view of the sparkling water that invited a variety of birds. Several large flocks appeared to pause there before heading south. It would be fun to learn the names of the migrating species native to the area. Jason and Camila joked around, having fun. Jason didn't have a lick of trouble with his riding, or the easy pace. They followed the edge of the water as much as possible.

"JJ," Camila said, "this area gets fairly busy in the summer months with family day campers and easy hikes in the area. There are a two corner stores around the road entrances for camping supplies and such."

"It's a pretty ride." JJ took out his camera and captured the view and smiling faces of their little party.

Jo pointed. "Wow, it looks like a few cabins might be available."

Camila chuckled. "Yep, there are four in total. For those who want to pretend they're roughing it. I heard those have limited electricity, beds, and doors, but no running water."

"My mom would camp there," Jason admitted.

"We need to head back, kids. I want to watch the progress. Jason, Jo and I want to talk with you about some help when we're away too."

Jason nodded, sitting up a little straighter. "Yes, sir."

They took a few turns heading back, getting closer to the road. A few cars zipped by; one caught JJ's attention. He made a mental note to mention it to Tommy.

They finished the horseback riding, letting the teens lead the horses back to Hank's. JJ and Jo were amazed that, by the time the sun was heading toward evening, how much got accomplished. The house was gone and the ground leveled. It gave them a new perspective on how their vision might be realized.

"Bill, I am amazed at the speed of the team. Everything worked like a concert."

Bill laughed as he helped lug the totes to the Mustang. "It's faster to bring it down than raise a new building. The barn structure is sound. I think we need to look at the slab tomorrow and see what you want to do with it. There aren't any cracks at least. I plan to be here around eleven in the morning to work on the fence with one of my guys, if that works for you to meet us."

"Eleven is good. I was hoping I might take Jo out dancing tonight, if she wants to."

"Really?" Jo bubbled with excitement. "I'd love that, but where?"

"LouAnn's Lounge has a dancefloor, and sometimes she has bands Thursdays through the weekend. My wife likes to go there now and again," offered Bill.

"Let's take Jason home and then get cleaned up. I'd enjoy a night out at a new place."

"I love it, honey. Bill, thank you for the great job your crew did. We'll see you around eleven." Jo reached out to shake his hand.

JJ locked up the barn, and they headed to pick up Jason.

While Jason climbed in the car, Jo told Ann they were going dancing and received advice on what to wear.

CHAPTER 33

# Dancing, Texan Style

**JJ** immediately noticed Lily pacing the foyer, talking on the phone. "Hon, why didn't you tell me sooner you were having a boot-scooting event? I'll let everyone know in eight minutes on my phone tree."

She gave each of them a hug. "You two have a treat in store for your date. LouEllen told me they're amping up their party atmosphere at the lounge to Dancing with the Stars. She selected a country band for a one-night-only boot-scooting night. LouEllen almost turned them down because of how scruffy they looked. Then the lead singer with the lusty look in his eye whispered in her ear that he could belt out most of Lonny Lupnerder's love melodies for tips. Claimed they were making their travel expenses from Nashville to Los Angeles for a recording gig."

JJ wanted a romantic night out with Jo, not a town event. "Lily, I'm not certain how you heard, but we like Magnolia Bluff for the quiet, not the hoopla. We might not even go. It's been a long day and…" He caught the bright eyed, beaming happy glow on Jo's face. "It's definitely thoughtful, but we need to cool it going forward. What do folks mean by the term Texas boot-scooting?" He sighed. "Will tennis shoes work? I have a clean pair."

Lily roared with laughter, and tears filled her eyes. "Oh, hon, you're gonna need some decent cowboy boots. His and hers, so you can clomp around to the fiddler."

Jo shook her head. "We didn't bring ours."

Lily patted Jo's back. "High-tail it over to Robert Joseph's Boot Barn out on Texas Highway 28 where it intersects the I-35 runway. It's a little driving but make sure to ask for Bobby-Joe. He'll get you outfitted with boot-scooting country dance footwear."

Lily took Jo by the arm and confided, "When you go to dance, keep yourself in between LouEllen and JJ. She doesn't mean any harm, but enjoys shopping. She can't control reaching for tight male bums to squeeze. I think she keeps a tally somewhere, if you know what I mean." Lily winked and chuckled with a knowing nod.

Smiling, Jo nodded at the advice and pulled JJ along to shower and change in record time.

JJ opened Jo's side and paused to watch her get seated. Her short skirt molded nicely to her shape, yet flared at mid-thigh. Jo whistled a favorite tune and found a country channel on the radio to set the mood. "Babe, I'm looking forward to Texas-made boots. I have my riding boots, but here they wear fancy ones with rhinestones. To go out dancing in a small-town lounge while they play Lonny's music is a nice addition to our plans, isn't it?"

JJ winked and reached for her hand. "Yes, beyond belief."

JJ pressed his hand against Jo's back to enter LouEllen's Lounge. Other couples also drifted in, so word of the band had spread.

JJ eyed her boots and grinned at her legs. She gave him the once-over too.

"I don't know why you didn't go ahead and get the hat. I thought Bobby-Joe was right, it matched the boots perfectly."

JJ laughed at the image in his mind. "Babe, the anaconda skin boots are unique and special. I didn't want a matching hat because I didn't want to look like a reptile. I wanted something less ostentatious. The black felt was too big."

Jo chuckled. "Agreed. I cracked up when Bobby-Joe said he stocks hats for fat heads. Let's find LouEllen."

LouEllen hollered, "JJ and Jo." She rushed to their side from the back, waddling like a duck on a mission. "I heard you were in town. Glad you came. I want a hug from each of you." Jo stepped in front of JJ to stay in between.

LouEllen frowned and griped, "Dang, Lily warned you, huh? I'm an aging frumpy woman barkeep. He's never leaving you for me. I know he is not available. But a nice fanny pat now and again is harmless."

Jo chuckled and swung JJ around for LouEllen to embrace. JJ frowned at Jo with a silent never-again message.

LouEllen disengaged with a beaming smile and fanned her face. "Oh my. You're a cutie."

JJ looked at LouEllen. "Can we get a table close to the dance floor, LouEllen?"

LouEllen pointed. "Big Boy, you and Jo can sit wherever you like. If a table is open, grab it."

He leaned in and brushed his lips across her cheek. "Thanks."

"I'll bring drinks. What's your poison?" LouEllen fanned herself a bit more with a happy expression that reminded JJ of one of the seven dwarfs.

He placed the order. Jo grabbed his hand and navigated them to an open table close to the dance floor. JJ pulled out the chair for Jo and took his seat across from her. Jo peered over his shoulder.

He heard a few snippets of discussion from the bar about the body Tommy found. Additional comments speculated an argument over leftover spoils from that lousy human trafficker and drug selling that hadn't been found. Jo cocked her head, her face contorting with confusion.

"Honey, what's wrong?" asked JJ.

The banter and misinformation continued. Jo leaned forward, yet kept her voice low and with a menu blocking her face. "I see a full set of backsides on barstools against the far wall. A lady on the far right is wearing a Destiny Fashion. I also smelled a whiff of the same parfum. Can you turn to see if it's Stacie?"

JJ looked and put two fingers on the menu, pushing it down. "Jo, the last seat on the right is empty. The rest of the drinkers are men, except for the twenty something young lady standing between the two guys. She's waiting for a free drink."

Jo dropped the menu and confirmed the empty seat. She looked at JJ. A guitar chord and voice announced over the amplifiers, "Folks, the band has entered the building. We play for you. You can dance, sit, listen, or sing along. We guarantee our music will have you shifting cheek to cheek. Hit it, boys!"

Music pulsed through the lounge. JJ spotted the enthusiasm in Jo's eyes and her shoulders keeping beat. He stood, bowing slightly with his hand extended. She sprang to the dance floor following his lead. They ignored the drinks placed on the table. Jo's delight was contagious. JJ spun, twirling her with grace and style, gaining applause from other patrons.

The crowd did a bit of line dancing, Jo insisted they join. JJ suggested they match a two-step including singing along, oblivious to the clapping. JJ swiveled around sensing someone watching but couldn't identify a source.

CHAPTER 34

# What's Your Emergency?

Lily took Renata home and returned to Flower to finish the last of her chores. The dinner menu included fresh rolls and baked potatoes; she wrote a note to start them cooking mid-afternoon. She made some ledger entries in the book at the check in desk when weird sounds from outside the front door got her attention. Thinking someone was delivering something unexpected, she opened the door and step outside. The impact of the falling man took her by surprise and cried out from the dead weight. "No."

Lily breathed heavy having exorcised herself from under Calvin. Prickles from splinters in her back worried her if they were to get removed with a burnt needle. The man was barely breathing, yet she found a pulse. She stood and danced in place, fishing her phone out from her front pocket. Relief swept through her as she punched a number and heard it ringing.

An alert commanding voice answered. "911, what's your emergency?"

Lily shrieked, "I wet my pants!"

The 911-operator released an exasperated sigh that sounded frustrated. "Ma'am, I'm sure this is an emergency in your mind, but this is not the place to report you need a fresh diaper. So let me recommend—"

"This is Lily Greenly at Flower B&B. One of my guests collapsed against me when I opened the front door. I want emergency people here now to help. He looks beaten, bloody, and is unconscious. But he's breathing."

Lily heard the demand in this order. "Stay on the line, please, while I alert dispatch." She heard him moving his wheelchair. The open line of communication let her know the dispatcher insisted on the EMT to come to the correct address.

"Ms. Greenly, in the future when you call 911, please leave your incontinent problems out of your request for help."

"Robert, don't use that tone with me!" Lily snarled. "The next time someone drops two-hundred-fifty-plus pounds of ex-football running back on you in surprise, let me know how that works for you."

The operator released a breath. "Lily, I'd probably wet my pants, too. Let me know how it comes out, please."

Several minutes later, Lily motioned to the emergency team parked in the driveway to come to the porch. Their intense activity had her watching everything. One attendant took the vital signs. The other scanned his body and cleaned a few of the open wounds.

The attendant hit their two-way radio. "Doc, the man is still unconscious, his pulse is erratic. His temperature is high, so likely infection, but nothing obvious."

"Transport immediately and start an IV. Get as much as you can on history from whoever is present."

"I honestly don't know him," Lily said. "He was a guest. He never revealed any medical conditions and ate like a horse."

One attendant monitored his vitals while the other retrieved the transport gurney.

Lily's eyes roved between the gurney and the bulk of Calvin. She tilted and shook her head concerned with the next steps. She stood to the side. One attendant groaned when the first attempt to set the man on the wheeled stretcher failed. "Good grief, he's heavy. Let's try again on the count of three. One, two, three!" Again, the effort failed.

Lily noticed Chief Jager's patrol car stopped next to the ambulance. He hurried to the porch. Lily could tell by his movements he was rapidly gaining perspective.

Tommy grabbed the side. "Here, let me help."

The extra pair of hands made the difference. They raised the cart and headed toward level ground to allow the attendants to roll the gurney to the ambulance where they loaded the patient. The wheels retracted as designed. One attendant stayed inside while the driver closed the doors.

He wiped his brow with his sleeve. "Thanks, Chief. Couldn't have done it without ya. For a minute, I thought we'd need to rent a crane to get him moved."

Tommy said, "With the bruising, torn clothes, and lump on his head, he looks a lot worse for wear. Anything you can tell me before you take him to the hospital?"

"I gave him a quick once-over. His vitals are weak. He may have broken bones, which we could have jarred loading him. His right side is bent in an odd manner. X-rays are needed. I suspect cracked ribs. We need to transport him and say prayers the almighty wants him to survive. The skin lacerations appear to be bite marks from the unforgiving Texas barbed wire plant. Like he went swimming in a large patch. Doc will assess after they x-ray and do some tests. I'd guess an hour 'til the hospital staff knows more."

Lily watched the EMTs back out and hit the siren on the road to the hospital. She hoped Calvin would survive. She wrung her hands watching Tommy return to the porch.

"Lily, are you okay or do I need to take you to emergency?"

"I felt fine once I got out from under his bulk and could breathe."

"So, what happened here?"

Lily shook her head as the noisy siren grew faint. "Wow, I knew he was big, but glad you helped. I don't know how they handle football players without hydraulic lifts."

"Looks to me he wasn't playing football. Maybe tackled a car." He pointedly looked at Lily and scratched his chin. "Well?"

Annoyed that Tommy wanted her story right this minute, she invited him in for coffee. No one was in the dining room so they approached a table. He sat and she poured them each a cup of coffee. Lily stood and recanted the events like related she related to Robert.

"I heard that Calvin and his accountant skipped out without paying. You didn't hunt them down to get paid, did you?"

"No." she snarled, giving Tommy the evil eye. "I didn't because I get a credit card numbers in advance for all bookings. Am I mad about them skipping out? Hell, yes. But not enough to hunt them down or hurt them. You know me better than that, Tommy."

"Did he say anything before he passed out? He looked pretty banged up. Whatever happened to him, he only thought to come back here. Any idea why he'd do that?"

Lily rubbed her face bouncing from one foot to the other. She sipped the coffee. "I don't know why he came here. He said two words before collapsing on me. Help me."

Tommy nodded thoughtfully, placed a five on the table for the coffee, and stood. "Thanks for your statement. You can go get changed now."

She closed her eyes, feeling her face turning scarlet. "Robert told you?"

Tommy let out a belly laugh. "No, Robert wouldn't do that. I simply listen to the 911 channel for all calls. Later, Lily."

She swatted his arm and grunted.

CHAPTER 35

# Puzzle Pieces Fall into Place

JJ and Jo finished a delightful breakfast. Lily told them about Calvin being in the hospital.

"Let us know when you hear something." JJ said. "I thought I saw his rental a couple of times yesterday. We want to talk to Tommy about that before we meet with Bill. You'd be amazed at how much has changed."

Jo opened her phone to photos and showed some of the newest she had taken yesterday. "I'm hoping you can come over this weekend. I'd like your opinion on placement of the garden areas, and a couple of other things. I'm so excited."

"As well you should be, sweetness. Now tell me about the dancing." Lily added a twist to her hips.

They regaled her of the fun at LouEllen's.

"I was glad you were pulling our leg about having everyone there. Next time this group comes to town, I think you need to join us."

"Har, har. I know how you two want a bit of privacy, which didn't happen last night. Everyone's talking about the cute couple, meaning you. Bobby-Joe said you made great choices, and he's gonna get a few hats for men in smaller sizes." Lily chuckled, tickled with her putting one over on them. "You two go have fun. We'll catch up later. If I get news of Calvin, I'll text you."

"Jo, let's drive to Tommy's then meet Bill. I don't think we'll need any food today, but we can always grab some to take to the work crew if Bill indicates they are staying for a while."

"Sounds good. Lily, wonderful breakfast as usual. Tell Renata she needs to come out to say hi now and again."

"That girl is in there making three different kinds of cookies to surprise me. She told me to leave the kitchen. Imagine that? My own kitchen. I'm going to clean your room and straighten up the front room. I expect two couples to arrive next weekend and she wants to practice."

JJ escorted Jo to the car. They took the short drive to Tommy's. They walked in the door, and saw him on the phone. He waved them into his office with a smirk on this face.

Tommy ended the call. He straightened the paper stack in front of him then handed it to JJ. "I received a copy of the court files from the district court in Springfield, Illinois. One Anastasia Daniels, aged fifteen, remanded to the Florida Teen Reformatory for girls. The record indicates she, along with three others, were caught stealing from a retail store. The others were adults and sent to jail. Her mother begged for leniency because it was her first offense. Her mother insisted on a legal name change, and it was changed to Annie Flagstone. Annie got released on her eighteenth birthday. She had five-hundred dollars and a notice that her mother had passed away leaving her nothing, though they corresponded while she was in the institution."

"What a shame," said JJ. "It explains the connection with the Stevenses. Anything else?"

Tommy grinned like the cat that grabbed the canary. "Yep. It seems they included not only her fingerprints, but also a record of her reformatory school achievements. Her first year in, she was picked on and hospitalized three times at the hands of two other inmates. Then she found a buddy and learned to fight.

She earned solitary confinement multiple times for senselessly beating other kids, including breaking bones and pushing one girl from a second-story window. They've since installed wire on the windows at the reformatory. That girl lived. Officials partied when Annie got released."

JJ gave Tommy a look. "What about the fingerprints?"

"Oh, yeah." Tommy slapped the side of his head and shrugged, appearing smug. "They match Stacie Duncan. Good instincts, son."

"Wow!" JJ and Jo exclaimed in harmony.

JJ related the possible sightings of the vehicle Calvin drove.

"I think I smelled the scent of parfum made by Destiny Fashions. Plus, I know Stacie wore one of the designs at Flower when I first met her," proclaimed Jo. "I thought I spotted a lady at LouEllen's last night in another of those creations. The fabric is fairly distinctive." Jo eyed him.

Tommy softened his gaze toward her. "Jo, you are a smart young woman with good instincts. It might be her. Won't know a lot more until I can question Calvin. Any other details come to mind?"

"Not right now."

JJ noticed Jo looked relieved. "Jo and I are headed to meet with Bill. If we spot the car, we'll let you know. Call either of us if we can help."

JJ and Jo arrived a little before eleven. They walked around the area where the house once stood. The foundation appeared level yet unimaginative. "Jo, what would you think of building a gazebo atop the old house foundation? We locate the new house toward the front at an angle to the barn. The gazebo dancefloor would be partially hidden."

"You mean like having a Brazilian grill area? It might be nice for entertaining. We could set up an entire area with refrigerator, double sink, wet bar, and counter. We could plant bushes at the border to act like a privacy fence."

"I bet we'd have enough room for tables and chairs for entertaining, or our own private dance floor. Jo, we could have a great sound system. It would be watertight inside the gazebo."

"We might look into screens or shades for sun or mosquito protection. Unless rain falls sideways, we'd be fine."

JJ observed Jo walking around with her index finger, tapping as she formed the picture in her mind. "What do you think, sweetheart?"

"I think it'll make a great entertainment venue. I like the idea of it behind the house. We certainly have enough room for a lovely flower garden. Plus, vegetables in the back might be closer. We love being outdoors back home, so why not?"

"I bet we could use indigenous rock and stone to create a lovely setting. Maybe a cherrywood bar; the grains and color shifts over time are vibrant."

"Let's ask Bill. I think he arrived." Jo pointed at the truck.

Bill and someone new got out of the truck. The man was as tall as Bill but younger, with longish light brown hair cut to the top of his collar. "Hi, there. Meet Jeff. He's my fencing expert. We picked up what we needed this morning. It shouldn't take more than a couple of hours for us to knock this out.

Jeff shook hands with them. "Thanks for giving me the chance to work on your fence."

JJ pegged him at twenty-five at the most, with pale blue eyes that looked straight at you. "Nice to meet you. Once we get the house up, we may want to have you put in some garden fences, and how are you at constructing a gazebo?"

"Handy, Bill and I can construct about anything out of wood. Can you show us what you mean?"

"This is the first I've heard of that, JJ," Bill said.

Jo giggled. JJ said, "We looked at the foundation and came up with some ideas. We'd like to bounce them off you and get your opinion."

JJ and Jo used the next thirty minutes to explain their thoughts. Bill made a few suggestions. Jeff contributed ideas about solar lighting and ceiling fans. Before they finished their discussion, they had a reasonable drawing, and something Bill said he'd show Stan the next day.

Bill and Jeff went to work on the fence. JJ left Bill a copy of the gate and barn keys, so they could enter when needed.

Jo appeared quite pleased when they got into the car.

"Are you happy with the changes?"

She threw herself into his arms. "These aren't changes, they are enhancements. As long as we can afford it and we both like it, then why not? Things are fitting together like they should. How about we park our car at Flower and walk to town for lunch?"

"Sounds perfect. We can relax for the night. Tomorrow, we plan the steps for the rest of our stay."

"Deal! I love you, JJ."

CHAPTER 36

# Hospital Drama

Tommy watched the duty nurse move from patient to patient across several rooms during his rounds. He punched the air when the board by the nurse's station lit green next to the name Montgomery. He sauntered down the hallway and watched the caretaker enter the room of Tommy's concern. Tommy peeked through a crack in the doorway. He had the perfect view of the unconscious patient. A hand extended showing a blue scrub covered arm and retrieved the patient's clipboard of information.

At the bedside, the RN flipped through the chart and checked vitals to record. "What I wouldn't give to work in a hospital with twenty-first century technology," he groused. "Look at this scribbling. I can't even tell what the doctor is trying to convey. We need digitally captured statements so the next nurse can decipher the instructions. I'd better call to—"

A clink sound on the tile floor caused the nurse and Tommy to look at that spot. A small pool of liquid had puddled from the patient's drip line. Tommy widened the opening to watch and intervene if needed. Concentrating on reconnecting the drip, the RN failed to notice the Calvin's large, powerful hands reaching toward him. The hand grabbed the nurse's clothing and pulled the caretaker closer. Then Calvin, eyes glazed, wrapped his left hand around the man's throat. "Where am I?" he demanded in a dry, raspy voice. "What happened?"

The RN was big. He gasped and wiggled, his fingers picking at the hand on his throat. "Ah, good. You're not dead. I am your nurse here to help. Maybe we'll get paid for your stay in our outdated hospital. As to what happened, the police are hoping you can tell us. Please unhand me before I ring for security."

Calvin relaxed and released the nurse, exhausted from the effort. The caretaker sidestepped and smoothed his medical coat. He rubbed gently in the area as if to massage the pain.

"How 'bout I call the police chief and let him know you're able to talk? I don't recommend you grab his neck. He might not take kindly to being assaulted."

Tommy let the door shut and leaned against the wall waiting for the nurse to finish. He nodded to the RN when he exited a few minutes later.

"Mr. Montgomery is no longer on the narcotic drip. His stats are doing well, and he's not hallucinating at this point. He's all yours, Chief."

"Mr. Montgomery and I will be fine. I'll buzz you if needed. Thank you."

Tommy looked at Calvin, keeping emotion from his face. The pasty dried look to his face and swollen areas on his arm above the cast suggested he'd taken a beating. "What do you recall? You look like you took a fall. According to your stats, you're dehydrated."

Calvin closed his eyes and turned his head away from the Chief.

"I can only guess that you weren't scrimmaging to get ready for the next game."

Calvin inhaled and faced Tommy. "That rotten Duncan bitch! She tricked me into a ride to Fredericksburg then threatened to barf on me. She pretended to heave. I stopped, threw it into park, expecting her to open her door. She didn't. I felt certain she was ready to hurl. I jumped out and ran around to help her from the car. I got played like an idiot."

Tommy shrugged. "What happened next?"

Calvin's hands flailed with frustration, illustrating his actions. "As I got to the front of the car, I caught sight of her behind the wheel. She slammed it into drive, floored it, and rammed me. Not just once, but multiple times. Every time she knocked me to the ground, she'd back up while I struggled to stand. Each time it was harder to rise. She's a psychotic bitch." He pulled the cup close, took a sip from the straw, then sat the container on the table. He paused, catching his breath. "It was worse than football two-minute drills. Don't know if you played, but when I was at the end of my strength, the coach would yell, Montgomery, you want to play or not? The bitch wouldn't stop hitting me with the car until I slipped over the edge out of her sight."

Tommy clucked his tongue. "I get she's a bitch. Leave out the color and finish your story." He saw the anger written on Calvin's face and in his eyes.

"The last hit sent me through the air and off the road into the barbed wire plant," Calvin snarled. "I was glad I blacked out for a bit. When I came to, it felt like a thousand needles in me all over, including places that never get pierced."

Tommy involuntarily flinched at the perceived sensation. "How'd you make it to Flower? Lily says you gave her two words after you collapsed."

Calvin shook his head with a look of confusion. "I made it to Flower? Is that where you found me?"

"Yes. The doctor will tell you all the details, but your chart indicated multiple broken bones, cracked ribs, severe lacerations, and a probable concussion that might cause memory loss. Anything else you can tell me, like why she turned on you?"

"Duncan and I met with Gunter. She brought me to this area to buy a bank, or a seat on the board of directors for my investment consortium. This bank was her number one recommendation, to the point of obsession. Gunter wasn't interested, so she lost it. He threw us out because she ran her mouth threatening him. I warned her to let me do the talking. I said she was fired. I got her back to the B and B and ordered her to get out of my sight."

Tommy nodded. "I guess she didn't warm to the idea of being fired. Thanks for filling in the missing pieces. I'll bring her in for questioning."

"She has my revolver. A .45. It was under the seat. If she has the car, she has the gun. She knew I had it."

Tommy clucked his tongue. "Good to know. I assume you'll testify?"

Calvin nodded fiercely.

Tommy left the room, pausing at the nurse's station. "Let me know if I need to speak to your supervisor, but I want Calvin's location in the hospital classified. I'll try to send a guard over, but for the time being, record him as being in another room. I'd prefer one unoccupied."

The nurse looked appalled. "Why? If we don't show him in the proper room, his medication and treatment will get screwed up."

Tommy laid his palms on the counter. "Give him a false identity then. I don't want him to get any visitors."

The RN muttered, "I wonder if the big city hospitals with their automation have this much drama."

CHAPTER 37

# Cat's out of the Bag

Tommy walked up as Gunter fumbled to find the right keys to unlock the front door. They'd spoken of it before so Tommy knew the banker's nerves were on edge each morning for the ninety-second race to disarm the alarm system. The keys jangled so loudly while he hunted the winner, he never realized Tommy was behind him off his right shoulder.

"Been opening doors long, Gunter?" Tommy's deep voice rumbled.

He snapped his head around in surprise, ready to get attacked. He chuckled.

"Why don't you color-code the keys with nail polish? Makes 'em easier to identify. While you're at it, put on those glasses crafted in the sixties. They add ten years to your appearance."

The man looked relieved to identify his first customer, as he gulped air. "Dammit, Tommy. I don't need the plaque blown out of my arteries, so don't be sneaking up on me! You've made my head hurt."

Tommy moved his fingers across his lips and turned the tips like a lock.

After a deep breath with a few quiet moments, Gunter opened the door and dashed to disarm the system.

The wad of keys slipped into his dress coat pocket. "What is it now? Changed your mind about the money, or do you just want to visit with those bundles? The time lock on the safe is ready to be opened." He headed toward his office with Tommy on his heels. He heard a teller enter through the back door and the click, click, click of her heels to her window. He closed his door, hung up his outer coat on the hook on the wall, and sat at his desk. His expression was smug as he waved Tommy toward a chair. "If you want it back, I don't have the combination."

Tommy clucked his tongue. "I guess it's good my meager salary isn't enough to store the extra in your bank. I need a favor, Gunter, and it has to do with the money."

Gunter studied Tommy with a red glow rising from his collar. "You want some coffee?"

He flinched. "The thin, weak brew you palm-off on the customers? No, thanks, I'll get the good stuff from Lily's, or Really Good."

"Yeah, I know, the coffee here isn't as good as theirs." He took a breath and sheepishly grinned. "That's why I put a healthy shot of bourbon in…to give it some strength. What's on your mind?" Gunter hit the single cup button and started a cup. It whirred as it brewed. He pulled out his special condiment from under the cabinet.

Tommy, distracted by Gunter's actions, collected his thoughts. "Gunter, I want to leak the news of you holding the found money. Someone's after it. If they know where to look—and the town gossips'll make sure of it—maybe they'll come prowling here. I can capture 'em in a place I know."

Gunter stirred his coffee, clanking the spoon in the mug. "I've already heard that Calvin got run down. Is that my fate if the world knows I've half a million locked in my vault?"

"If I can grab them here, I can question the person and maybe get the truth. To your point, allegedly Calvin got run down by his accountant after he fired her. You'll be at risk until I can bring Stacie Duncan in for questioning."

Gunter guffawed. "If you think I'm worried about me being at risk, forget it. Remember I'm married to Mary Lou Fight. That alone proves I'm used to danger." Gunter took an extra heavy swallow of the bourbon-flavored coffee and smiled as he closed his eyes.

Tommy chuckled. "All right, I'm gonna feed the gossip mill. Be on your toes until I get this mess under control. Call me if anything unusual occurs 'cause you're gonna be a target. The silent alarm still operational here?"

"Yep." Then he added. "If anything happens to me, no one will ride herd on Mary Lou. I love this town, so don't let me get killed. Please."

Tommy extended his hand to seal their pact.

Tommy pulled his cruiser into a parking spot at Flower. He marched in the front door hoping to catch Lily at the end of the breakfast meal.

She greeted him with a grin as he stepped inside and handed him a large hot cup of coffee. Not completely surprised, he smiled, accepting the beverage.

Lily eyed him and joked, "There're only two reasons a single male shows up mid-morning. Since you're not hitting on me, I deduced you were here for my second-best asset, coffee."

Tommy hooted. "Truth be told, I'm here for your first best asset: gossip and information. I need two things. First is the license plate of Calvin's rental. Second, I need you to cascade out to your infamous phone tree that the embezzled money got found and is stored in the bank's vault. I gotta catch our person of interest before anything else happens. I'm hoping this will flush her to me. Leave out the part of this being a trap, okay?"

Lily bustled to the check-in desk and the register. She flipped pages. "Great idea, Tommy. Let me give you what the car rental people told us." She handed him a piece of paper. "That is the vehicle plate number you wanted. They are trying to track it because of JJ's call. The LoJack device, with its software reporting capability, shows the vehicle located around Magnolia Bluff. They are looking for fixed locations, but it moves between towers, whatever that means. The rental folks suspect someone's trying to keep it off the grid."

Tommy rocked on his heels, stunned. He took the printout and read the details.

Lily appeared self-righteous. "JJ said you'd need this. He's kinda smart, isn't he?"

"Did Detective JJ and his apprentice, Jo, say how he knew I'd need this?"

"Not exactly. As soon as you showed up, he said I should be ready to light up the gossip waves with information. He wondered if you went to see LouEllen yet. She's a good blabber too. Most of her clientele aren't on my list. That way you can tell her to be on the lookout for that Stacie Duncan they spotted the other night."

"I like 'em," he grumbled, "but I can't wait for them to go back to their day jobs."

CHAPTER 38

# I'll Drive

The afternoon sun streamed through the windows. Jo and JJ flumped down in comfy chairs of the Flower B&B living room, relaxing from their busy day. Jo made notes in her phone of things to do tomorrow. She smiled at JJ, who looked calm after her silent pep-talk. Her thoughts raced from one thing to another.

"JJ, I feel something's wrong."

He smirked. "You mean besides dead bodies, shattered dreams of a young couple, and a lucky find of a half million dollars? Realizing Magnolia Bluff wasn't as easy as we hoped. Either this is the most crime-riddled city in this quadrant of the galaxy, or we're a magnet for crimes against humanity."

Jo softly chuckled. "No, I mean I don't feel safe with everything swirling. I want to borrow Lily's skillet, so I can defend myself with a weapon. I'll keep it handy in the delightful burlap sack we got while shopping. I love the colors swirling on the front."

JJ furrowed his brow. "I don't make you feel safe?"

"I didn't say that. I know you're a ninja-stealthy, karate-chopping, spin-kick enabled, two-legged assassin. I want something I can do if needed," Jo protested.

"I understand, sweetheart. Go ask Lily for your weapon of choice while I text Hank and Ann. We need to drop off Renata and show the property to Lily like we promised. I know Ann won't mind having Lily join us for dinner." JJ winked. "It'll give Camila and Jason time to visit before we take him home. I hope things worked out well today. I'd like them to keep an eye on stuff if their folks let them."

Jo smiled mischievously. "JJ, will you say it again please? I like hearing it."

JJ stood with his arms raised. "Now entering the combat arena, Jo, the iron-skillet-wielding maiden. The crowd roars in awe of this currently undefeated champion in the lightweight category, for clocking bad guys upside the head. The characteristic ring of the cast iron skillet against their noggin is Jo's winning signature. To fans who follow this goddess, give it up for Jo!"

JJ and Jo jumped and clapped, waving arms over their heads, and laughing uproariously. They turned to find Lily with her arms folded over her chest, and shaking her head. Jo felt certain Lily worried about their sanity.

She beamed. "Lily, may I please borrow the iron skillet?"

Lily moved her tongue back and forth across her teeth and shook her head. She returned to return to the kitchen for said item, she remarked over her shoulder, "You're right, I don't wanna know. Renata and I are finishing our chores. Can we all fit in your car without the sportscaster's dialog?"

JJ grabbed Jo in a hug and swung her around in a tight circle before landing her. They stared into each other's eyes, holding the moment as well as each other.

Jo held out her hand. "My turn to drive?"

JJ kissed her palm and deposited the keys. "You bet, sweetheart."

## CHAPTER 39

# Date Night

Tommy considered the day's accomplishments, making notes on priorities for tomorrow with staking out the bank. The man was a tough businessman; his homelife gave him a foundation to handle the worst customers, the best ones were easy. He chuckled recalling Gunter's comments when the phone rang.

"Good evening, Chief Jager here. How may I help you?"

"Tommy, this is Mary Lou Fight. Are you with Gunter?"

Tommy leaned forward then pulled out his notepad and paper. "No, Ma'am. Is there a reason he should be with me?"

Mary Lou growled. "Then where the hell is he? I'm stuck here all day long with no one to talk to. The only bright spot for today is going out to eat once a week. Granted, it's with that boneheaded husband, but at least I don't have to hear from the gossip tree that they rotated me to get some sun on my other side, like I was some plant needing sunshine."

"Wouldn't be so bad if I could at least socialize a little while trying to learn to walk again." Mary Lou signed. "He's MIA. I'm sure he's tossing a few back somewhere. Rumor mill said you paid him a visit this morning. Now I can't find him. Did you arrest him?"

Tommy drummed his fingers, suddenly nervous. "What makes you think I'd need to arrest him? Did you talk to him today? Or did you bark at him earlier like you are at me now?"

"Don't get smart with me, young man. I help pay your salary. No, I didn't talk to him because tonight is our date night. I try not to disturb him so he can finish his work and come home on time. He isn't responding but he never misses picking me up for supper."

Tommy covered put the phone on mute to decide how to proceed. "Unless he is with his emotional support group getting crocked because he's married to you." The wheels in Tommy's head turned. He unmuted the call. "Mary Lou, I haven't spoken to him since early this morning. As a courtesy to you, I'll drive by the bank to determine if his car is still there. He may be working late or had a customer meeting run over."

"Cut the crap, Tommy. Gunter doesn't miss a meal because of business. But yeah, look if his car is there. It doesn't explain why he's not calling me back. Something's wrong."

"I'll let you know what I find." After disconnecting, Tommy mumbled, "Gunter was right. Anything that happens to him means I have to deal with the witch on wheels."

## CHAPTER 40

# Dinner with Friends

JJ watched Lily and Renata in the flurry of activity as they finished cleaning the kitchen. Jo slipped in next to him, looping her arm around his. He leaned over and kissed her hair, inhaling her fragrant scent. "Honey, the sun is nearly set. I promised Ann we'd get there by dark."

"Lily, if you two don't finish in the next minute, JJ's cancelling dinner."

Lily looked like she'd spotted Dracula. "But-but…" She threw her hands in the air. "Never mind. Renata, we'll finish this tomorrow. I haven't seen Ann and Hank for a visit in a while. Your mama's a fine cook. Is your daddy up grilling yet? He knows how to flip the burgers, or heck, any meat, at the perfect moment. I'm getting hungry thinking about it."

"He's up some, but mama fusses if he stands too long, even with the crutch. I'll bring the cheesecake and my purse."

Lily grasped her bag and stared at JJ. "No cheesecake for Mr. Impatient here," she said as she blew by him toward the front door. "Come on y'all, we don't wanna be late."

JJ and Jo hooted and followed them out. "Lily," he called, "should I lock the front door?"

Lily turned and smirked. "Well, of course. The guests changed their arrival dates." She got into the backseat with Renata right behind. "It happens."

JJ opened the driver's door for Jo. He glanced at the fading light, satisfied they'd meet the promised arrival time. Jo smoothly pulled to the front of Hank and Ann's house. The sounds of greetings filled the air, and everyone exchanged hugs. JJ moved up to the porch to find Hank looking pleased with the onslaught.

"Hey, Hank, how are you feeling?" JJ took the seat next to Hank, noticing his foot up on the bench and extra pillows behind him.

Hank leaned over. "I'm good. I get extra cushions. Ann's fussing over me more than when we first got married. It's nice. I know it's short-lived 'til the doctor clears me, but I'll take it. Don't mention this to her."

Renata moved next to Hank and patted his arm. "Did you have a good day?"

Hank sighed. "It was a little boring, but I'm healing. How 'bout you?"

"We had a good day. New guests are coming day after tomorrow afternoon. I get to prepare the dinner menu."

Hank patted her arm. "It'll be delicious."

Noise of horses trotting through the gate disturbed the discussion. Camila and Jason waved as they slowed their mounts to a walk, headed toward the corral. JJ noticed Renata looked at Ann with a plea in her eyes.

Ann chuckled. "You go on, Renata. Help them with the horses. We'll be eating in half an hour or so."

"What can I do too, Ann?" asked JJ. "Hank mentioned he is on oversight duty, so I can barbeque if you wish."

Ann beamed. "That's sweet, JJ, but we've got this. Lily and I spoke earlier about finishing supper. I've had some chili heating. Do you prefer hot or not?"

"Oh, I like spice as long as it leaves the skin and doesn't dissolve the spoon."

"I have ribs, brisket, and chicken ready to grill. Hopefully enough for lunches tomorrow. Ladies, do you want drinks first, or to get the food out?"

Lily did a bit of a dance. "I've always been fond of both. If JJ gets him and Hank a drink, then we can have some wine or such while we cook." She splayed her hand at the outside area. "We're eating out here on the porch, right?"

Ann nodded. "Jo, if you would be so kind as to bring out the tray of placemats, dishes, and silverware from the kitchen to set up, Lily and I'll get started."

"No problem. I can also cook. I'd love to assist."

"She's a good cook," chimed in JJ.

Lily added, "She is great with a cast iron skillet too."

"Good, I have mushrooms that need sauteing," Ann said, missing the reference.

The ladies disappeared inside, leaving JJ and Hank.

"Hank, what are your plans over the next few years."

"Ann and me like what we have. Easy days unless I do something crazy." He pointed to his foot. "We enjoy the simple life and our friends. I'd like a beer if you're getting a wine." Hank waved a hand to the countertop to his left. "The bar is open. You might want to bring a few tumblers for the kids. You heard Lily, they'll get their wine inside, though I have extra bottles out here in the cooler."

JJ grabbed their beverages and set the tumblers on the table. He returned in time to meet Jo with the tray. "I'll help, honey."

They set the table with the bright southwest colors. JJ let her take a sip of his wine. "I know you'll get a glass inside, but this is a starter."

"That is a very nice pinot noir, sir. I hope they have more."

"There is. You take that glass, and I'll find another."

With goblet in one hand and tray in the other, she glided inside. JJ filled another glass and toasted Hank. "I think we're both lucky men."

"Cheers to that, son."

JJ noticed some bright solar lights dotting the area. He liked the variety of colors and patterns they emitted. "Hank, how long have you used solar lighting for decorating?"

"As long as they've been available. They last two or three years, which is about time for a color change for Ann. She has fun picking 'em out. Heck, it's nothing to install them. They stay bright 'til long after we go to bed."

Excited conversation from the teens advised they had finished their chores. Camila joined with hugs for both JJ and Hank. "We had so much fun today. Jason's riding is improving. And he likes country songs, too."

"Guess you're invited for dinner, Jason," Hank added. "Why don't you grab you a Dr. Pepper and find a spot. I want to hear all the details of your adventure." He leaned away from the kids and winked at JJ.

Settled with a beverage in hand, Jason related his misstep with the horse on the way out that morning.

Camila smirked. "You fell for the old horse inhale trick. The animal is smart enough to inhale and hold its breath when you cinch the saddle. Then when you think everything is okay, the animal goes back to breathing normal but the saddle is no longer tight enough to hold. You ride the saddle to the ground."

Snickers were chorused.

"How did the fencing appear, Jason?" asked JJ.

Jason pulled his phone out of his pocket to share the pictures while platters of food, brought by the cooks, were placed on the table. The ladies sat and everyone joined hands. Hank offered a brief prayer of thanks before everyone dug into the closest platter or dish, then passed to their left, like a ballet of plates. Everyone took a few bites and uttered compliments.

"JJ," Jason said, as he brought up the photos on his phone, "if you start at this picture and scroll right, you'll see the finished work."

JJ took the phone and flipped through the pictures with his finger. "You're right, these look good. Did you kids ride around the entire property?"

"We did," admitted Jason. "It was locked up tight. You can see the improvements with the clearing efforts from outside. It's taking shape. Any idea when building might start, or are you planning to redo the outside of the barn first?"

"Jo and I wanted to get the barn buttoned up. We decided the old house foundation has potential for an outdoor grilling area with a gazebo for entertaining. I was hoping we'd have time before dark today to take everyone to get an opinion. Perhaps we can plan that for tomorrow morning?"

Nods of agreement followed.

"JJ, something unexpected took place before the photos Jason took," Camila stated. "Some lady walked near where we stopped the horses." She glanced toward Hank then back toward JJ. "We stayed in the saddle and close to one another. She explained she was out walking, and asked about the activity on the property. Wanted to know what was going on with multiple days of activity. Asked if someone was fixing it up to sell."

"Jo, we may have a new neighbor we haven't met yet," JJ said between bites.

"I don't think so." Camila shook her head.

JJ cocked his head in her direction. "What did you say?"

"I told her my friends purchased the property and they've had an exciting week."

"True that." JJ considered her comment an understatement, listened intently.

Camila took a sip of her beverage. "Jason said a body was discovered in the barn. Then the lady leaned-in interested. I added that my friends found a bunch of money, but I didn't know how much. The lady stepped back appearing shocked, her face got red and her voice changed a little."

"Camila told her the money was locked up safe and sound in the bank until the case was solved," Jason added.

"Do either of you recall what time this was?" asked JJ, rapidly losing his appetite.

Camila looked at Jason who moved his fingers as if counting. Then he clipped the side of his head and opened his phone. He pulled up the first picture and handed it back to JJ. "Ten minutes before I took this first shot of the fence."

"Around eleven. Definitely before lunch."

Camila nodded. "She looked angry saying she had no idea Magnolia Bluff was dangerous, and that she better move on. She said thanks and turned toward the cabins we showed you the day we rode."

JJ noticed the fear reflected in the eyes of the teen and water glistening her eyes. "Thank you for remembering so much. Any other thoughts you think would be useful?"

"As she walked away, I thought the lady wore weird shoes for a routine walker. Rhinestone sandals are hardly useful to avoid the small stones and stickers on the route back to the cabins."

Jason nodded. "And she asked a lot of questions to folks she'd never met."

Jo calmly asked, "Can you describe her?"

Camila blinked a few times. "She appeared a little older than Mama. Lots of makeup, which is also odd for a serious walker in this heat. Her brown hair was twisted into a hairclip with rhinestones on it. Loose pants and lightweight blouse."

Jason added. "She also must use the perfume my mother tested last time we went to Austin. It smells like lavender and orange."

JJ ran his hand over his face and stood. "I need to make a call. I'll be back shortly." He strode to the corner of the house to gain some distance. He clicked Tommy's name and proceeded. While he waited for an answer, he tapped his foot thinking, Come on, answer, Tommy. He got voicemail and left a message. Next, he tried the office number and then called the cell phone again. Frustrated, he completed a detailed text to Tommy's mobile about his fears. Then he called Gunter. Again, no answer, so he left a message asking for a call.

JJ returned to the table and slumped into the chair, thinking of what else he might do.

"You have a problem, son?" Hank asked.

JJ explained he needed to speak with Tommy, but he wasn't able to reach him.

"Hand me your phone. I can help." Hank dialed a number and put it on speaker.

"911, what's your emergency?"

"Raymond, this is Hank. We have a serious situation and need to know if you sent Tommy to respond to any calls."

"No, Hank, I've had no calls today. I was hoping you might add some excitement to my day."

"Does he still monitor your channel?"

"Of course,"

Hank stated, "Tommy, if you're listening, I need you to head to the ranch and call JJ. I'll keep this broadcast up for every five minutes." He handed the phone back to JJ.

Camila burst into tears, and babbled, "Did I do something wrong?"

JJ reached across the table and snagged her fingers. "No, you did everything right. I could be overreacting, but Tommy needs to know about the conversation you guys had with the stranger. We'll get it sorted out."

Camila jumped up and ran into the house. Renata rushed right on Camila's heels, looking confused and calling her name.

CHAPTER 41

# Ominous Silence

After his call with Mary Lou, Tommy's thick grilled cheese and ham sandwich had cooled enough to eat. His sharp knife severed the crispy crust and a wave of pepperjack oozed onto the plate. He added a couple of dill pickles and sat thinking of the possibilities. Gunter might ignore her calls. I know I'd be tempted if I were him. He might have had work to finish before their evening out.

He stood, then grabbed his plate and empty milk tumbler, taking them to the sink. He washed and dried the dishes before putting on his gun to drive around town.

Juggling his phone, hat, and keys, Tommy secured the front door to his bungalow then went to the cruiser. Inside, as he turned on the ignition, his phone rang. He glanced at the screen, noting another spam call, the tenth in the last hour. He pressed the block caller icon and then silenced the ring tone, putting the cell in his top pocket. He made the drive to the First National Bank of Magnolia Bluff. The solar streetlights were growing brighter. These LED fixtures saved the town money, but between dusk and dark, visibility was dim. No cars remained in the parking lot or in front of the bank. The town rolled up the sidewalks early during the week unless there was some holiday or event.

Tommy decided to methodically drive the streets all the way to the reservoir. He hoped to get lucky and spot either Gunter's car or Calvin's rental. He knew the streets like the back of his hand, along with most of the vehicles that belonged in the various driveways.

Feeling a tinge of guilt, he pulled out his cell and hit redial on Mary Lou's number.

"Tommy, did you find him?" He caught the edge of concern in her voice.

"No, Mary Lou. Not yet. I am driving around to see if I can spot his car."

Mary Lou snorted. "Check LouAnn's Lounge. If you find him there, tell him not to bother coming home, ever."

"Now, Mary Lou. I'm sure he's not out carousing. It's a weeknight. He's always good about your date night. I've heard him talk about how much he looks forward to it." Tommy uncrossed his fingers, fearing they'd get stuck because of his lie.

"Really?" Mary Lou's voice softened. "He mentioned it? How sweet. Sometimes he can be nice."

Tommy raised his eyes toward heaven for a second. "Yes, he cares about you. Now try to relax and not worry. I'll find him and let you know."

He disconnected then systematically meandered several more streets, passing a parked car sitting at the end of two empty lots. He slowed, hit his lights, parked, then got out with his high beam flashlight in-hand. He approached the car, keeping the illumination where it would catch anyone in the car and stop them like a deer in the headlights. He felt the hood; it was cold. This car hadn't moved in a while. No one was inside. The unlocked door opened. He popped the trunk. The contents included a spare and some snack packs. He checked the license plate to the one he'd written down earlier as a match. Tommy called twenty-four-hour towing to arrange for pick up plus storage at their lot until the rental company collected it.

Tommy stomped back toward his cruiser with a sinking feeling. If Calvin's car was parked and cold, Stacie likely left it. Gunter and his car were nowhere to be found. He hoped she hadn't threatened him with the gun Calvin mentioned. He wondered where she might take Gunter. He was worried. He opened the door to his unit and had set down his belt when he heard his radio.

"Chief, this is Raymond. JJ needs you at Hank and Ann's ranch for something important. You're not answering your calls or text messages." Flustered, Tommy pulled out his cell and checked messages. There were five from JJ.

"Raymond, this is Chief Jager. Come in."

"Hey, Chief. Are you all right? JJ was panicked when he couldn't reach you. Hank knows you always listen. They need you at the ranch."

"Got it and on my way. Call Hank back. Let him know I should be there in fifteen. Thanks."

Tommy sped to Hank and Ann's, hoping they might have Stacie in custody. He slid slightly on the gravel at the turn and fishtailed a bit. Everyone was gathered on the porch when he parked and got out.

"Heard y'all needed some help. What's up? I was thinking you might have captured our person of interest, but apparently not."

"You'll need to hear all the story," JJ said. "Jason, relate the story to Chief Jager. Don't leave anything out."

Ann rushed inside for a tumbler of sweet tea and to see if she could persuade Camila to add her comments.

Jason twisted his fingers as he retold the events of the afternoon. A red-eyed Camila came outside and sat next to Jason. Tommy asked a few clarifying questions.

"You both did a good job. Very detailed descriptions, thank you. We'll see what we can find at the cabins across the lake. JJ, how 'bout you ride with me."

JJ nodded.

Tommy looked toward Lily. "I may have a new phone tree rumor for you tomorrow, but for the time being, can you go be with Mary Lou? She's been waiting for Gunter to get home from work. She needs someone with her."

"Lily, I'll drive you," volunteered Jo.

"Sounds good. I think, Ann, we'll need to postpone that cheesecake for another time."

JJ kissed Jo goodbye as he handed her the keys. "We'll keep in touch by phone, honey."

"Yes. I'll meet up with you later."

"Come on, JJ," said Tommy. "I want to check those cabins before it gets any later."

They got into the cruiser, and headed toward the reservoir.

Within an hour, they located the cabins' owner who said none of the cabins were rented but gave them a key to check. Tommy confirmed each of them were empty and returned the key.

"JJ, any ideas?"

"The whole mess is crazy. I suspect she searched our room looking for information on the property and to see if we were involved. Then the rumors started. She's desperate and dangerous based on Calvin's condition."

Tommy rubbed his palm on his forehead. "I agree. One tough cookie. I want to keep looking for a while."

"I don't know the area well enough to say where this woman would go in Gunter's car. I'm fine with being a second set of eyes."

They drove around for a couple of hours with no success.

"I don't think she'll hurt him until after she gets the money," Tommy stated.

"Seems logical, Tommy. But, based on the records you got, she has a nasty side."

"I know, and Gunter's heart's not so great. Let's go to Flower to rest. We'll position ourselves early to get them at the bank when it opens in the morning. That's her target at this point. She's armed."

JJ called Jo to meet him at Flower. Lily said she'd bring Mary Lou to stay, so she's not alone.

Everyone arrived. Tommy brought Mary Lou up to speed with as much as he could share, painting Gunter as a hero.

"Let's get some rest. Things will look better in the morning."

CHAPTER 42

# Closing Time

Tommy huddled with JJ and Jo before dawn. They knew Gunter and his car were missing. Stacie was suspected of kidnapping him after he locked up, because Gunter closed on time according to his staff. He hoped Duncan would bring Gunter to get the money. Different scenarios of how they might have eyes on the bank from multiple vantage points got outlined, discussed, and planned. They agreed to get into position before sunrise, knowing the lock vault wouldn't release before nine.

Tommy pointed to the diagram of the area. "I'll be behind the building adjacent to the bank. I'll bring the tarp, to keep my cruiser hidden until they arrive."

JJ nodded. "Agreed. It makes sense they'd pull up right in front to minimize the distance to travel with the money. The area is fairly quiet at that time of the morning."

Tommy wiped his chin with his knuckles. "What we don't know is Gunter's condition or Ms. Duncan's state of mind."

"We're going to set up behind the dense scrubs near the end, right JJ? That's a short sprint if we need to block them," noted Jo. "If you can distracter her, we can get fairly close, I bet."

"I'm concerned that she has Calvin's gun and likely knows how to use it. I'd like you to both wear flak vests, like me. I suspect she'll be anxious and frazzled. Gunter, will try to help too if he's able." Tommy looked at the table and shook his head. "I hope he has some mobility. No doubt, she'll have a gun on him."

"I like the plan. It gives us a good chance," said JJ.

"You're still sworn in deputies." He looked at his watch. "We leave in ten, so do the last-minute stuff. I'll be outside getting your protection." Fastening the vests was easy.

Tommy drove to town with no lights. The sun would show on the horizon in a quarter of an hour. He parked in the designated spot and JJ helped position the cover. Jo, the designated spotter, had no traffic or movement to report.

"You two get to your location. Put phones on silent and keep texting at a minimum."

JJ nodded and grabbed Jo's hand. Keeping low, they spider-walked to the spot, verifying to visibility from any streets or sidewalks.

"We're settled and watching."

"Perfect, thanks."

"Who's that walking alone?" Jo whispered and pointed to a figure on the back sidewalk, clip clopping in heeled boots.

"Gunter's head teller. I'll let Tommy know."

"Glady's is walking in the alley toward the back entrance. No sign of our target."

"Got, her. Don't move. Gunter's car pulling around. Wait for my signal."

Tommy ripped off the covering and started the car. He rolled down the windows to hear possible conversation, grateful for the quiet engine. His eyes followed the vehicle as Stacie slid into the handicapped parking. She noticed Gladys. Her face contorted and she pounded the steering wheel. Gunter sat in the passenger seat.

The door opened and he wiggled his frame out with Stacie right behind. She had a wide scarf on that almost covered the gun in his back. She said something Tommy couldn't quite hear and used the muzzle of the weapon to get the banker moving. Gunter plodded toward the door.

Gladys hailed, "Good morning, Mr. Fight. I trust you had a pleasant evening. Ready for another riveting day in the banking world?" She frowned when she noticed Ms. Duncan.

Stacie angled the gun from Gunter's back to shove it into Gladys' ribs.

Tommy flinched.

Stacie snarled, "Open the door. I'm on a tight schedule, and now so are you. Move it. Disarm the alarm. Anything else and Gunter gets shot. No funny business, Gladys."

The teller nodded and they dashed inside.

"Tommy, do you want us to enter?"

"No hold your position. She has to come out. Her voice was high-pitched, like frazzled. I'm going to reposition my vehicle."

"Yeah, from our spot her eyes look wild."

Tommy saw them at the door. He thought about calling back up but was afraid the radio would be too loud. He had a view to the vault and saw it opening with all three people visible.

"I think they're coming out. Get ready."

Stacie pointing the gun at Gunter stayed close as they walked out with the footlocker between them. She opened the trunk with the key fob, then jumped as a police cruiser screeched to a halt behind her. Gunter and Gladys dropped their load, ran inside the bank. Tommy prayed they locked the door just in case.

Heart pounding like a jackhammer, he circled the front of his cruiser with his hand on the hilt of his weapon. His eyes watched her every move while her eyes darted between the chest and him with the gun wavering. "Stacie Duncan, I need you to come with me for questioning. You're a person of interest for more than bank robbery."

Stacie's eyes blazed like a rabid dog. Her face reddened and her mouth twisted. "It's my money I found out he was stealing and he said I'd get half. Then Thomas wanted to give it back. He said he'd go to jail or spend his life making restitution. I refused to quit. It was going right until Marissa ruined everything by dying. I even tried to seduce him, thinking we could live in Mexico. Mister Righteous refused me. Months of work in vain. Me, broke, again."

Hands sweating, Tommy tightened his grip and inched closer. "You killed him thinking you could take it all? He must have suspected you'd turn on him."

Stacie spat. "How was I to know the rotten bastard buried the money? I dug on and off for years but never found it. I left and got my education in finance to get a high paying job in a bank, so I could buy the property. It had to be there."

Tommy watched tears stream down her cheeks and edged forward. "How did Calvin figure into all this?"

Stacie smirked. "That clown. I had him thinking this was a prime investment area. I wanted to get a look at the books and determine the legal the status on the property. He was too stupid to execute on my ideas. But then the bastard fired me."

"Okay," he calmly agreed. "When did you hit on the idea of pressing Gunter into giving you the money?"

Stacie smiled; hatred flashed across her face. She pulled back the scarf, pointing the gun at Tommy. "I think I've told you too much." She turned and pulled the trigger. In the same moment, an object soared between them. Tommy flinched, bracing himself for a direct hit.

There was a ping-thud sound, then Stacie screeched and clasped her face. "What the—"

"No one hurts our police chief," Jo screamed. She secured

the skillet with both hands and swung with all her might at Stacie's head. A resounding glong echoed, followed by Stacie crumbling to the ground with a thump.

Tommy noted Jo's satisfied expression and suddenly the situation made sense.

She gently touched his face. "Tommy, are you okay?"

Tommy swallowed and inhaled to regain his composure. "I'm-I'm okay."

JJ used his foot to dislodge the weapon from Stacie's hand and scooted it toward Tommy. The gun was bagged and tagged in seconds.

Then he hugged Jo close. "Nice shot, honey. Really cool how the bullet ricocheted back to hit her." With a quick snap of his head and a smile, he raised her arm in the air and announced, "Still undefeated."

"Thanks, you two." Tommy grinned and extended a hand.

CHAPTER 43

# Close Call

Tommy drove Stacie Duncan in the squad car to his office, storing her in the holding cell. He alerted the EMTs to come by and look Gunter over. Then he formalized the arrest with paperwork, and alerted his county counterpart to come get her.

Meanwhile, JJ drove Gunter's car to the chief's office with Jo and Gunter. They waited in his office until he could talk to them.

Tommy called Mary Lou. "Mrs. Fight, I have Gunter and he is fine."

"Oh, Tommy, thank you."

He heard sniffles and nose blowing. "He's a hero, ma'am. I need to take a full statement before I bring him and the car to Flower. Please sit tight and get a little rest."

"Can I call him or text?"

"Not right now, ma'am. He's not certain where his phone is at this point. If you're worried about being home tonight, have Lily set up a room there for you two."

"I'll think about it. Let me know when you're headed here."

"I will. It won't be too much longer."

The EMT attendant stopped at his office and said Gunter had some bruises and cuts but nothing requiring emergency services. He wanted to get Gunter back to Mary Lou.

Tommy opened the office door. "Why don't you come sit in the conference room where we have more space. I have some water in there too. They found seats.

"Gunter, I'd like Jo and JJ to stay and listen if you don't mind. Right now, they are sworn deputies and want to help. I need to know what happened while you were missing. We were worried about you. By the way, Mary Lou knows you are safe."

Gunter raked his hair back with his hands. "I'd like a cup of coffee and any additives you might have available."

Jo rushed out to get coffee and Tommy retrieved a small flask from the drawer behind him. "Help yourself, Gunter."

"Tommy, it was unbelievable."

"Take your time and tell me what you recall."

Gunter gulped the hot coffee and closed his eyes for a moment. "I gazed out the windows watching the staff head toward their cars. Shadows increased with the fading sun. You know that short period before the streetlights brightened. The trees appeared still and peaceful. The last person out waved the all-clear. I gathered my stuff and armed the system. The ninety-second lag permitted enough time to get outside to do the final door lock. That part is always a stressor for me. When all three tumblers locked, I relaxed and looked forward to date night. It always makes Mary Lou happy."

He took a breath and sighed. "A cold nasty-tempered voice echoed in my left ear. It was low enough to not be overheard, yet sent a cold chill to my heart. I didn't panic until I felt an object poke my ribs hard enough to make me freeze. It was the worst Simon Says command of all time." He shook his head and gulped more coffee, offering the empty cup to Jo for a refill. "Duncan told me we needed to go back inside to complete some unfinished business, saying I should unlock the door and disarm the system. You were right, Tommy, she wanted the money."

He nodded thanks for the refilled mug and poured a little courage inside. "I got mad as a hornet and told her, 'Ms. Duncan, how nice of you to drop by. In case you forgot, I told you I wouldn't even sell you a chair, so get out.' I probably should have been nicer—" he shrugged— "but, hells bells. The gun got pressed harder and her demands didn't end. She said she waited twenty-five years, which was long enough." Gunter rocked in the seat and Tommy noticed his hands relax some.

"Gunter, do you want something to eat? I think I have some food in the refrigerator."

"I told her the time-lock was engaged until this morning at nine. She swung her hand with the gun and whacked me on the side of the head." He pointed to the small lump, not yet bruising. "She demanded the keys and said we had date night. I would-a laughed if my head hadn't hurt so much. I dropped the keys and earned a kick in the knee, which is sore, too. The car had a full tank so we drove for hours, then stopped for a bit to rest."

He sipped some more coffee and ate the sandwich Jo located. "I tried to find out when she killed Thomas, but that question made her madder. With the sunrise, we headed back toward Magnolia Bluff. When I looked at her face it was contorted with anger. I saw the city sign and a sense of dread took me over. I made some offhand quip so I could get a chance to get out and pee." His hands shook a little as he took another bite of food. "She kept threatening to shoot me. She hadn't slept all night… looked like a ragdoll the dog drug in. She kept watching the time and didn't want to arrive too early. When she spotted Gladys, she said it was time to get out. The rest you know."

"Good job, Gunter. I'll get this typed up tomorrow so you can review it before you sign in case something else comes to mind." He patted the arm of the man who needed rest. "Let's get you back to Mary Lou and we'll find out if she wants to stay at Flower or have us drive you home."

"Sounds good."

Gunter rose and shuffled out the door to the bathroom. Tommy indicated with his head that JJ should follow and make certain he didn't fall. JJ took off to catch up.

"That is such an awful story. He'll have nightmares for weeks." Jo grinned. "At least you saved him, Tommy."

"We all saved him." Tommy looped an arm around Jo's shoulder as a thank you.

## CHAPTER 44

# Friends and Foes

Jo and JJ focused on surviving the whirlwind of house plans, contractor discussions, supply chain issues, and impromptu meetings with insurance investigators, as well as attorneys to close the open issues in the remaining two weeks of their vacation. Today sleeping in was task number one. Lily had other ideas.

The soft knock on the door brought JJ awake.

"Kids…time to get up," Lily called. "I've got breakfast almost ready so you can get to your property early. You said last night there were questions outstanding on the construction of your dream home. I know this has been anything but relaxing, so I've left a small pot of coffee and cups by the door. I made it extra strong in case you want to run over there rather than drive."

Bleary eyed, JJ rocked up to a sitting position and laughed. "Do we need to drink it fast before it eats through the cups?"

Lily hooted. He heard her retreating steps as she went downstairs.

Lying on her stomach, Jo cocooned herself in the covers with her head half-buried under the pillow. "JJ, I'm gonna pass on her coffee. The last time she made strong stuff it took days to get my back teeth to stop wiggling."

JJ patted on her affectionately, scooching the covers closer to her body. "I'll go shower first so you can doze a bit more. For my part, I'll have her Mach I coffee so I can run to our place.

Speaking of that, I think, because we're in Texas, our spread needs a name."

Jo chuckled.

When JJ finished, he kissed her forehead. Jo smiled at him, ready to get up and take her shower. He shook his head hearing Lily mischievously banging a spoon against a large pan, sending shock waves through their room.

JJ leaned out of the door. "We need fifteen more minutes, please, warden," he hollered.

"Har, har," she called.

The couple scampered into the dining area with eight seconds to spare, stifling yawns.

"JJ," Jo whispered. "I'll never complain again about Lara rousting us out of bed for an early morning shoot again."

"Just think, sweetheart, when the house is done, we can sleep in 'til whenever."

"Note to self, no roosters on our property."

He grinned at Lily. "We're looking forward to breakfast. I swear, we'll never oversleep again."

Lily sighed. "You made me promise to help get you out the door early. It'll be okay. Have the contractors to confirm everything you want in writing. Answer the myriad questions. Come back for a nice afternoon nap. Don't try to boil the ocean to achieve a six-month build cycle if it compromises the end results. Besides, I'm planning a close friend celebration for getting the yucky part behind you for tonight."

JJ and Jo snapped their heads and stared at each other. JJ interjected, "Lily…"

Lily chuckled. "No, it won't be like your arrival. Just your immediate friends who want to thank you. Tommy said he'd attend." Lily listed on her fingers. "Then we have confirmations from Hank, Ann, Renata, Camila, Jason and his mom, along with Gunter and Mary Lou. Oh, LouEllen said she wanted to come too. Jo, you'll have to watch her. She said JJ was guy candy."

Jo chortled. "We'd enjoy that small group, Lily. What an honor. They mean a great deal to us."

Breakfast consisted of waffles and eggs. JJ bagged up a couple of waffle sandwiches with the hot sausage, syrup inside, and the leftover eggs in case they got hungry later. "Thank you again for your alarm clock efforts. Your breakfast was amazing."

"JJ, I'm bringing shorts in case we want to cool off. Lily, can we take some waters too?"

"Yes, Jo, the cooler is by the door. Grab 'em on your way out. Oh, Ann called and asked if you could swing by on your way. She needs to ask a favor."

"No problem," replied JJ.

JJ navigated them to Hank and Ann's, parking near the porch.

Ann walked out, all smiles. "Good morning, you two. Today is a big day for you to set your plans in motion. Sorry to bother you, but I need to take Hank to the doctor to have his foot checked. I was wondering if I might borrow your car as it's easier for him to get in and out of than the pickup."

"Of course, no problem."

"Maybe we could borrow the ATV to go to our place," Jo suggested.

Ann nodded. "Fine with me. Let me get you the keys." She disappeared inside and returned in minutes with Hank ambling right behind her. "Here you go, JJ. Doc is in Fredericksburg, so we shouldn't be too long. Camila said you could call if you needed her. I expect her to finish her chores within the hour."

"She can ride over if she wants, or I can come back and bring her on the ATV."

"Thanks again." Ann waved and drove off with Hank.

Meetings with each of the contractors went well. The drawings were updated with the current changes. Stan planned weekly calls on Fridays to summarize the completed projects and to outline the next week of activities. Jason committed to taking confirmation photos which he'd get paid to complete. JJ and Jo signed a couple of addendums.

Jo's smiles and little dances as a task got completed made it fun. Things looked great until JJ noticed Tommy's cruiser pulling in the gate. He parked and walked over to them.

"Hi, Tommy. We weren't expecting to see you until tonight at Lily's."

"I wanted to see how it's going with the town troublemaker."

Jo sashayed next to JJ and grinned.

Tommy continued with a touch to his hat, "And the iron skillet maiden. Glad you found your dream. You look happy."

Jo did a small two-step. "I'm delighted."

"Good. JJ, I have one small detail I'd like to clarify with you, if Jo doesn't mind me borrowing you."

"Go right ahead. I'm going to see if I can get Jason to help me pace out the gazebo one more time. I have this idea, honey."

JJ shrugged and grinned. "Go for it."

The two men stepped into the barn away from everyone.

"JJ, we've got a problem. Where's your car?"

"Ann borrowed it to take Hank to Fredericksburg to the doctor for his foot. Why?"

"Some out-of-towners were driving around near Flower this morning acting like they were lost. I pulled them over and offered to help. Two guys and one very pretty girl got out. The guys wouldn't look me in the eye but assured me they were fine. I pressed them for where they were going. They grew more uncomfortable the longer we talked."

JJ listened, trying to think of where this was headed.

"I asked to see what their GPS application was saying and noticed the license plate number at the top of the program. I asked if they were detectives working a case. The fidgety one finally blurted, 'We're looking for a Brazilian super model to interview for our media publication.'"

JJ flinched and clenched his fists, anger raging inside.

Tommy continued, "I laughed it off. 'Here in Magnolia Bluff?' I said. 'Doubtful. Supermodels belong on the Riviera, right? Ha!' It was your rental license number on screen. It was doing intermittent tracking by the LoJack device. They said they got proximity feeds every few hours. It brought them to the center of town, but they couldn't spot your car."

JJ ground his teeth as he closed his eyes.

"Then the lead mouth tossed in, 'We believe she may have been abducted from her work location by an unknown assailant. We want to get to the truth of her departure and make sure she hasn't fallen into harm's way.'"

"We thought we sent them on a wild goose chase to southern Mexico. Bummer."

"I don't have a good reason to arrest them or run them out of town. I've seen people like this before. They won't stop until they get what they want. No one in our town would rat you out even if they knew, which they don't. People respect you both too much."

JJ's thoughts raced through options. "Do you have their license plate?"

Tommy nodded and pulled a folded piece of paper from his pocket. "Did I ever tell you about my friend at UT Austin? He creates leading edge electronic solutions for law enforcement and has me test stuff. He likes to use solar and miniature speakers and batteries."

"No, but it sounds interesting."

"He and I have talked about you some. He'd like to meet you."

"Thanks. Happy to talk to him, Tommy. See you tonight." He shook his hand.

JJ went to the garden bench to access his laptop. He used his cell to get an internet connection. He read Tommy's note and laughed aloud. Several encrypted programs got launched. With this new twist courtesy, JJ's fingers went to work on the devious plan he'd hatched.

Jo hip-bumped him fifteen minutes later. "Are you working?"

"No, honey, just shutting down."

"Good, I think we are ready to go take that nap. Stan wanted to let you know he was going."

JJ walked up to Stan. "Stan, looking forward to working with you. I know we are in good hands. Let me or Jo know if there are issues. We are not unreasonable."

Stan nearly choked on his water. "You are the nicest customers I've ever worked with. It's a pleasure getting your business." He extended his hand, and they shook.

## CHAPTER 44

# Now What?

**JJ** enjoyed watching his wife look so relaxed. He scooted from bed, feeling refreshed, rubbing his hands together, hoping he could put the troublesome interlopers in his review mirror. With laptop and earbuds in-hand, he quietly left the room, sat on the floor leaning against the wall. Seconds later, his laptop connected. He navigated to the application he'd created in the barn, delighted that several audio files were stored.

He pushed the oldest one but the sound wasn't quite clear. Fiddling with the setting of volume, base, and background suppression, he started the file at the beginning. A woman's voice said, "Rickey, are you sure we're closing in? Seems like we're going in circles. Are you reading this right?"

"Of course, I know how to read it. I've gotten us this far, haven't I?" a man's voice replied. "After that cop in Magnolia Bluff wasted our time searching our car, the next feed indicated our target vehicle was headed toward Fredericksburg. A day driving around in the hot sun, yuck. Small town Texas works on country roads. We're getting close based on the tracker."

JJ heard a different man's voice. "Rickey, she's right. Every time they turn left or right, we are spot-on. Why aren't we seeing their vehicle? Where is the damn red Mustang convertible?"

"We should have seen them by now. Oh crap! How did they do that?"

The file size ended per JJ's program instructions. The next file played.

"What's wrong?" an angry man demanded. "You said, how did they do…what?"

"We aren't tailing their vehicle anymore. We're tailing ours. Look at the license plate number on my screen. I'll bet the VIN I'm seeing is the one on this van."

"S-some-someone was smart enough to change the target vehicle I entered, and replace it with ours. We've been chasing our tail for I don't know how long. At least an hour."

JJ nearly giggled at the exchange enjoying the way he messed with these guys. He pulled out his cell phone and after masking his number he sent a text.

"Reload the original license number. We'll find 'em. I want the payday on this job."

All three of their mobile devices sounded an incoming message.

> This is the end of the lesson. Recommend you go home.
> We know who you are.

Minutes passed before another audio file dropped into the storage area of his laptop.

"Do like I tell you and reload the program! No one makes a fool of me!"

Rickey said, "I suggest we head for Austin and that Mexican restaurant with those terrific frozen margaritas. The message is a generous 'get out of here and don't come back' offer. Anyone who can reprogram our tracking program without us noticing, and text all of us at the same time has more skills than we do. This game is over. Checkmate. No payday is worth facing off against a digital assassin who seems capable of swatting us like babies. I don't want to be digitally erased like you read about in the Enigma Book Series."

JJ heard the siren. A minute later.

"It's that cop again." Ricky said. "Keep quiet, I'll roll down my window to talk to him.

"Hi again. I'd take the advice and leave Texas, period. You'll have better luck anywhere else. Nothing here but grief for you."

JJ chuckled. He looked forward to shaking Tommy's hand.

Following their afternoon nap and shower, JJ watched Jo get ready for the evening's festivities. Her graceful movements reminded him of yet another reason he wanted her in his life. "You look ravishing, but inside beats the heart of a woman of conviction. I liked how you knocked the items off our list. We are at a point where we can somewhat relax before we return to work. I will attest to Aunt Lara you haven't gained an ounce." He winked.

Jo pirouetted in the soft vibrant colors of Brazil, with the flowing skirt swirling around her long legs. "You like?"

He waggled his eyebrows and raised his lips. "And then some, sweetheart."

"I thought perhaps we might create a picture story of our time here and what we've done to share with the family. If you think of it, can you take a few candid shots tonight to include? The folks Lily invited are nice, though quirky people." She laughed.

"I hope she doesn't make it too crazy."

Jo rolled her eyes and took one more glance in the mirror. "Let's head down. I'm ready for snacks and a glass of wine."

JJ stood and angled his elbow after a short bow. "This way, my dear."

The dining room sparkled with candlelight. Outside the windows, the garden was alive with tiny white lights showing off the blooms of Lily's backyard garden.

Jo leaned against JJ and whispered, "I look forward to making our gardens this inviting."

"I have no doubts." JJ headed toward the buffet to get wine and stopped, stunned. "Stefan…Marta. I didn't know you were coming."

Stefan swallowed the morsel he'd taken from his plate. "When we checked in, Lily asked us if we wanted to join. We figured we could meet more people."

"Jo, you look stunning. Maybe you can schedule another massage," Marta suggested with a gleam in her eye, "before you and this charming husband of yours leave."

Jo leaned in for a quick hug with Marta. "I will."

Marta took a sip of wine. "Lily thought a little cross promotion would help both our businesses. We get a romantic getaway, and Lily gets a full-day pamper in exchange." Her fingers wiggled in the air as if writing an advertising slogan. "The romantic couple power package, Bed, Breakfast, and Pampering."

JJ nodded. "I like it."

Lily popped in greeting folks and filling serving dishes. "Would anyone mind if I turned on some music?" No objections were voiced so she played jazz. "All y'all can dance if you want."

Hank and Ann arrived with the girls looking quite spiffy. Hank was using a four-pronged cane.

JJ watched his movement. "Looks like you're making progress, Hank."

"I am, son. I need to not overdo too much, so no dancing for me tonight." He eyed JJ. "I wouldn't turn down a beer, however. Ann wants a red wine."

JJ realized he was the resident bartender until Tommy arrived. "No problem. Pick a table and I'll bring it."

Hank and Ann selected a table while their girls went to the buffet to select some food. JJ returned with their drinks.

Ann smiled. "Perfect timing. What a day. Thank you for the loan of the car, JJ. Though you might want to check it before that long drive back. When we arrived at the doctor's office, the dashboard flashed oddly, like it was receiving a software update. But it didn't cause us a lick of trouble."

"Glad to hear it helped."

Jo sidled up to him. "Honey, Gunter and Mary Lou arrived. Are you bartending?"

"That I am. Talk later."

JJ clapped Gunter on the back, and squatted to get eye-level with Mary Lou. He grinned. "Glad you two joined us. Find a spot. What may I bring you to drink?"

Mary Lou's face softened just a bit. "We're celebrating our date night so a glass of champagne each." She reached up and squeezed Gunter's hand for a moment. "Let's take the table by Ann, Gunter." She rolled off.

As he turned, he was enveloped in an embrace as he faced LouEllen. She grinned. "I promised your wife not to grab, but a hug seemed perfect. And you're a bartender, too. Let me know if you ever want to work at my place part-time. I have great benefits."

They both hooted.

"I'll take your best whiskey neat," she added.

"Of course. Be right back. Find a seat."

JJ noticed Jo engaged in a conversation with Joyce. Jason was cutting up with Camila and Renata like old friends. JJ delivered LouEllen's drink in time to see Tommy enter in jeans and a Don't Mess with Texas tee shirt.

Lily rushed to Tommy's side. "Why are you so late?"

"I had a small chore to take care of. My apologies."

"Harumph," she growled. "JJ's been filling drinks. I'll take a white wine, and food is on the buffet. I want you to do a toast."

He saluted and went to fix the drinks.

JJ followed him. "You planted some slick technology that worked like a charm. The solar powered transmitter and speakers in the center of the vehicle were perfect, following cell towers like a homing pigeon. I look forward to meeting your friend. Do you have another of those devices?"

"Nope, I only had the one. I'll ask him for another though if it worked."

JJ clapped him on the back. "I heard your final warning. Did they seem to take it seriously?"

"I'm not certain how you pulled it off, and I don't care to know, at least not tonight. They were hightailing it toward Austin when I left. They won't return or admit their defeat to anyone."

"Good to know. Glad we teamed together, Tommy." JJ shrugged. "Let's get our drinks, and I'll do the toast if you don't mind."

Tommy looked relieved, rushing to hand Lily her glass.

Jo magically materialized at JJ's side. He raised his glass. "To friends, new and old, and my lovely bride. Cheers!"

Tommy hollered, "To J & J. Friends, trusted advisors, and protectors who always bring trouble to light. Prost!"

Wide-eyed, Jo grabbed JJ's arm. "JJ! That's it! Our property name—J&J Ranch and Skillet."

JJ clucked his tongue. "A great start, babe."

Jo leaned into him and whispered. "Have noticed, gossip is the number one industry in Magnolia Bluff."

They giggled and high-fived.

Discussion Questions for
# The Killer Enigma

**Book Club Leaders** … contact Breakfield and Burkey to participate in a special meeting to discuss the book, the concepts, and the evolution of the series. We always encourage readers to post individual reviews on *Amazon.com*. And thank you.

In-person gatherings are possible if you are in Texas and either author is available. Otherwise, Zoom is always an option.

## Discussion Questions

**Did the ending pull you in? Did you want more?**
- Were you satisfied or disappointed with how this story ended?
- How do you picture the Magnolia Bluff citizens feeling after the end of the story?
- If you were to identify the most important theme within *The Killer Enigma,* what would it be?

**What do you think of Jo and JJ wanting a home in Magnolia Bluff?**
- Do you think they can fit in, even part-time?
- Would you enjoy having them as neighbors and friends?
- Do you think it's important for a woman to feel empowered and capable like Jo?

**Do you think the sadness from the prior owners will haunt JJ and Jo?**
- What would you like if you had the opportunity to make a significant change in your life to escape your obligations now and again?

- What did you think of Jo and JJ's reactions to the Stevens background?
- Do you think they will be happy and why?

**How will the town receive them when they return?**
- Will Jo and JJ isolate themselves or remain interactive in the community?
- Do you think the rest of the town will discover Jo's secret?
- What is your favorite memory of Magnolia Bluff?

**Would you help a stranger like Jason and Camila did?**
- Where should people draw the line on helping others?
- What is the best way for teens to learn responsibility?
- Did you like Jason and Camila?

**What themes surfaced in the story?**
- Have you ever been in a situation where you needed someone to save you?
- Have you ever been in a situation where you did not want someone to save you?
- Have you ever had to step in and help someone out of a dire situation?
- Have you ever allowed yourself to cut off others you knew well because you felt they lied to you?

Enjoy an excerpt from Joe Congel's
Book 17 of The Magnolia Bluff Crime Chronicles
# Second Chances

CHAPTER ONE

Brandon Turner guided his truck off the interstate and pulled into a small rest stop outside of Austin, Texas. He'd been driving for three days and was ready for this road trip to be over. He was tired of chasing shadows. Or at least that's how it felt the direction his career and life had been headed these last few years. As a former narcotics detective for the NYPD, he was fed up watching the bad guys use the courthouse like a revolving door in a swanky hotel on 5th Avenue. He knew the system wasn't perfect, but a solid conviction was becoming more and more elusive. Seemed that nowadays every drug dealer in New York had a powerful attorney on speed dial. So, after twenty-three years on the job, he'd decided to pack it all in.

Retiring was a simple decision to make after what could've been a career-ending accusation had been made following what he knew was a clean bust. He didn't steal those drugs or that money. He was raised better than that. All he knew was that he was supposed to be innocent until proven guilty, not the other way around. And even though in the end he was completely cleared of any wrongdoing, the job had just become too hard. He knew when he'd been beaten.

Cleaning up the drug-infested streets on the east side of Central Park all the way down to 110th was a younger man's job. He knew when it was time to move on, so he put in for his retirement, packed up his life, and headed south.

He'd grown up in the city and now just wanted to get out, and he really didn't care where he went as long as it wasn't New York. Maybe somewhere he'd never been before. Leave everything behind. Start fresh. Spend his retirement years doing a little fishing in some sleepy little town a million miles away from the Big Apple.

As random as it sounded, he'd purchased a map of Texas, spread it out on his kitchen table, closed his eyes and touched his forefinger on its smooth surface. When he opened them, he was pointing at the name of a place he'd never heard of before. He bent down and scratched his dog behind the ears. "Well, Max, I guess we're headed to Magnolia Bluff, Texas."

It was a twenty-six-hour drive from his apartment on the west side of the city to Austin, and then it would be a quick hour to Magnolia Bluff. He had planned it as a three-day trip, no need to drive straight through. He certainly wasn't in a hurry. He may never be in a hurry again.

He stepped out of the four-wheel-drive vehicle and stretched his arms high above his head. Leaning back inside his truck, he clicked a leash on his two-year-old black Labrador and coaxed him from the back seat of the cab. "Come on, Max. Time to do your business." He stroked the canine's head and then they both strolled over toward the grassy area marked for dog walking. Turner bent down so he could be face-to-face with his best friend. He smiled. "If you get this done quick enough, I'll bring you a treat when I'm done doing *my* business."

"You're pretty far from home, son."

Turner looked over his shoulder to see who had the stones to address him in a rest stop in the middle of nowhere. It surprised him to see a man dressed in all black, except for the white collar poking out of the top of his shirt. "Hello, Father," he said, with a bewildered look on his face. "What makes you say that?"

The priest nodded over at the New York tag affixed to the rear of the four-wheeler. "I saw you walk from the direction of the truck. I made an educated guess. Am I wrong?"

"No. Well, yes, actually. I guess I'm closer to where I'm hoping my new home will be rather than my old home."

"And where are you hoping that new home will be?"

"A small town about an hour from here. A place called Magnolia Bluff. Ever hear of it?"

The priest's eyes widened. "Well, isn't this a coincidence?" he said. "I just left Magnolia Bluff this morning. I spent a few days there visiting a very good friend of mine." He took a step forward and offered his hand. "I think it's time I introduce myself. I'm Father Frank DeLuca."

"Brandon Turner. Nice to meet you," Turner said, shaking Father Frank's hand.

The priest smiled. "So, Mr. Turner, what makes a Yankee want to pack up his life in the big city and move all the way down here to the Texas Hill Country?"

"Let's just say I'm looking for a new start." Turner sighed and then gazed off into the distance for a moment before refocusing. "Please, Father, call me Brandon," he said, managing a smile. "This will be my first time in Magnolia Bluff. Is it as sleepy a little town as I hope?"

Father Frank's eye twitched and Turner detected a slight hesitation in the priest before he answered him. "I'll tell you this… Brandon," he replied, choosing his words carefully. "It's a beautiful little town. The people are nice, and the air is clean and fresh." He leaned over and patted the dog on the head. "Good-looking dog. He's been a very patient boy. I'm going to let you get back to walking him. And besides, I've kept you long enough. You have a new life to get to and I have a congregation anxiously awaiting my return back in Pine Tree."

Turner gave Father Frank a tired smile. As a cop, he was trained in reading body language and facial expressions. He could tell that the priest was holding something back but decided not to push. "Thank you. His name's Max. And you're right, he's been a pretty good boy… this entire trip, actually." He leaned over and scratched Max's head and smiled. "I think I owe him a treat." He straightened himself back up and the two men shook hands again. "Safe travels, Father."

Father Frank smiled back. "You too, Brandon. By the way, I'm not sure if you're a man of Catholic faith, but I get into Magnolia Bluff to visit my friend Father Lee every couple of months. He's a good man and is the pastor at Christ the King Church. You should look him up. And perhaps we'll run into each other again the next time I'm in town."

**Less than ninety minutes later,** Turner drove past a billboard that read *Welcome to Magnolia Bluff, Texas. Home of the Burnet Reservoir.* He stroked Max under his chin. "Well, boy, looks like we made it. We'll have to check out that reservoir and see if it's a good place to fish. But first we need to check into our room at the Flower Bed and Breakfast. Get a good night's sleep and then head to the local real estate office in the morning."

Turner had done a little pre-game investigating by Googling Magnolia Bluff's visitors page on the internet. It was a wealth of information. He learned the Flower was located close to the center of town, which he preferred, and that they were pet friendly, which he needed. He also found a list of places to eat and the information for the real estate office. When he called the bed-and-breakfast, the good-natured tone of the woman who'd helped him with the reservation struck him immediately. A far cry from what he was used to in the city. It's not that the people who run the hotels in New York City aren't friendly, it's just that the woman at the Flower seemed more genuine to him, like she really was looking forward to having him and Max stay there.

All the tension and pent-up frustration seemed to lift off his shoulders the minute he pulled up to the B&B. He sat in his truck and took a full look around before going inside. The building was right out of a storybook. It was a two-story gray clapboard house with white trim and beautiful matching curtains adorning all the windows. The colors of the rainbow popped into his head as the fragrance from the beautiful floral decor stretched out on either side of the steps leading up to the porch tickled his nose.

There was an elderly woman sipping a glass of iced tea, easing a rocking chair back and forth with her feet. She stood to greet them as he and Max approached the stairs. Turner noticed there were touches of gray starting to invade her blond locks, and the deep wrinkles beneath her eyes exposed a lifetime of stories. "Mr. Turner, I presume?"

Turner bent down and scratched Max under the chin. He looked up at the light-haired woman and smiled. "What gave us away?"

The woman crinkled her nose and offered a crooked smile. "Well, let me see," she said. "It could be the fact that you pulled up in a truck with a New York tag on it, or it could be it's been a little slow here lately and you're the only guest I've got booked who's arriving today." She smiled down at Max. "Or maybe it's that beautiful dog ya got there."

Turner laughed. "Well, ma'am, we'll go with the dog then," he said, climbing the steps. He glanced down at his furry friend. "This is Max."

"I'm Lily," she said. She leaned over and gave the dog a pat on the head. "Nice to meet you, Max." Then straightening back up, she smiled at her guest. "You, too, Mr. Turner," she said, before turning toward the front door. "Follow me, boys. We'll get you checked in."

Turner followed as Max bounded up the steps and entered the B&B. They walked down a short hallway, passing a dining room on their way to the registration desk. When Turner saw the nicely appointed seating area, it reminded him he hadn't eaten a proper meal in a while. "Say, Lily, would it be possible to get something to eat? It's been a long trip, and I didn't realize how hungry I was until just now."

"I reckon we can figure something out," she said. "You ever have chicken fried steak?"

"What do you think? You know I'm from New York, right? For as long as I can remember, most of my meals have been Chinese takeout, street vendor hot dogs, and pizza." He gave her a slight shrug. "What can I say? Curse of the single guy who's all about the job."

"Well, Mr. Turner, you're in the south now. And even more important; you're in Texas. Chicken fried steak is a staple 'round here." A grin broke across her face. "We need to sharpen up those taste buds of yours."

"I don't know, Lily. I'd put up a good New York pepperoni and sausage pie against your chicken fried steak any day." He paused and inched out a smile. "But it does have three of my favorite things—chicken, fried, and steak—so I'm guessing it's probably pretty good."

Lily let out a snort resembling a laugh. "I'll tell you what, Mr. Turner… you fill out this registration card and get settled into your room." She pushed a white card about the size of a half sheet of paper in front of Turner. "Then you both meet me back here at the desk. I'm going to introduce you and Max to Renata. She helps me out around here. She'll make sure he gets fed properly and will keep him company until we get back. That is, if you're okay leaving Max here for a spell. I guarantee he'll be in fine hands with Renata."

Turner had a puzzled look on his face. "Get back from where?"

"I'm gonna take you over to the Silver Spoon Café and introduce you to the best chicken fried steak with all the fixins you'll ever have."

"Sounds like a plan, Lily. And please, it's Brandon." He wrote all the pertinent information on the card and slid it back across the desk.

"Here's your key, Brandon." She handed him a vintage, decorative brass key on a blue ring in the shape of a flower. "You're in the bluebonnet room. Turn left at the top of the stairs, look for the door with a blue flower painted on it."

Turner smiled at the old-fashioned key. "Can't remember the last time I rented a room that had an actual key… or a name, for that matter."

"I like to think it's part of the charm of this old place," she said, smiling back.

"Totally agree. There is certainly a lot of charm here," he said, gazing around the room. "Your place is beautiful. Much better than the skyscrapers and brownstones I'm used to seeing back in the city." He looked down at his best friend. "C'mon Max. Let's get ourselves settled."

**CHAPTER TWO**

The Silver Spoon had a decent crowd for a weeknight. Lily introduced Turner to Lorraine Dillard, the owner of the café.

"Well, Brandon," said Lorraine, in a much more pleasant tone than he would've expected, given the hustle and bustle going on around them. "What do you think of our little corner of the world so far?"

Turner smiled. "I've only met you and Lily," he replied. "Oh, and Renata. If everyone in town is as friendly as you all have been, I'm sure I'll love it here. Nice change of pace from Manhattan."

"Not quite what you're used to in New York City, I suspect. But I believe you'll fit in nicely," said Lorraine. She leaned over to Lily and added in a mock whisper. "We don't want to burst his bubble about how friendly the town folks are, Lily. We need to keep him away from Graham Huston." The two ladies shared a laugh.

"Graham Huston?" Turner said. "Not as nice as you ladies are I gather?"

"He's the editor of Magnolia Bluff's newspaper, the *Chronicle*. He seems to have an opinion about everybody," said Lorraine, rolling her eyes.

"I know the type," said Turner. "Where I'm from, not only do these guys have an opinion about everybody else, but they'll also argue their point until somebody gets hurt."

Lorraine looked over at Lily. "Well, I don't think Graham

would ever take things that far. He's pretty harmless, even though he can be a sarcastic blowhard at times."

"Oh, don't listen to us, Brandon," Lily said. "You'll meet him soon enough and you can judge for yourself on how nice a guy he is."

"Enough of this talk. You look like a man who needs to eat," Lorraine said, looping her arm around Turner's. "Let's grab some menus and get you seated." She guided them over to a booth that had just opened up and got them situated with a couple of tall glasses of iced tea. "I'll give you a moment to look at the menu and then I'll be back to take your order."

Lily handed her back the menus. "No need, Lorraine. I told Brandon that you served the best chicken fried steak on the planet. We'll have two orders with all the fixins."

Turner caught the proud smile on the café owner's face as she went off to fill their orders. He turned toward Lily. "You know, it's unnecessary for you to stay and eat with me," he said. "I'm sure you have better things to do than eat dinner with a complete stranger."

"You were only a stranger until you pulled up to my B&B. Now you can consider me your first friend in Magnolia Bluff," she said, offering him that crooked smile again. "And besides, I want to see the look on that face of yours after you bite into a piece of heaven on earth."

*Friend,* he thought. *That's a good one. Any friend I had bailed as soon as I was accused of being a dirty cop.* His lip curled and his brows arched downward.

"You're frowning. Are you okay? I didn't mean to overstep with the friend thing. Sometimes I just run my mouth."

"What? No, it's not that. I guess I'm more tired than I realized. Long trip," he said with a tight smile, then added, "I'm happy to consider you my first friend." *If only she knew how true that was.*

Minutes later, two heaping plates filled with chicken fried

steak, mashed potatoes, and green beans all smothered in southern gravy were placed in front of them. They passed the time with some small talk while they ate their food.

"So, Brandon, why Magnolia Bluff? I would think that a big city feller like yourself wouldn't stray so far away from the bright lights and all that action. You might get bored living in our little town. It's a big change."

*All that action is why I needed to get away,* he thought. "I wanted to retire somewhere away from all that," he said. "Maybe buy a small fishing boat and while away my days dropping a line in a lake." He smiled. "Boring is what I'm looking for."

"A long way to come just to go fishin'. You could've done that on one of those beautiful lakes in the Catskills or Adirondacks."

Turner gave her a surprised look.

She smiled at him. "What? I'm country, not stupid."

"It's not that," he said, returning her smile. "It's just most people not from New York immediately think the city is the entire state. There's some beautiful country in upstate and northern New York. And you're right. I could've moved to a cabin in the mountains of New York and fished there. But like I said, I needed a change. And for me, that meant an entirely different part of the country." *Nowhere in the state of New York would've been far enough away for what I went through and how I was treated,* he thought.

Their conversation was interrupted when a woman riding one of those mobility scooters approached the table. "Hi Lily," she said before turning her sights on Turner. "And who do we have here?"

"Oh, hello, Mary Lou," Lily said in a less than enthusiastic tone. Turner noticed she didn't seem very pleased by the woman's presence. "Did you just arrive, or were you just leaving?"

"You're so funny," replied Mary Lou in a sarcastic tone

sweeter than the iced tea they were drinking. She readjusted herself and offered her hand to Turner. "I'm Mary Lou Fight. I'm the founder of the Crimson Hat Society and I produce a very popular podcast here in town. And you are…?"

Turner stood up to greet the woman. He was good at reading people, and he could already see that this woman could be trouble. "Brandon Turner, ma'am. Nice to meet you."

"Do I detect a Yankee accent, Mr. Turner? What brings you to our small little Texas town?"

"I'm recently retired," he replied, ignoring her comment about his accent. "Max and I—he's my dog—thought Magnolia Bluff would be the perfect place to slow down, do some fishing, and enjoy life."

Mary Lou gave Turner the once over. "You look much too young to be retired, Mr. Turner. What line of work were you in before showing up on our doorstep?"

He understood why Lily didn't sound pleased when this woman approached their table. She had all the makings of a busybody who was full of herself, and he was not about to give her something for the rumor mill… or her podcast. Best he didn't mention he was a former narcotics officer from the Big Apple. Besides, he wanted to leave his past in the past. He didn't need this woman digging into it. "Let's just say I was a servant of the great City of New York and decided it was time for a change."

"You seem to be avoiding the question, Mr. Turner." She glared at him with a furrowed brow. "What exactly are you hiding?"

"I think you've grilled our newest resident quite enough, Mary Lou."

The three of them turned to see a man standing there, scowling at the woman. "Oh, Huston… *get a life!*" she said before turning her scooter around and driving off in a huff.

The man turned his attention to Turner. "Hi, I'm Graham

Huston. Couldn't help but overhear. Be careful what you say around that one," he said, pointing at the departing Mary Lou. "She thinks anything is fair game for that damn podcast of hers."

Turner, who was still standing, shook hands with the editor of the *Chronicle*. "Good to meet you, Graham. Brandon Turner." He shot Huston a grin. "And how do I know that whatever I say to you won't end up in the headlines of your newspaper?"

Huston laughed. "I see my reputation proceeds me." He glanced over at Lily. "Are you telling tales out of school about me to our new friend here, Lily?"

"Nothing that isn't true to form, Graham," she replied.

"I'll bet," he said. "I'll let you two get back to your meal." Addressing Turner, he added, "Don't be a stranger, Brandon. A bunch of us meet every morning at the Really Good Wood-Fired Coffee shop. Great coffee. If you've never had wood-fired coffee, you're in for a treat. I know the owner, Harry Thurgood, personally. If you stop by, I'll introduce you."

Turner nodded at the newspaper editor. "Maybe. I'll see if I can fit it in. I've got a lot going on tomorrow."

"Understood. It'll be worth your time. If you can make it, we meet around nine o'clock."

After he left, Lily said, "He's such a pompous ass. Always trying to sound more important than he actually is. *Everyone* in town knows Harry Thurgood, personally." She sighed and then added, "At least as personally as Harry allows, anyway."

"What do you mean by that, Lily?"

Remembering his veiled response when Mary Lou asked about his former line of work, she leaned in across the table and said, "Let's just say you're not the only one with secrets, Brandon."

Turner started to respond, but Lily put up her hand, stopping him. "Not to worry. It's your business and I'm not asking." She gave him a warm smile. "But as your first official friend in

# Second Chances

Magnolia Bluff, if you ever want to talk about it, I'm a pretty good listener."

Turner nodded. "Thanks. I'll remember that."

They finished their meal without further interruption. Turner leaned back in his chair and patted his stomach. "That was incredible, Lily," he said. "I haven't eaten like that in forever. I'm used to mediocre Chinese takeout and overcooked hot dogs. I think my stomach's about to explode."

Lily smiled. "Told ya you'd enjoy it." She reached across the table and gave her new friend a motherly pat on the hand. "Let's get you back to the B&B so you can check on Max and get settled in for the night. I know you've got a long day ahead of you tomorrow. Moving's never easy. Especially a long-distance move."

"Sounds good, Lily." Turner waved at Lorraine, trying to catch her attention from the folks she was currently engaged with. She returned his wave, said something to the couple she was talking to, and headed over to their table. When she got there, Turner said, "This was the best meal I've had in years. I wanted to thank Lily for bringing me here and you for proving her right—the best chicken fried steak on the planet."

"Well, high praise like that just got you your meal on the house, Brandon."

"I couldn't," Turner said, protesting her generosity.

Lorraine dismissed him with a wave of the hand. "Consider it a little welcome home gift. You're going to be a part of our community now, so this first meal is on me." A grin widened across her face. "Course, if you're wanting to make it up to me, come on back again and I'll make sure I charge ya next time."

Turner laughed. "You've got a deal."

After thanking Lorraine one last time and promising he would bring Max by for her to meet, Turner and Lily made their way back to the Flower.

"So…?" Lily said as they walked along the sidewalk towards the B&B.

Turner smiled. "You know I liked it. It was good," he said. "Actually, it was better than good. But better than a nice hot slice from Joe's Pizza on 14th Street in the East Village?" He had his hands out in front of him, moving them up and down as if he were weighing something in each. "Eh? Let's just say there's room in my life now for both."

"After what you said to Lorraine, I thought you'd concede," she said, glancing over at him.

"What are you talkin' about? That was me conceding."

Lilly rolled her eyes and laughed as they walked up the steps to the porch.

Max was curled up on a fluffy doggy bed by the front desk when they walked in. The commotion caused him to pop his head up and as soon as he saw who it was, he stood, stretched his body and then danced his way over to greet his owner. Turner leaned down and rubbed Max behind his ears. "Well, boy, you seem to have settled right in," he said, smiling. He looked over at Renata. "He give you any trouble?"

Renata smiled at Max and then looked up at Turner. "No, no, Mr. Brandon," she said in a thick accent. "He was a lovely gentleman while you were gone. He ate, I took him outside for a walk, and then found him this nice doggy bed and a chew toy. Maxie and I got along just fine. It was my honor to watch him for you. He is a wonderful dog."

*Maxie?* Turner chuckled under his breath.

Max lay on the floor, gnawing away on the chew toy while Turner spoke with Renata. Glancing down at his dog, he said, "He certainly likes that thing. Okay to let him keep it?"

She smiled. "It is his to keep. We have a box full. And feel free to use the bed for him while you stay here."

Turner collected the dog bed and then thanked Renata with a generous tip for taking such good care of his buddy. He said goodnight to her and Lily, and then, smiling to himself, said, "C'mon, *Maxie*. Bring your toy and follow me. Time for bed."

## CHAPTER THREE

Turner felt the warmth of the new day rolling across the bed until the sunshine finally hit his eyes, persuading them to open. Morning arrived earlier than he'd expected. He breathed in, and let the air slowly escape as he swung his legs to the floor. Max was lying in his new bed just inches away from where his owner's feet landed, his eyes laser focused on Turner.

Turner stretched his arms high above his head. "Morning, Max. Did you sleep well?"

The dog hacked loudly, sneezed, shook his head, then sneezed again.

"I'll take that as a definite maybe," he said, laughing. "I'm not so sure how well I slept either, old buddy. Always harder to fall asleep in a strange place, but hopefully it won't feel strange for long." Taking in a deep breath, he added, "Something smells good. What do you say I get myself cleaned up and dressed and we'll go investigate?"

Turner had packed a small bag of dry dog food before leaving New York. He removed the bag and two bowls from a duffle. He pulled on his robe and took one bowl down the hall to the bathroom and filled it with water. Once back in the room, he placed a towel on the floor, set both bowls on the towel, and filled the empty one with the kibble. "You enjoy your breakfast, Max. I'm gonna take a quick shower while you eat."

By the time Turner was back in the room, Max had finished

his breakfast, jumped up on Turner's bed, and was snoozing away. He couldn't help but laugh at his dog spread out across the mattress. "C'mon, Max," he said, coaxing the black Lab off the fluffy comforter. "You'll have to catch up on your zzz's later."

Max opened one eye and slowly wagged his tail. And then, dropping his front paws to the floor, he sluggishly dragged the rest of his body off the bed. All Turner could do was smile and shake his head at the dramatic antics of his dog.

The dining room was fairly crowded, which threw him off when he walked in. Lily and Renata were bustling around the tables, laying plates filled with pancakes, sausage, eggs and toast in front of happy patrons.

Lily spotted him, and once she positioned the last plate of food down on one of the tables, she went over to greet him. "Good morning, Brandon," she said, smiling. She bent down and scratched Max behind the ears. "You too, Max."

Seeing Lily speak to Max, he realized he should have left him outside of the dining area. "I'm sorry, Lily. I wasn't thinking. Let me get Max out of here."

Lily sighed. "You're right. Normally I wouldn't mind since he's so well behaved, but since we're so busy this morning, you never know who might have a problem with him being in here."

"No issue," said Turner. He walked Max out and over to the front desk, told him to stay, and then went back to the dining room. "You've certainly got your hands full this morning. I thought you said there weren't that many people staying here."

Lily pulled a napkin from her front pocket and wiped her brow. "Oh, there's not." She pointed at two tables near each other with five men who looked like construction workers. They were responsible for half the people in the room. "That's Jeff Peterson and some of his crew. They're fixin' a stretch of highway out by the reservoir. They come by every morning for breakfast when the road crew is working an early morning job."

Turner nodded. "So, you don't have to be a guest at the B&B to enjoy your breakfast? It smells delicious, by the way."

"I couldn't stay in business if I didn't open the kitchen to people who wanted a quick bite to eat without having to put up with all the gossip that flies around Harry's coffee shop and the Silver Spoon this time of day." She sighed. "To tell you the truth, Brandon, our little town has suffered some bad press over the last few years. How should I put this without scaring you off on only your second day in town?" She paused to look around, making sure no one was eavesdropping on their conversation. "We've had more than our fair share of people dying lately."

Although surprised by this information about his new hometown, as a former police detective, her admission didn't faze him. "By dying, you mean murdered?"

"Yes," she said, and then quickly added, "But, rest assured, the police department is headed up by Chief Tommy Jager. Between him and Reese Sovern—he's Magnolia Bluff's homicide detective—there's nothing to worry about. Tommy and his team are pretty good police officers. And Reese?" She glanced down at Max, who appeared bored with the conversation. "Well, he's like a dog with a bone when he's brought in on a case."

"Pretty good?" Turner said, frowning. "I didn't hear the word effective in that explanation." As a career cop, he knew that any cop being referred to as 'pretty good' was probably not that effective. "What's their track record on solving all these homicides?"

Lily narrowed her eyes and frowned. "Let's just say that even if those guys have never actually been the ones who solved any of the homicides, they try hard." She crossed her fingers. "Here's hoping no one in our little town needs their services again anytime soon."

He smirked at the innkeeper. "Doesn't instill a lot of confidence in Magnolia Bluff's police department, does it?"

She shook her head. "I guess not, huh?" A concerned look crossed her face. "It does seem like the citizens of our little town have been better investigators than the actual investigators."

Turner stood silently, contemplating what he'd just learned. The last thing he needed was to live in a town with an inept police force. Well, chances were, he wouldn't have to worry about it. It couldn't be any worse than any other small town. How many homicides could there possibly be, anyway? He could guarantee the murder rate in the Big Apple would put this place to shame. He looked at Lily and smiled. "Don't worry about me. I'm a big boy from the big city. I've seen things on the streets of New York that would make your toes curl. You can't scare me off that easily. Now, how about a plate of those pancakes?"

**After stuffing his face** with a four-high stack of blueberry pancakes, two scrambled eggs and bacon, he caught up with the innkeeper, who was back at the front desk. "Lily, would you mind if I asked Renata to watch Max for about an hour?"

"Not at all," she replied. "While I get the kitchen cleaned up from breakfast, Renata's gonna be outside working in the garden for a bit." She glanced down at the dog, who was sitting there waiting to see what would happen next. She smiled. "He can spend some time outside with her."

"That would be great. I want to pop into the Really Good Wood-Fired Coffee shop before my appointment at the real estate agency. And since it's close to nine AM, I thought maybe I'd run into Graham Huston. Maybe get that introduction to Harry, the mystery man."

Lily let out a snicker. "By the way, the locals just call it the Really Good. If you're fixing' to be one of us, just call it that. We'll all know whatcha mean." She paused, then said, "You sure you want to run into Graham? That could be like entering the belly of the beast."

"Trust me. I'm pretty sure I can handle Huston," he said with a sly grin. He bent down and gave his dog a pat on the head, then glanced back up at Lily. "See you in about an hour… and thanks."

It was a beautiful morning outside. The sun had yet to start baking the tar on the sidewalk, so he decided that a walk across the town square to the coffee shop was a nice way to start his day after that big, filling breakfast. He wanted to bring Max along but wasn't sure if the owner allowed non-service animals inside the coffee shop and he didn't want to tie Max up out front. *Better safe than sorry,* he thought.

As soon as he walked inside, he was greeted by a man whose accent was closer to his own than everyone else he'd met so far, and he immediately pegged him as a fellow northerner.

"You must be our newest resident," the man said, offering his hand. "I'm Harry Thurgood, the owner of this little coffee shop."

"Brandon Turner," he replied, clasping Harry's hand. "Nice to meet you."

Graham Huston waved from a booth across the room. "Turner! Glad you could make it," he roared. "Come join us."

Turner returned his wave and he and Harry made their way over to the booth. Alongside Huston sat an attractive woman. There was another man sitting across from them. They were all sipping mugs of coffee. He had to admit; if what he was smelling was wood-fired coffee, he would need to try some pronto. The aroma was incredible.

Huston looked at the man across from him. "Scooch over, Father," he said. Then, addressing Turner, "Sit down, Brandon. Coffee? It's on Harry."

"Hold on there, Graham," said Harry, who was standing on

the side of the booth closest to the woman. "I've got this."

Huston laughed. "That's what I just said."

Harry stared across the table at the newspaper editor. "It's my shop, so I'll make the offer, if you don't mind."

"What's the difference? Turner here still gets a free cup of coffee," Huston said, still laughing.

Harry slowly shook his head and then turned his attention to Turner. "What would you like, Mr. Turner? As a brand-new addition to our town, this one's on the house."

"Yeah, Brandon," grinned Huston. "The first one's free, and once he's got you hooked, you'll be here every day begging him for his coffee."

A smirk formed on Turner's lips. If Huston only knew how often he'd heard words like that in his former line of work. And all the drug dealers he'd busted who got rich using those words.

He was sitting directly across from the woman, and the aroma from her mug was slapping him squarely across the face. Turner smiled at her and then glanced up at Harry. "I'll have whatever she's having. It smells fantastic. And please call me Brandon."

Harry smiled and went off to fill his order. The man sitting next to him turned towards Turner and said, "Well, it's obvious that Graham is not going to make the introductions. I'm Father Lee Gorman." He nodded at the woman across from them. "This is the Reverend Ember Cole. And of course, you've already met Graham."

"Nice to meet you both." Turner cocked his head at the priest. "Father Lee… hmm. I met a friend of yours yesterday at a rest area somewhere between here and Austin. I believe he said his name was Father Frank, and he was on his way home after a visit with you. He told me to look you up, and now… here you are."

"Ah, yes," replied the pastor. "He's a good friend. I've known him for a long time. We met at seminary."

Huston smiled. "What are the chances you'd run into a priest at a truck stop who tells you to look up Father Lee? It must have been some sort of divine intervention."

The reverend rolled her eyes. "Oh, shut it, Graham."

"I'm just saying," persisted Huston. "Maybe Brandon needs to get something off his chest, and it needs to be with a priest." He smiled at Turner. "I'd take this as a sign if I were you."

Harry arrived with a steaming hot mug of coffee and a plate with a large, warm pastry covered in white icing dripping down the sides. He placed both in front of Turner. "I thought you'd enjoy one of my cinnamon rolls to go along with the coffee. It's fresh out of the oven."

Turner picked up the roll and took a bite. The icing oozed down his chin as he chewed the pastry. Harry waited patiently while Turner washed down the confection with his coffee. After wiping the sticky icing off his face and hands, he looked up at Harry. "I think I've died and gone to heaven. This is one of the best cinnamon rolls I've ever tasted. And combined with the coffee… just amazing." He took another sip from his mug. "So, this is wood-fired coffee? Why have I never heard of this before?"

"It's a longer process to roast coffee using the wood-fired method. Most shops nowadays will not take the time to slow roast their beans using a wood fired roaster. But I believe in the process and won't offer my customers anything less."

"And besides," added Huston. "That big city you come from is way too fast-paced. People up there aren't going to slow down enough to enjoy this kind of coffee. I'm betting there's a Starbucks on every corner in New York. It's all about the profits up there." He gave the shop owner the side-eye. "Harry doesn't care what it costs to make wood-fired coffee. He doesn't need the money. It's all about the experience for him. Ain't that right,

Harry?"

Harry shook his head at Huston and sighed. He nodded at Turner. "I'm glad you like it, Brandon." There was a jingle from the door as a couple of women came into the coffee shop. "Duty calls," he said. He smiled at Ember. "Will I see you at lunchtime?" The Reverend Cole gave Harry an affirmative nod. "Good. We'll have time to talk then." He said his goodbyes to the rest of the table and marched off to greet the new arrivals.

"I really have to be going, myself," said Turner. "I've got an appointment with a real estate agent to see a few homes this morning." He stood, pulled his wallet out, and threw a couple of bills on the table.

"What's this?" asked Huston.

"Tip. Good service and free food and drink. It's the least I can do."

"Keep your money," replied Huston. He picked up the bills and handed them back to Turner. "I wasn't kidding. Harry really doesn't care about the money. Apparently, he has plenty stashed away somewhere. If you leave him a tip, he'll just consider you prepaid for your next coffee."

"Well, then," said Turner, stuffing the bills back inside his wallet. "Nice to meet you, Reverend. You too Father."

"Will we see you at mass on Sunday?" asked Father Lee.

"Pretty presumptuous, Father," said Huston. "You don't even know if he's catholic."

"I was raised catholic, although I haven't practiced in years," answered Turner.

Father Lee smiled. "Well, then… maybe?"

"Probably not this Sunday, Father. But I'll make you a deal—once I get settled into my life here in Magnolia Bluff, I'll come check out your church. No promises beyond that, though."

"Fair enough," said Father Lee. "All I ask is that you give

Christ the King Church a chance. You may be more ready than you think."

Turner blew out a breath and nodded. *You just may be right, Father,* he thought.

## ABOUT THE MAGNOLIA BLUFF CRIME CHRONICLES

"What is a multi-author crime novel series?" is the question CW Hawes got when he proposed the idea to our fellow Underground Authors.

We collaborated on a short story anthology, and CW was interested in taking the idea of collaboration to the next level. A multi-author series is what happens when a group of authors decides to write a series of novels. In the case of the Magnolia Bluff Crime Chronicles, the Underground Authors created a fictional town that would be the common denominator for each of the books throughout the series.

Each author has his or her characters and perhaps uses characters the other authors created. The action takes place in the beautiful little Texas Hill Country town of Magnolia Bluff. Nine authors showing us nine different sides of the town in 2022. The authors are growing to twelve, with more cozy mysteries in 2023, Season Two, and again in 2024, Season Three.

Each author writes in their genre to allow readers to experience humor, dark dilemmas, suspense, romance, thrills and spills — all told through a whole lot of good storytelling. The kind that will keep you up past your bedtime, or make you miss your bus stop. Stay tuned. There's lots happening in Magnolia Bluff. And you don't want to miss any of it. Breakfield and Burkey signed up for season three, too. More fun to come.

# MAGNOLIA BLUFF CRIME CHRONICLES

# MAGNOLIA BLUFF CRIME CHRONICLES

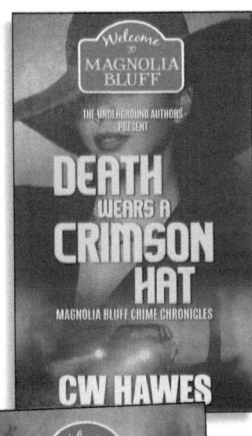

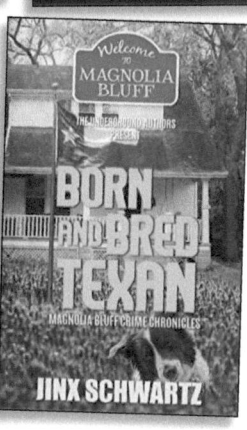

## About the Underground Authors

An email from Caleb Pirtle III and discussions resulted in our joining the author co-op he organized to support a group of writers he knew. The purpose of the group would be to promote each other's books. Writing, after all, is easy. Marketing, on the other hand, is difficult. But many hands make light work, and that's what we were hoping for.

In addition to promoting each other's books and keeping each other up to date on what's happening on the business side of writing, we collaborated on a short story anthology, and are now working on a crime fiction series set in the lovely little Texas Hill Country town of Magnolia Bluff.

The current Underground Authors participating in the Magnolia Bluff Crime Chronicles are Caleb Pirtle III, Linda Pirtle, Cindy Davis, James Callan, CW Hawes, Kelly Marshall, Richard Schwindt, Jinx Schwartz, Joe Congel, Kay McNiven, Rob & Joan Carter, and Breakfield & Burkey. They are all fine writers, and we're honored to be associated with them.

# About the Authors

**Breakfield** – Works for a high-tech manufacturer as a solution architect, functioning in hybrid data/telecom environments. He considers himself a long-time technology geek, who also enjoys writing, studying World War II history, travel, and cultural exchanges. Charles' love of wine tastings, cooking, and Harley riding has found ways into the stories. As a child, he moved often because of his father's military career, which even helps him with the various character perspectives he helps bring to life in the series. He continues to try to teach Burkey humor.

**Burkey** – Works as a business architect who builds solutions for customers on a good technology foundation. She has written many technology papers, white papers, but finds the freedom of writing fiction a lot more fun. As a child, she helped to lead the kids with exciting new adventures built on make believe characters, was a Girl Scout until high school, and contributed to the community as a young member of a Head Start program. Rox enjoys family, learning, listening to people, travel, outdoor activities, sewing, cooking, and thinking about how to diversify the series.

**Breakfield and Burkey** – started writing non-fictional papers and books, but it wasn't nearly as fun as writing fictional stories. They found it interesting to use the aspects of technology that people are incorporating into their daily lives more and more as a perfect way to create a good guy/bad guy story with elements of travel to the various places they have visited either professionally and personally, humor, romance, intrigue, suspense, and a spirited way to remember people who have crossed paths with them. They love to talk about their stories with private and public book readings. Burkey also conducts regular interviews for Texas authors, which she finds very interesting. Her first interview was, wait for it, Breakfield. You can often find them at local book fairs or other family-oriented events.

The primary series is based on a family organization called R-Group. Recently they have spawned a subgroup that contains some of the original characters as the Cyber Assassins Technology Services (CATS) team. The authors have ideas for continuing the series in both of these tracks. They track the more than 150 characters on a spreadsheet, with a hidden avenue for the future coined The Enigma Chronicles tagged in some portions of the stories. Fan reviews seem to frequently suggest that these would make good television or movie stories, so the possibilities appear endless, just like their ideas for new stories.

They have book video trailers for each of the stories, which can be viewed on YouTube, Amazon's Authors page, or on their website, *www.EnigmaBookSeries.com*. Their website is routinely updated with new interviews, answers to readers' questions, book trailers, and contests. You may also find it fascinating to check out the fun acronyms they create for the stories summarized on their website. Reach out to them at *Authors@EnigmaSeries.com, Twitter@EnigmaSeries,* or *Facebook@TheEnigmaSeries.*

**Please provide a fair and honest review on amazon**
and any other places you post reviews. We appreciate the feedback.

Other stories by Breakfield and Burkey in
The Enigma Series are at www.EnigmaBookSeries.com

We would greatly appreciate
if you would take a few minutes
and provide a review of this work
on Amazon, Goodreads
and any of your other favorite places.

Other stories by Breakfield and Burkey in the Heirs Series are at **www.EnigmaBookSeries.com**

www.ingramcontent.com/pod-product-compliance
Ingram Content Group UK Ltd.
Pitfield, Milton Keynes, MK11 3LW, UK
UKHW041303180426